Black Bloods

Black Bloods

Denis Gray

BLACK BLOODS

iUniverse books may be ordered through booksellers or by contacting:

iUniverse
1663 Liberty Drive
Bloomington, IN 47403
www.iuniverse.com
1-800-Authors (1-800-288-4677)

ISBN: 978-1-4917-7651-3 (sc)
ISBN: 978-1-4917-7652-0 (e)

Library of Congress Control Number: 2015914356

Print information available on the last page.

iUniverse rev. date: 10/02/2015

De Wolfe let Fagan look into his eyes, and Fagan saw a man who had grown older by some years, as if the world had fallen in on him, and the dark bags under his eyes had dragged him down to being a mere mortal, a man who would never recover from the fall.

—*Maxwell Engelbert De Wolfe & Fagan Dooley*

Chapter 1

Maxwell Engelbert De Wolfe was drunk after the opera at the New York Metropolitan Opera House, not before. The production was *La Traviata*, a grand opera by Giuseppe Verdi.

Maxwell Engelbert De Wolfe had gotten drunk at the Limelight on Fifty-Sixth Street, a fancy "drinking hole" for the rich. Men of extravagant wealth gathered there nightly. Money in 1923 was an object of excess, not restraint or caution. New York City, not Hollywood—a town of movie stars and movie palaces and bright lights and glitzy promotion and cheap entertainment—was a city of big business and Wall Street and gritty finance and an overzealous press that fed the average citizen of its time a strong sense of its reportorial curiosity, envy, politics, and profound hatred of the deep-pocketed, roguish, black-hearted men who controlled the nation's wealth with a powerful sense of kingship.

It was the Gilded Age.

The luxury Packard had crossed Fifth Avenue and was moving eastward on Sixty-First Street. De Wolfe's body was slumped in the Twin Six Touring car's backseat. De Wolfe was a smart drunk, for his mind absorbed every detail of any information spooned to him in the Limelight by men who loved money as much as he did. It's all they talked about, even while surrounded by beautiful women with carefully flipped hair, who smoked from twelve-inch-long diamond-studded cigarette holders and whose hysterical laughter lit the air to match that of a pack of hyenas.

Maxwell Engelbert De Wolfe was a New York–based financier. He came from tough, savvy German stock. His father, Florentz Klaus De Wolfe, a brilliant financier himself, had built the investment banking company of De Wolfe & Kaiser, and through a succession of two or three name changes that covered several years, in the year of 1918, it became the company of De Wolfe & Fitch. Florentz Klaus De Wolfe died in 1906. Maxwell De Wolfe inherited a healthy, well-managed company with zero debt, and he hoped for even better prospects and profit for the future.

De Wolfe felt the late October's dark night press on his bearded face, his head as light as a cork bobbing out at sea. The opera was a pleasant pastime for him. He was not only an aficionado of opera who rented out a luxury box but also a huge donor to its financial coffers. He admired songs and the artists who sang them. Particularly the soprano's and tenor's powerful voices soaring above the orchestra pit jolting De Wolfe with one spine chilling thrill after the other.

De Wolfe slumped more. He wished Eva had been with him tonight in the New York Metropolitan Opera House and at the Limelight, but this was an impossible wish. But oh, how he wished it to happen—the diamonds and the furs he would lavish on her for the occasion, the impassioned stares that would reflect off Eva's luminous skin by jealous men who envisioned her holding to their arm, not his.

De Wolfe laughed at the thought.

THE MANHATTAN SKYLINE HAD A priceless look at midnight. It had a cold, distant wintry glow De Wolfe loved. Or maybe it typified a day of negotiations, when cold-eyed businessmen tried to beat him out of the same dollar he was trying to beat out of them in the continual war to grab and get as much money out of a business deal to make it worth his time and patience.

It was that coldness in his office that drove today's big deal. He'd sat down with Felix Huber, a media mogul, a man who prided himself on driving a hard bargain, someone whom he'd dealt with before. Huber had come to the table with solid facts and figures that would impress probably anyone but him. But he knew how to deal with Huber, how to bring him to his knees. He had his own facts. And fact number 1 was no man was smarter, or more devious, than him or had as much personal information on powerful people. Some business deals he consummated reached beyond business and into personal revelations. He had facts and figures on Felix Huber's personal life that could jeopardize Huber's personal reputation if they ever got in the wrong hands.

In the privacy of his office, his cold eyes looked into Huber's narrow, faintly gray ones to inform him that he was aware of a son, Adam, whom Huber had sired through his Negro mistress, Rosetta "Rosie" Cobb, some fifteen years ago.

"Adam, your son," De Wolfe had whispered in Huber's ear, "only knows his mother's told him his father (whom he does not know) is rich and sends money to them monthly to maintain their living standard. It is enough, it appears, to keep them well contented.

"You are no cheapskate, so it seems, Mr. Huber, when it comes to your Negroes. In actuality, a damned pushover."

De Wolfe laughed again, his brain no longer drunk, drowned by liquor, but, instead, pleased by the anguished look that was on Huber's face: first a look of shock, then of resignation, then, finally, of shame.

The event had made De Wolfe's day.

"A Negro whore. How convenient." De Wolfe laughed under his breath. "It is far too amusing but sad. This high-pitched fever rich white men seem to possess when chasing these Negro women in their mansions. Who turn their beds. Scrub their floors. And clean their toilets. But the ultimate service, it appears, is sex, sex, and lots of it."

There's no need for me to exaggerate or to expound upon the point, De Wolfe thought. *I find it both accurate and just to state, this perfervid, jungle relationship they maintain with their Negro whores.*

"Huber must look a damned ghastly sight with his drawers down!"

Sobering even more, De Wolfe's eyes narrowed in on Fagan Dooley's black bowler in the Packard's front seat.

"Fagan, I was having a hell of a good laugh here in the backseat," De Wolfe said.

Fagan Dooley, De Wolfe's chauffeur, smiled like his heart had just hugged Ireland's sandy shores. A land where the sun set brightly and wind-tossed emerald-green grass blew like giant waves rolling over knobby, hilly fields.

"Ain't it the God's honest truth, Mr. De Wolfe, sir." Fagan laughed loudly, this jolly little Irishman with the walrus mustache that always gave the impression it was too large for his ruddy, pudgy face—until Fagan Dooley grinned.

De Wolfe pulled himself out his backseat slump, taking in a full measure of breath. "I was thinking of Felix Huber just now, Fagan."

"Why Mr. Huber, sir?

"Oh, have you ever witnessed a rich man with his drawers down at his ankles, Fagan?"

"No, not that, sir," Fagan said, playing along with De Wolfe. "Ain't a practice I'd likely take to, sir. Not under any circumstance."

De Wolfe howled.

Of course Fagan Dooley had not expected De Wolfe to explain himself: never had he in their twelve-year relationship. De Wolfe often said outlandish things for him to respond to. It was not meant to be a two-way dialogue between them to determine the nature or intent of those remarks.

The Packard was nearing De Wolfe's destination. De Wolfe's anticipation grew whenever the Packard reached this particular location of the long block, Michaels Street, and then branched off onto a much shorter block, Ballad Street. The black Packard was moving toward a building at the end of Ballad Street De Wolfe owned. He put money into the building to restore it. It's where, three nights of the week, De Wolfe came to do personal business, not financial.

The Packard began slowing down, and Fagan Dooley said, as always, "We're here, Mr. De Wolfe."

"Yes, Fagan!" De Wolfe bellowed. "The opera. The Limelight. And now home!"

Fagan Dooley hopped out of the Packard and opened the passenger-side door for De Wolfe.

The two-story brick building the men faced had a short concrete stoop *sans* a handrail. It led up to a solid black metal, off-putting front door. Above the door hung a wrought iron night lamp, casting dull light. Windows appeared on the second floor, not the first. There were six in total: three windows on the left side of the building and an identical number on the right. The building was once a factory that De Wolfe had converted into a residence. Its lack of appeal was due to the building's façade and location, Ballad Street. Ballad Street was short and narrow, practically deserted during day and night hours. It was why De Wolfe had carefully chosen it.

De Wolfe walked with a bad limp and with the aid of a tapered mahogany cane. He was wearing a velvet-collared Chesterfield topcoat and a stiff black top hat.

De Wolfe handed Fagan the door key.

"Thank you, Mr. De Wolfe." Fagan inserted the fat key into the door's metal lock. He opened the solid black metal door for De Wolfe.

"Thank you, Fagan."

There was no light, not until Fagan turned on the electric lights in the broad, barely furnished vestibule, and then the succession of lamps that would eventually light De Wolfe's way up to the second floor landing, but not beyond. The trail of lights led to, and then up to, a plain wooden stairwell. Fagan, by now, had bounded up the steps to turn on the lights despite his chubby frame and the late hour.

De Wolfe looked up the stairs and then began climbing them. Besides him not fully recovering from his Booth's gin (his favorite liquor) served at the Limelight tonight after the opera and the bad limp that permanently burdened his step, De Wolfe moved slowly up the stairs, his feet making such lumbering sounds as to wake the dead as Fagan patiently awaited him.

There was another solid door at the top of the stairs but made of thick wood, not metal.

Fagan, when De Wolfe had reached him, unlocked the door with a slender key on the same metal key ring this time. He opened the door for De Wolfe, and De Wolfe brushed past him. Fagan returned the key ring to De Wolfe who slipped it back inside his coat pocket.

"Thank you, Fagan. And good night," De Wolfe said, after huffing and puffing up the eight stairs.

Fagan smiled, tipped his bowler, and then turned.

"See you in the morning. The usual time."

"Thank you, Mr. De Wolfe," Fagan replied softly. He turned back around to shut the door.

De Wolfe was in a hallway of gorgeous Italian marbled walls. And it was as if the interior of the building had turned overnight from a bohemian's humble dwelling to a rich man's Versailles. De Wolfe was treading on a plush Oriental carpet as he passed one closed door after the other, still out of breath, winded from the single flight of stairs.

"Max, is that you?"

"Who else," De Wolfe said a few feet from the open door.

The laugh was bright and sexy. "Oh, Max!"

And when De Wolfe entered the huge bedroom, the creamy-complexioned young woman with the long pitch-black hair, attired in a red sheer peignoir, threw her arms out at De Wolfe, hugging him.

"Eva, Eva, my darling, Eva!"

Eva kissed De Wolfe's cheek not once but twice. "Here, let me take your coat, Max!"

De Wolfe handed her his cane and top hat. He began unbuttoning his Chesterfield coat, eagerly.

The bedroom's tall windows were covered by long flowing silk drapes. The wall facing the Regency Walnut queen-size four-poster bed contained an array of large and small mirrors neatly arranged but drew suspicion as to why so many mirrors for one woman (Eva Durant) to gaze into.

"You're so beautiful," De Wolfe said, looking into Eva's dark eyes as she took his coat. "Do you ever grow tired of me telling you that, Eva? Of me indulging myself in this manner—opinion of you?"

"No," Eva said, not looking directly into De Wolfe's eyes but into one of the mirrors she faced. "Not at all. In the least, Max."

She'd smelled the gin on his breath. But what was new in that regard? Eva realized there was no mystery to Maxwell Engelbert De Wolfe. He was a brilliant but sad man. A man who kept her in this building at the end of the quiet block. She was his mistress. It'd been a little over two years, this relationship. No, there was no mystery to this man who kept her: he loved gin and sex and was lonely as hell.

De Wolfe sat on the four-poster bed as Eva attended to his coat, cane, and hat. De Wolfe lay back on the bed. He stroked his neatly trimmed black beard, simultaneous to him shutting his eyes.

"Are you tired?" Eva Durant asked, her beautiful breasts heaving urgently inside the sexy peignoir.

"No, Eva. Hell, I was thinking about us."

"Us?" she asked, approaching him cautiously.

"The opera."

"Yes, the op—"

"You in attendance with me in that staid setting of aristocrats. The rich. The privileged. The goddamned captains of industry," De Wolfe said mockingly, his fingers still calmly stroking his beard, "and their bejeweled, boorish women who flit away their fortune.

"But not you, Eva," De Wolfe said, quickly rising off his back and grabbing her and hugging her hard to him. "Not you. If you were on my arm at the opera house tonight, I thought coming over here in the car with Fagan, damnit, all eyes would be set on you.

"All of them would be held captive by your uncanny beauty," De Wolfe said with a maddening feeling pumping inside his chest. "They would cower … all of them. Shrink."

"Yes, I know, Max. I know."

And after De Wolfe's enthusiastic hugging of her, he fell back on the bed.

"Max, you *are* tired."

And she didn't let him reply, for she was on her knees, spreading his legs open and unzipping De Wolfe's zipper. "I-I'll help you to relax … Max."

"Oh yes, Eva, of course you will …" De Wolfe said, his white skin turning pinkish.

Eva's head bent down to meet De Wolfe's fattening penis.

Chapter 2

The next morning, seven o'clock.

De Wolfe leaned heavily into his cane. He was in his office. He'd been picked up by Fagan Dooley in the Packard at six thirty and whisked over to 11 Broadway, the southern tip of Broadway, where the location of his office, De Wolfe & Fitch, was established. Keeping with the area's architectural refinement and patented grace, the grouped buildings' structures were ornate and marvelous to view, down to the last brick and cobbled pavement. De Wolfe's building was no exception. Eleven Broadway exuded power, blended to architectural perfection by high-priced builders who knew this class of men and how to build their buildings to further exude and elevate their extraordinary power.

De Wolfe had not eaten, for he was not a breakfast person, but as a rule, he ate at eleven o'clock on the dot. Last night's hangover was long gone. There was no special need for a "concoction" the following day to cure his hangover. It was his will to work, to make or break deals that drove his day, that sobered and absorbed him. He was a financier, a moneymaker; it was his life and his soul.

Eva, De Wolfe thought. *What a great hump!* He laughed. That thought would routinely persist after a night of sex with her, and of what he possessed, this beauty of a young girl whom he kept and who brought the only true joy to his personal life. He bought the building for his sexual romps, exploits, the many women he'd bedded. There were the one-night stands and the mistresses. But none of his mistresses had lasted long, not like Eva Durant. He'd been keeping her for over two years by now. She—

De Wolfe looked up from his desk.

"Good morning, Cyrille."

"Good morning, Mr. De Wolfe."

Cyrille Otto Fitch was a thin man with an unattractive face. A man in his midfifties who had heavy dark eyebrows, a fussy look, and mutton chop sideburns. He was a brilliant man, peculiar and particular. He spoke quickly and assertively, leaving no room for doubt or confusion.

"I—"

"This morning's principal players should be in the conference room by eight o'clock sharp," Fitch said to De Wolfe.

De Wolfe rubbed his chubby hands together. "It should be juicy fun this morning, Cyrille."

"More like a killing, don't you think, Mr. De Wolfe," Fitch said, his eyes squinting, then glinting through horn-rimmed glasses, his posture straight and rigid as a New York lamppost.

De Wolfe sat back in his leather chair, balancing the cane against the large cherrywood desk. "You have such a delicately sweet way with metaphor, Cyrille." De Wolfe's hand touched his heart. "It warms my heart."

"Mine too, Mr. De Wolfe." Pause. "Excuse me then," Fitch said with impatience.

"Of course, of course."

Cyrille Fitch left De Wolfe's office. It was a private chamber in the rear. As partners of the firm, De Wolfe and Fitch maintained separate quarters. Mostly all of De Wolfe's office furniture was imported from Germany in not only pleasing De Wolfe's personal taste but also championing his native stock.

"That damned Fitch!" He stood when he'd said it, using his hands down on the desk to brace himself *sans* the cane. Fitch was a man who, over time, had grown on De Wolfe. And once that occurred, De Wolfe made him a partner. He'd immediately ascertained Fitch's brilliance and exceptional intellectual talent, but ultimately, it was his ruthlessness, in De Wolfe's mind, that won the partnership for Fitch.

"He has the goddamned heart of a snake, that man!"

This was not a new way De Wolfe had used to describe Fitch; only he loved repeating it, just as he loved thinking of Eva Durant, this young, sexy "thing" that made his blood boil like the fresh deal awaiting him and Fitch this morning in the conference room.

EIGHT O'CLOCK, IN DE WOLFE & Fitch's enormous conference room.

A veil of silence sat in the room, not until Fitch called the meeting to order with an officialdom to rival that of a British Parliament of parliamentary procedure and regulation. There were powerful men in the room, especially Joseph Castle of JC Industries, a railroad magnate who was tightfisted and cautious but knew how to convince and persuade to his advantage upon listening to all sides of any negotiation or points of argument before he struck.

By now, the conference room was clouded by cigar smoke and filled by a rough stock of rich men who had been fighting over principle, profit, and their profound stake in it.

All eyes turned to Castle who had just extinguished his cigar in the enamel ashtray, who had been making crude grunts for the past few minutes of the heated meeting.

"You have pushed your point particularly well, Mr. Fitch," Castle said, clearing his throat, his large face strained. "Are you playing some kind of game with me, or—"

"You heard the terms, Mr. Castle. We want you to put more skin in the game."

Castle's skin turned red. "Do I need not tell you, I brought this deal to you, initially. And it is all of you who owe me a great debt of gratitude for—"

"We owe you nothing, Mr. Castle. All of us are in this jointly," Fitch said, looking at the other heavyweight investors in the smoky room. "All of us are owed equal participation from you and your company's funding. An equal amount of your company's money in the financial pot."

Castle was stunned. His eyes turned in the direction of De Wolfe who was seated at the top of the table, staring at him, as it were.

"What about you, Mr. De Wolfe? Is this your recommendation, counsel to me too? That of your partner Fitch and the rest of the ungrateful men in the room? These men of profit, but little else of status?"

De Wolfe's shoulders took on the exact relaxed posture of his lax face. "You are not above the pack, Mr. Castle. Nor your company's money. It does not spend any differently than ours. You feel more on the fringe of this investment"—De Wolfe sighed— "than in its center we all genuinely agree."

Castle, this tall, sturdily built man, seemed to physically shrink at the long, wide conference table. "You are greedy men, every last damned one of you!" he said sonorously.

"You will—"

"Pardon me, Mr. Fitch, but …" De Wolfe spread his hands over the table as if sweeping dust from it. "I beg you let me continue this with Mr. Castle."

"Of course, Mr. De Wolfe, sir."

De Wolfe took his sweet time before directing his attention to Castle's concerns, again.

"Mr. Castle, with all due respect, you will not preach of greed to us. Not from a man who would make Cornelius Vanderbilt, the 'Commodore,' blush.

"You'll put more of JC Industries' money into this potentially lucrative enterprise, or the whole goddamned venture will collapse." De Wolfe drew back his hands from the center of the table. "We will stand to lose a lot of money, of course. But you stand to lose our confidence for any future financial dealings with you.

"We are a band of powerful men, sir, who lean on each other whenever our instincts require us." De Wolfe paused and patiently stroked his trimmed beard. "When what is in our best interest is not to compete with each other but, rather, engage. To strike the proper chord and balance.

"You do comprehend fully our joint resolve and seriousness here today, don't you, sir? In order to move the ball forward and advance it to its greatest monetary worth that is standard."

BACK IN DE WOLFE'S OFFICE, at nine five, De Wolfe and Fitch were laughing up a storm.

"As usual, Cyrille, you laid the necessary groundwork, and I, dear fellow, the coup de grâce. Hell, Castle's face was a goddamned bloody mess when he left the building."

"He left enough blood behind, to suggest he'd been gorged by a raging bull."

"What a damned pity."

Suddenly, De Wolfe paused. *Are Fitch and I cowardly men?* The thought had suddenly hit him. De Wolfe had no idea where such a thought had come from. But how could they be *cowardly* when they always looked their rivals straight in the eye and then cut them to shreds, and if it left a "trail of blood," as Fitch had so succinctly summarized it—then so be it, GODDAMNIT!

In the past, he'd suffered the same bloodletting in cutthroat negotiations, just not this morning. This morning, it was Joseph Castle's blood that stained the conference room's rug.

Cyrille Fitch had left De Wolfe's office over an hour ago. Marilyn Ochs, De Wolfe's secretary, had just dropped off papers for De Wolfe. He wasn't a hands-on boss; Fitch was. De Wolfe reviewed reports his crack staff prepared for him. They pored through financial figures and then presented them to him in neat, handwritten copy.

Rarely in his workday did De Wolfe engage with his staff. It was only Fitch, fundamentally, who had this privilege of access to him, and, of course, Marilyn Ochs. But De Wolfe, through Fitch's reporting, knew the strengths and weaknesses of his staff, who was doing a good job as opposed to a poor one for the firm.

Bored, De Wolfe looked up from another meticulously formalized report on his desk and then at his gold-plated wristwatch. Ten after ten. It was time for him to check in with his wife, Alexandra Bauer De Wolfe, De Wolfe thought.

He glanced down at the telephone just inches removed from his right elbow. He had not eaten, but now it felt as if he had and that everything sitting in his stomach had turned to stone. De Wolfe shut his eyes and thought about today's nasty negotiation with Castle, and last night's sexual romp with Eva, and then picked up the telephone.

"Good morning, Elsa. May I speak to Mrs. De Wolfe."

De Wolfe waited, as he knew he must, for Alexandra De Wolfe was never immediately available to him when he called the mansion no matter the time of day. It'd been this way for some time now, and by now De Wolfe would define it to be calibrated on her part, not innocent or unfettered, but freighted with much psychological baggage.

He waited and waited until finally Alexandra De Wolfe was on the other end of the telephone.

Alexandra De Wolfe always spoke first.

THE BLACK PACKARD WAS ON Washington Place and Mercer and Greene Streets east of Washington Square Park. This fashionable urban district was immersed in huge amounts of New York lore and history in its grand old bones.

De Wolfe's residence was a four-story, double-wide house of red-brick with brown-stone trimming. The house, needless to say, cost De Wolfe a pretty penny. He bought the property, only to raze the old structure and construct a new one under the skillful directorship of Lewis Calendar, an "architect of the rich." At the time, money paid a vital role in obtaining Calendar's professional services. It seemed Calendar had previously committed himself to another client De Wolfe quickly outbid. That transaction cost him a pretty penny too, but every cent spent, De Wolfe thought, was well worth it.

De Wolfe looked out of the car window and wished people didn't think him a humorless man (cynical, yes; sarcastic, yes), but he knew he had no one to blame but himself in casting this shadow of an implacable, impenetrable persona. But it was too late for him to pull back the curtain, to reinvent Maxwell Engelbert De Wolfe. He was fifty-six. Literally, he'd run out of time.

"Fagan, where does the damn time fly off to?"

"It's something I certainly ask myself, Mr. De Wolfe."

"I suppose it is an age-old question, with no answers, just the interest of the mind to muddle through."

Fagan Dooley had never heard it put quite like that whether he agreed with De Wolfe's remark or not. He chuckled, and it seemed to please De Wolfe. Fagan kept the chuckle alive to soothe De Wolfe's spirits.

He was the chauffeur of one of the richest men in the world and, in a way, every day, felt privileged. He came from a poor Irish lot, the New York City slum. A tenement life, where food, daily in the Ronan Dooley household, was at a shortage; clothes, hand-me-downs; and sharing a bed with his older brother, Malachy, until age fifteen.

Dooley laughed inwardly: he didn't know if he liked De Wolfe more when he was drunk or sober, but he didn't have to like him at all. It wasn't a job requirement: he was under his employ. But seeing how De Wolfe lived, he, on occasion, wondered if one person was in reality better off than the other: rich or poor.

Now Fagan Dooley eased the Packard into an underground garage that housed ten cars—all beauties. Coming out of the darkness and into a bevy of garage lights didn't brighten De Wolfe's mood; ironically, it made it worse. De Wolfe knew he was home, and after the requisite demand of moving out of the garage and onto the built-in elevator in his thirty-two-room Washington Place mansion, De Wolfe knew what was in store for him, the usual dismal state of affairs and duty.

When both men reached the underground elevator, Fagan pulled down on a brown braided cord at the right of the elevator there to alert the mansion's staff that De Wolfe had arrived. As soon as De Wolfe exited the elevator, Helga, a tall, big-boned, blue-eyed, beautiful blonde German girl with braided hair, greeted him.

"Good evening, Mr. De Wolfe."

"Good evening, Helga."

Fagan remained in the gold-finished elevator.

"Good evening, Mr. De Wolfe."

"Good evening, Fagan."

The elevator's doors then shut with Fagan Dooley in it.

Helga took De Wolfe's black top hat and Chesterfield coat, which she helped remove from his shoulders. He leaned on his cane and looked up at the mansion's grandiose foyer that looked practically as if he'd stepped into a Catholic cathedral, the fifty-foot domed ceiling maintaining its stable, serene beauty and the marbled walls ordered from Sienna, Italy, and arched windows of stained glass. De Wolfe stood on a burgundy broadloom.

De Wolfe, with the master interior decorator, Edwin Marten, had put all the pieces of the mansion's magnificence together over a period of one year of active, intense buying and unrestrained creativity. There were times when the two men bumped heads, Marten, on occasion, being as stubborn as De Wolfe regarding their individual taste. For De Wolfe, the constant haranguing and bickering brought greater passion and exuberance to the project. It meant to him, that both cared deeply about the mission's stated objective.

It was his evaluation of commitment consistently evidenced in the office, and at play. He wanted to work with someone as competitive as him (Cyrille Fitch, for example). Edwin Marten had his aesthetic of beauty and he his, and so when the two forces collided, out of the collision came a new aesthetic, one that was pure, original, and unspoiled; one not to be copied or imitated by anyone, no matter their great wealth or designing talent or ambition.

Helga was De Wolfe's personal maid in the De Wolfe mansion. She drew his bath, ironed his clothes, performed all practical functions for him.

"How has your day been, Helga?"

"Quite good, Mr. De Wolfe," Helga said in a soft, soothing voice.

Even in flats she was much taller than De Wolfe, and De Wolfe liked this about her. It rendered her a sense of authority, a regalness that lent itself well to the mansion's tone, expanding its dimension, De Wolfe had at one time considered.

Helga turned and stepped away from De Wolfe. De Wolfe followed her. This was how De Wolfe trained Helga, to follow this simple protocol of him following her so that nothing was ever out of order or balance in his mansion. That he, Maxwell De Wolfe, was in control of everything, from the smallest to the most extreme details of the occasion.

ALEXANDRA DE WOLFE'S BEDROOM WAS elegant but dark and cheerless. It was elegant because of its fine furnishings. Cheerless, because of who Alexandra De Wolfe was, this woman without a light in her soul, a source to feed her in ways that were not only depressing but also self-fulfilling.

"Mrs. De Wolfe," Elsa said in a lightly tempered voice, "Mr. De Wolfe has arrived to the mansion, ma'am."

It was Elsa's responsibility to tell Alexandra De Wolfe this bit of news even if Alexandra De Wolfe had heard the bell's chime that had signaled, to her, the obvious.

"Thank you, Elsa."

Elsa stood behind Alexandra De Wolfe, angled just off her right shoulder.

Alexandra De Wolfe stared into a beaded, silver-plated hand mirror. She was powdering her longish face and pale, spiritless cheeks; she had red hair. Her hair ended at her shoulders. It was long, strict, and straight. There was light at the vanity table where she sat, but the darkish room helped to swallow much of it. She stood, and her silk, flared evening dress was dark blue, stopping at her ankles. A double string of lovely pearls lay across her chest. She was a thin, brittle woman but tall and maintained an erect, aristocratic posture no matter her apparent weakness of spirit.

She turned and took Elsa's arm, her personal maid, someone who was short and stocky and as physically unengaging as her. "Thank you, Elsa."

This was ritual for them whenever De Wolfe was home in the evening from De Wolfe & Fitch to dine with Alexandra De Wolfe, his wife of thirty-one years, if not pressed by other outside activities calling him away from the mansion.

Alexandra De Wolfe and Elsa began their walk out of the huge bedroom, the interest the room provoked alarming. Maybe it was because of its funereal gloominess, of just how much of it hung heavily in the room. This could be the curiosity, the single thing alighting attention.

DE WOLFE WAS AT THE head of the table, fiddling with the glistening Birks's silverware when he looked up at Alexandra De Wolfe as she passed him. He said nothing but looked farther up at the neoclassical sixteen-light silver chandelier with the gadrooned ceiling rose.

It's when Alexandra De Wolfe was finally seated by Elsa at the bottom of the dining room table that De Wolfe and Alexandra De Wolfe's eyes made instant contact, and Elsa and Helga were dismissed by De Wolfe from the dining room.

It was just the two of them at the broad-sweeping rosewood dining room table. De Wolfe was at the top of the table and Alexandra De Wolfe at the bottom.

"Good evening, Maxwell."

"Good evening, Alexandra."

And as if on cue, Yvette, the French chef's petite wife, with the rosy red cheeks, entered the dining room from the side door with her husband's (Jules Le Mon) lovely delicacies on a Tiffany glass serving platter.

Alexandra De Wolfe smiled along with De Wolfe at what was present on the platter.

They had eaten in silence, as was customary. A bottle of Bauer's wine had been unsealed and poured, and each was partaking of it after a meal of two small soups, pigeon cutlets in olive sauce, filets of beef with mushrooms, and an assortment of sweets for dessert.

De Wolfe sipped leisurely from the white crystal glass.

"The opera last night …"

"Yes," De Wolfe said. "*La Traviata*, you know, Alexandra, is quite compelling. What I like to call: Verdi's triumph of the heart. Oh, how the man plays to our damned heartstrings. The true passions of young lovers. When one loves too much and is defeated by forces unbeknownst to them.

"A deathbed we do not see, nor can we ever imagine, but is all too clear to us, our pending doom."

Tighter, Alexandra De Wolfe clenched the crystal white wineglass in her hand. "Is it the reason why you enjoy *La Traviata* so much?" Alexandra De Wolfe's tepid voice queried.

"Yes."

"It, what you like about it," Alexandra De Wolfe said hesitantly, "is its cynicism wreathed in gorgeous music and heavenly voices?"

"Illusionary, yes, I do agree, Alexandra. But oh so real in the final act. Act 3. When fate crushes the human heart under its ponderous, graceless foot."

"Love, you mean," Alexandra De Wolfe said, placing the glass of wine back down on the decorative place mat.

"Love. Yes, love. Its eternal uselessness," De Wolfe said bitterly. "What usefulness does it ultimately serve, when love dies as quickly as it is ignited?"

De Wolfe laughed at his remark, picked up the silk napkin, and then threw it back down in the same spot on the table for what seemed dramatic effect. "Hell, Alexandra, this is what I think of love, goddamnit!"

Alexandra De Wolfe, for reasons she could not fully fathom, did not enjoy opera but did enjoy ballet. Maybe it was because opera had such a deeply visceral, engrained honor in it, its librettos so intently committed to love. Ballet, in a way, themed love too, but the dance did nothing to caress her heart like the human voice when plunged far down into her private, personal emotions. The great singers of opera singing it from a naked, bared soul that, intimately, she felt; it wildly gesticulating and near bursting like a flame when the tenor or soprano reached for the high C or C-sharp to climax the scene and release it in a torrid shriek. The unleashing of hell from their hearts. The final scream.

De Wolfe stared at Alexandra and pondered just what it was she was thinking. And then he shrugged his shoulders and returned to drinking the delightful Bauer white wine from the wineglass.

De Wolfe and Alexandra De Wolfe's bedrooms occupied the same floor. De Wolfe and Alexandra De Wolfe had slept in separate bedrooms for six years, four rooms apart. Alexandra De Wolfe slept in blinders. Rarely did she fall off to sleep immediately but went to bed every night of the week on perfect schedule, eleven o'clock. Mostly, she couldn't wait for the day to end. All of Alexandra De Wolfe's days felt long, but some that felt longer than others.

Elsa had turned off the bedroom lights. Alexandra would open the drapes to let the moon shine in to the bedroom. It was comforting to her even if she wore blinders. It comforted her mind and her mood in knowing the moonlight was in the room with her. That she was not alone.

Alexandra always slept on her back and was immovable, like a giant log. This is the way she had slept since small. Alexandra was born into a rich family, Otto Rudolf Bauer, a wine merchant who purchased land, cultivated it, and produced wines and built a wine company, Oscar Bauer Winery. He became a friend of Florentz De Wolfe, and it's when the arrangement between the two wealthy, powerful families solidified.

It was a European story like feudalism, the architect of this free, fierce forging of powerfully aligned families to rule over peasants (the proletariat) and keep vast sums of money in the hands of one class of people, its self-anointed nobility. It had always made Alexandra feel uneasy about her breeding, but she never exhibited the gumption nor the verve to abandon it. She eased her conscience by making substantial donations to charities. How much it had assuaged her conscience in her fifty-fourth year, Alexandra had no estimable knowledge, but it was her crusade and dedicated mission.

But charities couldn't absorb all of her waking hours. It's what made the days long and, at times, insufferable. Physically speaking, she did not leave the Washington Place mansion unless, routinely, it was her charity work or clothes shopping. Otherwise, it's where her days began and ended. The mansion touted a huge, one-of-a-kind ballroom, but she and De Wolfe no longer entertained in the mansion, nor did they have a social calendar, where dancing and gaiety abounded among the rich.

When did Alexandra realize her life had bottomed out and that this would be its end result? It occurred in her early thirties. She recognized then the style and shape of her life, of what it had turned into. Maxwell De Wolfe was a man she thought she loved, but she soon discovered that an arranged marriage between families is as deadly a sin as any man-made circumstance could possibly construct and control.

The very thought made her body shake and her anger rise.

She was a woman in a place where women, not until recently (1920), voted in America. She would have been a flaming suffragette but was too cowardly and afraid to join this strong, vocal political movement. Surely De Wolfe would have repulsed her to a point where her marriage suffered more of his emotional abandonment and distance from her.

"I know where you were last night, Maxwell. After the opera and the Limelight," Alexandra said in the moonlit bedroom. She'd often speak to herself in this manner, in her bedroom, in her bed, before falling asleep when the quiet floated in her ears, not roar in them like one crashing wave after the other drowning her during the day.

De Wolfe's mistress was no secret to her.

"Only, she's been around now much longer than all the others combined."

Those affairs were cheap ones De Wolfe quickly folded and gladly discarded. This was the plight of most wealthy women like her: men of unlimited power and sexual drive, one vice bound tightly to the other. Men married to women who will not divorce them but bathe in their money and prestige while admirably adorning the nature of a lifestyle these men created for them.

She could well divorce De Wolfe and live off her inheritance, but then she would live with the embarrassment of a soiled, degraded divorcee's reputation. A woman socially ostracized in her world of wealth and opinion. And then who might be the next man in her life, someone as immoral as Maxwell De Wolfe: untrustworthy and unfaithful and unloving?

"Don't make me laugh. Please ..." Alexandra said with thick sarcasm.

Once she learned how to mistrust her parents she mistrusted everyone.

Eighteen months ago when Alexandra discovered he'd purchased the land and the building on Ballad Street, she knew De Wolfe was looking for a permanent setting (no longer the Carleton Hotel) for his sexual trysts. The execution of this arrangement, of him using the Ballad Street building for further business-related activity away from his office, in an ideal privacy (according to him), away from his two studies in the mansion, made her loathe him more for thinking she was such a fool as to believe his bald-faced, asinine lie.

Alexandra had had sex with only one man in her life: De Wolfe. He had not touched her now for the past twelve years of their marriage. She had not enjoyed sex with him when they had sex and did not know if it was because of her or him. And because she'd never had sex with another man, Alexandra did not know if he was a good lover or not. She had no means of comparison. They'd produced one child, Emilie Renata De Wolfe. Emilie was twenty-three.

Sex between her and De Wolfe had stopped suddenly like a scream in the dark. She didn't need nor want sex and had no sexual fantasies. If she had to live the rest of life untouched, without sex, barren, it would mean nothing to her. What she had now was all she knew and all she wanted in regard to sex.

It's why an opera such as *La Traviata*'s theme was so totally alien to her, of a woman dying in a man's arms and in love with him. To think that there could be a future when all she ever knew was a cold shiver whenever De Wolfe's chubby hands touched her, held her, kissed her, and injected his penis inside her for just those limited times and minutes in their marriage when he wanted sex from her, possibly finding her attractive or thought she finding him the same.

But all she waited for when she and De Wolfe did have sex was for the few minutes of it to end. For she would lie there in the bed as he frantically (huffing and puffing) fucked her thinking only of its ending, nothing more.

But she didn't feel in any way guilty that she had driven him out of their bedroom and into other women's arms or that he sought other women to fulfill himself sexually or that they had not shared the same bedroom in so many years. De Wolfe would be having affairs with different women with or without her help, she'd assumed. This was the sinful ways of rich men, her father included. It was steeped in her family, and her mother suffered. But Johanna Bauer loved her father, Oscar Bauer, in her own odd way now that, as an adult, she looked back at what she'd seen in their relationship.

But De Wolfe, maybe no woman could truly love him. Maybe he desired that. Maybe he understood love better than what she thought. That what he said in the dining room this evening, for the first time in their thirty-one-year marriage, actually came from De Wolfe's heart.

Alexandra shut off her mind and then adjusted the blinders covering her eyes, for a second.

Chapter 3

Eva Durant was waiting for De Wolfe in her luxurious bedroom on Ballad Street.

How had her day gone, it was the same weekly routine. It was the same profound look into her life and wondering if she was getting the most out of it. It was why she was on top of the bed with her back against the wide headboard, her legs spread apart, and her eyes shut questioning who Eva Durant was or, maybe, who she wanted Eva Durant to become.

She was college educated but had not finished college. She was an honors student at every level of her education. She was praised for her intellectual gifts by her teachers and professors, but when the acting bug bit her, she called on her other more racy talent, dancing (to make money), to become a showgirl, live a glitzy, glamorous life surrounded by dancehall dames and the men who squired them, and then hopefully audition for acting roles until she landed on the Great White Way.

"I want to be celebrated. An actress of my time. Set a mark of excellence in the theatrical world," Eva Durant said with deep conviction.

It's how she met De Wolfe: at the World Stage. He was a man who was known among the World Stage's regular male patrons, Eva giggled to herself. Her old roommate, Amy Dawkins's ex-roommate, Francine McCourt, had been De Wolfe's mistress. She was but one of many De Wolfe circulated through during his earlier days of debauchery at the World Stage.

They too began their affair at the Carleton Hotel like all the others. But she was the woman responsible for the building on Ballad Street, who broke the mold. De Wolfe gave it to her as a gift. "I do hold that particular status, don't I." Eva smiled, her dark eyes sparkling.

When De Wolfe bought the property for her and furnished it with all the beauty she adored, the care and attention he gave it, unmistakably, she saw the power she held over him, and how he would meet all of her creature comforts.

De Wolfe removed her from the showgirl circuit and secured a job for her as a proofreader (through her suggestion) at Masthead Publications, a publishing company. The pay was lousy, but she loved to read, so the position was a perfect fit. Besides, she had De Wolfe's wealth ensuring her financial status. So working a day job was merely an escape for her.

Being what this life as a "mistress" meant, she had no friends. And when she told Amy Dawkins of how far De Wolfe had pushed the relationship, Amy knew she'd be cut out of the picture too, that Eva's life had crossed over to a life of total privacy, and secrets, and that De Wolfe's name and reputation demanded protection at all costs.

"My secret." Tears ringed Eva's eyes. "I have held on to it for so long. With such fear, focus … trepidation."

But what she was doing was worth it. Being this sexual person for De Wolfe. Delighting him but not stealing him from his life or his wife. But she and De Wolfe having this perfect setup, this perfect place where a man with De Wolfe's power can relax and not feel pressured.

But *her* secret had politics embedded in it, a social history as if it were a running documentary of the status of America and forces out to create a liberal, progressive democracy while still, by way of the status quo, at a stumbling pace. But she felt liberated from it in this world she was a part of, that one day might bring her the fame she aspired.

For in time, she would go back to auditioning herself as an actress. As one who could command the Great White Way, Broadway, and then film, Hollywood, silent movies.

But right now she was waiting on De Wolfe. He said he'd be there by ten o'clock. It was eight forty-five. And so she got up off the bed and walked over to a table of books. She'd brought a new book in from Masthead Publications to read. But she wouldn't read it tonight. She was rereading old literary novels. She had no more than an hour to pick up where she'd left off with Charles Dickens's *A Tale of Two Cities* and then further prepare herself for her night with De Wolfe.

Before picking up the Dickens book from the small pile of books on top of the delicate table, Eva paused and thought of De Wolfe's secret, but then with sudden terror, her own.

"POLLY, YOU SHOULD KNOW EVERY crease in my top hat by now."

"You think so, Mr. De Wolfe?"

De Wolfe was going to wink at Polly, Alfredo restaurant's hat check girl, but thought of Eva, for he had not flirted innocently or otherwise with any woman since he and Eva had been together.

"I trust your instincts, Polly."

But Polly took De Wolfe's stub anyway, as she went to retrieve his items in the stuffed coat room.

De Wolfe's coat was halfway on him, when he felt a strong tap on his shoulder.

"Max!"

De Wolfe's head turned. He was looking at Jim Hawkins, a plumbing magnate.

"Hi, Jim!"

"Since I didn't get to talk to you after the meeting the other day, Max. Hell, we certainly shoved it up old man Castle's ass, didn't we!"

"Every inch of it, Jim!"

Jim Hawkins's face was craggy. He wasn't old but looked it, from his sloping shoulders to the slip of his spine. He handed his coat over to Polly and then waited for the stub. He turned back to De Wolfe.

"I had heard about him before, but it's the first time I was in negotiation with him." His face turned red. "He's an asshole! Trying to pull a quick one over on us, but you put him in his goddamned place, Max."

De Wolfe smiled.

"They call the lot of us robber barons, Max, but Castle is the worst of the lot," Hawkins said, practically choking on his cigar.

"And so what do you mean by that, Jim?" De Wolfe said, ducking a missile of smoke.

"The bastard robs from his own!"

DE WOLFE WAS IN THE black Packard.

De Wolfe was thinking of what Jim Hawkins had said back at Alfredo's. What he said and how he said it tickled him to no end. What the hell does he think rich men do! Does he think there is some sort of ethics in this circle of rich men they both navigated in and out of every single day, whether at work or in social settings? They were all thieves but on a larger scale. Being called robber barons applied to them, defined them, was more of a compliment than a curse. To deny what they did daily would deny who they were and how they made the stock market tremble from either making or not making deals, of managing the life of the nation by controlling the capitalist system to where catastrophe, collapse, or calamity lurked just around the corner if the stock market was destabilized. Men like him could sink the country by one major slip of their tremendous fortune. They could cause the stock market to reel out of control like a teetering giant.

"Did you know, Fagan, we're all asses?" De Wolfe said, as if his mouth had released a curse.

Fagan froze behind the Packard's steering wheel.

"What, no reply, Fagan. Or, my dear fellow, does it warrant one?"

Fagan Dooley looked in the Packard's rearview mirror guardedly. He knew De Wolfe wasn't tipsy, that whatever liquor he drank at Alfredo's was absorbed by his food intake. Thus, De Wolfe's eyes were clear and alert when he'd opened the car door for him.

"I do what I do, Fagan, because I am a bastard too. It's generational. Passed down from father to son." Pause. "But of course Mrs. De Wolfe and I don't have a son. A De Wolfe heir. So the De Wolfe lineage is at an end. No more bastards from the De Wolfes to spring onto the world.

"But bastards roam the earth, Fagan. Ripe, vile, alive ... and particularly savage."

Fagan Dooley never thought his job difficult—chauffeuring De Wolfe around Manhattan. Long hours was a standard part of the job (De Wolfe paid him well), but he was the personal driver of Maxwell De Wolfe. He was, in his lowly capacity as chauffeur, what seemed to him, De Wolfe's sounding board, and this exclusive function, he performed well. Being with him day after day, he was still painting a portrait of De Wolfe. At one time he had wondered if the canvas would ever be completed, but there De Wolfe was in the car's backseat calling himself a "bastard" and his father a "bastard" and practically rejoicing that the De Wolfe lineage would end in this century with him.

What men of his stature thought like him? Fagan thought. What percentage of them? But De Wolfe had just revealed another important side of himself, the side that was begging to be understood, who was trying to unwrap himself from his wealth, for he could be seen as a "bastard," but also, as a man with a heart and soul no matter how downtrodden each was.

Fagan took in a big source of air, lowered his head, and then let the air out his lungs, expeditiously.

He was driving De Wolfe off to Ballad Street, to a building he could enter with De Wolfe, but only so far. Not beyond the door at the top of the second-floor landing. Any point beyond that was off limits, was forbidden, verboten territory for him.

He had seen the other young women in De Wolfe's life, but not this one. This one was stashed away in the Ballad Street building like a hidden treasure, a gem, too exotic and wonderful to view, so all he could do was use his imagination and let it wander off to wherever, at the time, it took him.

They were on Ballad Street, and the building's light, the dull lightbulb, could be faintly seen, but for some reason, Fagan looked forward to it. Possibly this mystery was the most intriguing part of his relationship with De Wolfe, trying to figure him out while, in an odd way, trying to figure out his own fascination with his interior fantasies.

As soon as Eva got to him, coming out of the bedroom's en suite bathroom, De Wolfe kissed the back of her neck. As soon as he did, Eva began wiping his body off with the towel. His penis was sticky with scum from the sex, and she used the washcloth to attend to it. De Wolfe was spread out on the large bed whose mattress was as soft as a cloud, he'd often say. From the waist down, Eva was naked. She wore De Wolfe's white dress shirt. He touched her in her wet spot, and she reacted with a light moan.

"I can never get enough of you, Eva. I was born to fuck you."

"I believe that, Max. Fuck me ... yes."

"You do, really do?" De Wolfe said like a young, eager schoolboy.

"Yes, I do."

"I still can't believe my lucky stars," he said, his hand stopping hers from cleaning off his penis. "Considering the tramps I once bedded."

This Eva took exception to. She knew Francine McCloud, and they were not tramps as De Wolfe had just defined them.

"Eva, what's wrong?"

"Oh, nothing, Max," she said, now wiping De Wolfe's soft, chubby penis with the towel.

"Oh, I thought—"

"I'm just glad I'm here to please you, since you've done so much for me over the years."

This was another thing De Wolfe loved about Eva, her gratitude. She was vocal regarding it, making him want to do even more for her if possible.

"I'm going to return these to the bathroom," Eva said, looking at the towel and washcloth.

"Of course, Eva."

"I'll shower, Max. I won't be long."

"Take your time."

She stood and walked out of the room. She closed the bathroom door.

De Wolfe lay back on the bed but then looked at his cane. He didn't want to fall asleep, because after one good romp of sex with Eva, he easily could. He looked across the floor at the books on top of the table. De Wolfe reached for his cane, which was in easy access. He was still naked when he stood and walked over to the small pile of books.

"Hmm ..." he said, grabbing onto Beecher Stowe's *Uncle Tom's Cabin*. He carried the book back to the bed. "I wonder why ..."

De Wolfe lay back down on the bed and began scratching his beard with his pudgy fingers and then rested the book on top of his puffy stomach, balancing it there, and then laughing at what he'd done.

Minutes later Eva opened the bathroom door and was back in the bedroom. She looked across the room and saw what De Wolfe had done, the book perching perfectly still on top of his stomach.

"Why, Max ..."

And De Wolfe began laughing so hard, the book toppled off his stomach and onto the bed.

"You did look a sight," Eva said, now in a white skirt and De Wolfe's white shirt but without undergarments beneath the free-flowing black skirt.

"I must have, Eva. Hell, why not."

She cuddled up in his arms. He picked up the book with his left hand. "A slave book, Eva? Since when—"

"I'm reading old classic novels, Max. Dickens, Tolstoy, Harriet Beecher Stowe, and a few others."

De Wolfe looked at the frayed book. "This damned thing!"

She propped herself up. "You don't approve, Max?"

"Approve ... why, no, no, you know I don't interfere with anything you wish to do, Eva," De Wolfe said wide-eyed. "There's not a damned thing about you that I disapprove of." Pause. "But isn't this woman a moralist? Preaching for mankind to heal itself of its past sins induced by the very sins of slavery and white men's eager engagement in it?

"This nation's damned because of it. But what was a white man, whether he be a Southerner or Northerner, to do?"

"Yes, *Uncle Tom's Cabin* does favor that general tone, Max."

"All because of slavery and niggers?"

"Yes, Max, slavery and niggers," Eva said.

De Wolfe slammed the book down into the mattress. "I have no goddamned use for them. I wouldn't hire them for any service of any kind, even if most rich white men like me do. I just won't fucking do it!"

This kind of talk was new to Eva, but she was glad *Uncle Tom's Cabin* had sparked this kind of exchange between her and De Wolfe.

"They are a lazy lot of people. And as far as brains go ..." De Wolfe paused, for the struggle on his face suggested he was trying to organize a witty remark. "They don't go far. Not far at all." He laughed.

"By the way, Eva," De Wolfe said, picking up the book, "what do you think of them?"

"They're a strange breed, Negroes. Their race," she said, looking into De Wolfe's eyes.

"Why do you say that?"

"The little I've seen of them. It's how I'd describe them ... Negroes. Not that I know them, any, but—"

"But what you've seen of them ...?"

"Yes."

"Hell, it is a damned honest way of, to describe them. The whipping of them, now that I don't approve of. The cruelty of it. Savagery. But you do have to control, find a way of controlling them en masse, not unlike any animal. Any beast, Eva."

"'Breed,' it is the right word—"

"Yes, it is."

"Of ... in describing—"

Eva spread open her legs and rolled the white skirt up to her full, firm hips.

"Damn, if I'm not hard, got a hard-on, Eva. Damn!" De Wolfe yelped.

She rolled on top of him. De Wolfe began unbuttoning his dress shirt Eva was wearing. When he finished, and her shapely breasts with pink nipples were exposed, he knocked *Uncle Tom's Cabin* off to the floor.

Eva laughed at De Wolfe's violent slap of the book.

She understood he would come inside her again in just a matter of seconds, and then she would wipe his sticky scum from his penis with the towel and washcloth hanging on the gold-plated bar in the bathroom.

He called her a good "fuck," but he certainly wasn't. But it didn't matter, as her buttocks began rotating quickly, evenly on top of him.

"Ah ... Ah ... Ahhh ..."

She was there to satisfy him, to take the pressure off of De Wolfe after a rough day in the office, she thought. She fully understood her role in De Wolfe's private life and why it was necessary, the sex conducted between them.

Chapter 4

De Wolfe was off the elevator, Fagan Dooley still on it heading down to the car garage, and De Wolfe had handed Helga his articles of clothing.

"By golly, where is she, Helga? Ms. Emilie!"

"In her bedroom, Mr. De Wolfe."

"Of course, of course, where else!"

De Wolfe charged out of the foyer and toward the mansion's grand staircase. It was a staircase that curved seductively as if following the wall's masterly paintings of great art leading to the second floor's long hallway. Now on the second floor, De Wolfe's ever-present limp was not hindering his movement either mentally or physically, for De Wolfe had a huge appetite to see his daughter, Emilie Renata De Wolfe, a dynamo of a girl.

Rap.

"Father!"

"Emilie!"

Emilie Renata De Wolfe was a homely girl of twenty-three but had a knock-out figure. She was taller than her father, gaining the edge from her mother's lineage, not De Wolfe's. She blinked excessively, abnormally so, and spoke with a terrible lisp. Emilie De Wolfe had a brilliant mind. She had Alexandra De Wolfe's blazing red hair.

"Come in, Father!"

It was another enormous room of abundant fineries and exquisite taste. Vases, Emilie De Wolfe loved vases, small and tall. Vases at the foot of her bed. Vases in various corners of the room. They were imported from around the world and gave the room an enormous sense of presence. Flowers bloomed from each vase. The room's aroma, a variety of sweet, captivating scents directed from different locations in the room.

"You're back from your trip abroad, Emilie!" De Wolfe said, holding on to his daughter's hand.

"Yes, Father. And there's always such a thrill when I leave New York for adventure and then upon my return back home."

"But Paris again, Emilie, I thought Spain—"

"I'm still the romantic," Emilie said, she and De Wolfe sitting on a settee near the bed that occupied the center of the room. "I can't get Paris out of my blood, Father."

De Wolfe kissed his daughter's hand and then held her face, kissing her cheek.

"Oh, Father, you make me blush so."

The one good thing De Wolfe would quickly admit that came from his marriage to a Bauer was his daughter Emilie. She was born into fortune and measured up to the prestige and privilege of it quite naturally. She was born to be a rich man's daughter, the aloofness she could dispatch to any social gathering, and her tempered charms vainly displaying (like a Hope Diamond) she was Maxwell Engelbert De Wolfe's daughter.

"Did you fall in love while there, Emilie?"

"Many times." Emilie giggled. "It is a habit of mine, I'm afraid, Father."

De Wolfe laughed too. "All rich young ladies like you, Emilie, fall in love at least five or six times a year." De Wolfe laughed. "Am I not mistaken?"

Emilie giggled again. "At least as many, Father. But to count accurately would make the exercise mundane, not fun or at all exhilarating."

"And it must be fun, mustn't it, Emilie. Exhilarating. Particularly at your tender age."

She was a meticulous dresser, one who favored jewelry, gems, and sapphire worn around her slender, swanlike neck, on her thin wrists, in her large earlobes. Her face was as pale as a ghost's, but with lots of makeup and dazzling adornment, Emilie De Wolfe flirted with the illusion of appeal.

"I missed you," De Wolfe said, his chin dropping down onto his hands holding the cane. "I always do when you leave on your three-week holidays abroad," De Wolfe said, with sad eyes.

"Thank you, Father. I always need that encouragement of my value to this family. It certainly does not come from Mother."

"Yes, your mother," De Wolfe said, clearing his throat. "She never had your advantages, Emilie. The money, yes," De Wolfe said, staring blankly out into space, "but not the advantages you modern young ladies of the twentieth century have and take for granted."

"But she shouldn't be jealous of me, should she, Father?" Emilie said, pouting.

"No, she shouldn't."

"Then you do agree."

De Wolfe mulled over his answer, but only for a second or two. "Yes, I do, Emilie. Of course it's at play. Of course jealously influences her relationship with you. Your course of interaction with her."

"She's a, a damned iceberg, Father!"

"Now, Emilie," De Wolfe admonished her, "we mustn't be too harsh with your mother."

"Well, I saw her," Emilie said, standing, "and we exchanged hugs and kisses, the superficiality of the moment. Then I came to my room to wait for you. After Carla brought the luggage up to the room."

Carla, an older German woman, was Emilie's private servant.

"And what time was that?"

"Oh, a little past four."

It was six fifty-six.

37

"So that's over with," Emilie said.

De Wolfe knew Emilie would make it feel like duty, the courtesy she had passed on to Alexandra, her mother, after three weeks abroad.

"You must be famished then," De Wolfe said, charging to his feet.

"I am, Father!" Emilie said, grabbing De Wolfe's arm.

THEY'D EATEN ANOTHER FABULOUS MEAL prepared by their chef, Jules, and served by his wife, Yvette. The net of silence was about to be broken, no matter that Emilie was eating with them, it made no difference in the rigid ritual of the De Wolfe family at the broad-sweeping dining room table.

"Emilie, your trip," De Wolfe began. "Tell your mother and me all about it. Everything. All of it."

"But I must warn you, Father, I can't sit too long. I will spend the night with Rosalind."

"Rosalind! But why, Emilie? You spent three weeks abroad in her company every—"

"There are things that we have yet discussed, Father," Emilie said cryptically.

De Wolfe threw his napkin down on top of the table. "Women, young or old, gossip is your chief motivation. The unfinished conversations, thoughts, sentences …"

"We are philosophical creatures, Father. Even if it is nothing but sheer gossip and repetition at stake." Pause. "To us, it does matter, dearly."

Alexandra sat at the table dabbing her mouth with the napkin, her quiet presence unchanged.

"We must catch up with items back here in the States. It will not only be Rosalind—"

"But the others too," De Wolfe said, as if he were speaking of a herd of sheep.

"Yes, we all take a part. It is such fun," Emilie said, clapping her hands. "When we come off one of our overseas jaunts."

"I will pardon myself, if you two don't—"

"Stay, Alexandra. There's no reason for you to leave."

Emilie sat in the middle of the dining room table. A guilty feeling struck her, for with all of her heart she wished she had a good, personable relationship with her mother, a loving one. She knew her heart was good, a generous one, but her mother was an iceberg, she laughed to herself, someone she couldn't unthaw.

"Yes, Mother, stay, I will highlight the trip, if nothing more. The sights and sounds of it. The loveliness of each encounter."

ALEXANDRA HAD RETIRED FOR HER bedroom, but De Wolfe and Emilie were still at the dining room table. It was eight five. Emilie said she would ring her chauffeur, Xavier, in a matter of minutes to dispatch her to Rosalind's doorstep. Rosalind Le Grand was an uptown rich girl, Fifty-eighth and Fifth Avenue.

They were laughing practically as if they would die from it, and then the laughter receded.

"Emilie, can't you call Rosalind, tell her tomorrow night. That tonight's too special for us."

Panic gripped Emilie. "No, Father, I …"

"But, Emilie, darling …"

"I'm sorry, but Rosalind is so much looking forward to my company tonight, along with the other girls. They're all so excited by us being back with—"

"New tales to tell." De Wolfe laughed. "Oh, go ahead, my bleeding heart can wait until tomorrow night when I'll have you all to myself."

Emilie got up from the table and ran to him, hugging De Wolfe around his shoulders.

"I love you, Father!"

"And I you, Emilie!"

D<small>E</small> W<small>OLFE</small> <small>KNOCKED ON</small> A<small>LEXANDRA'S</small> door. Elsa opened the door.

"Would you tell Mrs. De Wolfe that I'd like to see her in my bedroom, Elsa."

"Yes, Mr. De Wolfe."

De Wolfe moved down the hallway. He was smoking a cigar, and suddenly he let the pain in his left leg erupt, for he wished to feel it throb, to remind himself of how it was damaged on the White Star shipping line's ship, the *Teutonic*. Eight years ago he took a misstep on the ship's gangway that spilled him. His knee jammed into an iron railing. The accident permanently damaged the leg, putting De Wolfe on (illegally) opium. But there came a time when De Wolfe had had enough of opium and set his mind on defeating the searing pain in his leg, which he had.

The pain in his leg he was feeling in his heart. It's why he would talk to Alexandra in his bedroom. Clear the air with her, as it were. Do something he should have done long ago, but tonight he felt more of a responsibility to it than he ever had in the past.

De Wolfe's bedroom was imposing. A double pedestal cherrywood desk was in the room (even if it was small, it was still elegant). De Wolfe moved over to the desk, for he expected Alexandra to sit in the velvet striped cushioned chair. The shaded desk lamp provided a shaft of light that sat on De Wolfe's baggy face, his eyes focusing in on what was at hand.

A knock he anticipated came from the door.

"Come in, Alexandra."

Alexandra entered the room after dismissing Elsa. She made her way across the room, her back straight, supported by a supple spine that had not lost its fitness or authority no matter her sallow skin and aging unhappiness.

De Wolfe's hands were folded out in front of him, planted solidly to the desk.

"I've come as you asked, Maxwell," Alexandra said in a dry, controlled voice as slowly she took to the chair.

"Thank you."

Silence.

The shaft of light shone on De Wolfe's bearded skin. He scratched at his dark beard and then settled back in the chair.

"We do have a daughter, you know, Alexandra." Pause. "She does have two parents in this household, not one."

"She loves you, not me."

"How outrageous!"

"Outrageous, I find it nothing of the kind," Alexandra said, her eyes bearing in on De Wolfe.

"You are a mother. You bore a child. When does the motherly instinct begin, if not at conception?"

She didn't expect this subject matter or for it to be so direct. To be honest, she didn't know what to expect, to be called into De Wolfe's bedroom at this hour and to talk of all things Emilie, their daughter.

"I am a cold person. Your daughter calls me an 'iceberg,'" Alexandra said matter of fact. "It's no secret in the household. It hasn't been kept from you or—"

"I have grown tired, exhausted of this estrangement between you two, Alexandra. Simply tired, disgusted by it."

"Your daughter's happy, Maxwell. Emilie has her friends, her life. She's gone off to be with them tonight. She doesn't suffer from—"

"You must do better with her. I will no longer stand for this in my—"

"You, Maxwell"—she glared at him—"will not order me to do anything. Of how to use my time—not anything!"

41

He rushed to his feet, and his face was out of the light, and he looked at this cold woman with this cold heart of hers and suddenly wondered how much he, Maxwell De Wolfe, had contributed to it.

"Have you ever loved me?" He'd sat back down.

"Don't ask me that."

"Have you ever needed love, Alexandra?"

"Must I recite some poem to you, when you are as callous regarding love as me? We've both lived in a soulless, godless world, Maxwell. You and your money, your great wealth, and me, and ..."

"And, and!"

"I have no feelings. I just count my days." Her eyes angled away from De Wolfe. "I count them like you count your money. Like my father counted his. But I am not saddened by the fact. Because I have never imagined another life, Maxwell. An alternate version.

"You must understand this. My mother tried too, but it failed. It all collapsed around her like a great house of cards." Alexandra laughed aloud. "You and I have witnessed the great failure of other people's lives. Our parents, Maxwell, firsthand.

"They lived this life too, the trashiness of it. We all die the same in the end. Our final days when death penetrates us. When we are summoned."

ALEXANDRA HAD LEFT DE WOLFE'S room. De Wolfe was in a sweat. Alexandra had left him pot-boiling mad. But once his temper had cooled, a different mood surfaced to afflict him: he became afraid. What had he and his father Florentz De Wolfe built but a financial dynasty. But what had Alexandra left him with, something that felt, to him, like ruin, rubble sifting through his fingers.

"She is an iceberg. An old hag."

But how could he dismiss her lightly if she had looked into the heart of his wealth and found there was no God there? That it shone like the desk lamp's light he stared into, like the gold De Wolfe & Fitch traded on the stock market trading floor daily? But like any man's life, it rose and fell. But he, Maxwell Engelbert De Wolfe, would one day die.

De Wolfe fell back in the chair. "I feel alone, and lonely."

One day, De Wolfe thought, every man must look back at his life. "When do I? Now? Later? On my deathbed? Just when?" Pause.

"She travels through life haunted. She is a hollow woman. She spends all of her awake time inside the mansion. In her room. Alexandra De Wolfe. S-she lives like this and is unafraid of the unknown.

"All I wished for tonight was to discuss Emilie's place in this family. To bridge the gap between them and breathe new life into this old, stale, miserable mansion."

De Wolfe squeezed both hands together.

"But so little of my time is spent here. De Wolfe & Fitch, Eva, social activities, and here, here in my room. My room ..."

He was afraid of what Alexandra was not: old age, infirmity, and ineffectiveness. "She wants to die. Dying does not matter to her. This cruel thing that befalls us."

De Wolfe was afraid to die, to one day be forgotten. It did have clarity. It did render rot. It did end expectation. It did matter.

EMILIE HAD BEEN DISHONEST WITH her father, but it in no way upset her. She loved him, but lies were what a family such as hers, the De Wolfes, did. The De Wolfes negotiated with each other; it's the practical wisdom she'd come away with living under her parents' roof. Truth can be compromised, she thought. Lies, though, could never be overvalued. She'd lied to him tonight for good reason. It was not Rosalind Le Grand she was to visit tonight to gab with her girlfriends, but someone dangerous, erotic, exciting.

Xavier, her chauffeur, had the address where she was to be driven. Since he was under her supervision, he answered to her, no one else in the De Wolfe family. He had no contact with her father or mother as she had none with Fagan or Reinhard (her mother's private chauffeur). These private chauffeurs were not permitted to converse with each other, and if ever it was discovered they had, they'd be fired posthaste, without recourse. So tonight's adventure would not be compromised or whispered about.

Her heart beat wildly. Her plan, until now, had worked delightfully. She felt so alive and clever, so much in love with her life and what she had found in Paris, in a small, quaint bookshop that held no pretension of fortune or treasure for discovery inside its walls, but there was, and it shone gleamingly at first sighting, this—

"We're here, Xavier. The Martinique Hotel," Emilie said, as if she had to say it to someone, her excitement ablaze like a house on fire.

Xavier was waved forward by the Martinique Hotel's valet dressed in a blue tailored uniform with a hat to match, with bulked gold braiding laced across its short, shiny bill.

Xavier, a tall, alert man, stepped out of the car and opened the passenger-side door. He removed Emilie's small piece of luggage. He handed it to the valet and then walked with a certain rigidity and grandeur to where Emilie sat waiting in the car and opened the door for her, and when she exited the car, Emilie's face exploded like a pile of fireworks.

"Thank you, Xavier."

"You are welcome, ma'am."

"You'll return by noon tomorrow."

"Yes, Ms. De Wolfe. By noon tomorrow."

"That will be all, Xavier." Emilie turned her head to the young valet holding her bag. "I'm in good hands."

On the hotel's third floor, in a hotel only the well-to-do could afford, she was a whirlwind of extreme emotions, and she felt the long dress that hugged her hips hug them even tighter.

"You may put the suitcase down on the floor," Emilie said. She and the bellhop had reached suite 306.

"That is all, ma'am?"

Emilie opened her purse and handed the bellhop his tip.

"Thank you, ma'am," he said, not looking down at the money, knowing he'd been well tipped.

Emilie stood at the door until the bellhop cleared the floor.

Now her heart began beating insanely, one big timpani-loud sound after another.

"Oh … oh …"

Emilie glanced at the lion-headed brass door knocker.

Knock.

The door sprang open.

"Juan Manuel!"

"Emilie!"

Emilie grabbed Juan Manuel Pagan before he could lift her luggage off the floor.

"Darling, darling!"

The door shut quickly. Juan Manuel Pagan, when he set the luggage down on the plush midnight blue rug, turned to her again, and his dark Spanish eyes bore into her eyes, and Emilie thought she might faint, but instead, she grabbed him again, this six-foot, athletic-looking Spaniard who spoke five languages.

Emilie quickly kissed his handsome olive-skinned face, a face that any century of man would desire to own to conquer a continent of women, as did Don Juan (the Seducer of Seville), for seduction and myth and legend.

"Come into the living room, Emilie!"

They coupled their hands and walked over to the sleigh couch and sat.

"Your fur, Emilie, it is mine to take from your shoulders."

"Yes, my fur," Emilie said as if it had become an annoyance.

"I do not have to find the closet," Juan Manuel said, removing her sable off her shoulder. She handed him her Ivanhoe deep-purple colored hat.

"Then you have settled in, Juan Manuel?"

"Very much so, Emilie. Where I stay," Juan Manual Pagan said, looking around the vast room, "this place, it is a dream for me."

"For you, my darling. All of this is for you and only you."

"Pardon."

"Of course."

Juan Manuel Pagan went off with the two items in tow.

They'd met in Paris in the Le Figaro bookstore. She looked up from a book she was holding, and his eyes, and his long, silky black hair, drove her mad from the start. When he smiled, it crushed any thoughts of her ever forgetting him. And since she spoke French too, she began to converse in the Romance language, but Juan Manuel knew she was an American right off, and so he spoke in English, not French, and it drove her more mad the more he spoke.

Coffee in a café and several nights together had now led to this, of Juan Manuel Pagan traveling back to the States with her and Rosalind. Of Juan Manuel becoming her lover, for they'd had sex in Paris—a lot.

Juan Manuel was dressed in a black suit Emilie had bought him in Paris. His white dress shirt's three top buttons were unbuttoned. A tiny nest of black hair sat on his broad chest. He wore two gold rings on each hand.

"I come back to you, Emilie," Juan Manuel said, returning to the elegantly arranged room.

Emilie swooned. "I am a schoolgirl now, Juan Manuel," she said, her eyes blinking furiously.

"You are no different than me: an innocent schoolboy in short pants."

He was holding her again.

"But we are not innocent, Juan Manuel, we are in love."

"Qui, Emilie. Qui."

"How did I find you?"

"How, I do not know. It is my mystery too, I think."

Her hand ran through his soft silky hair. "I am elsewhere tonight, Juan Manuel, not here with you."

"Yes, you tell me—"

"My parents will not know of you, not until I tell them. Of course they would not—"

"Approve. *Mais qui.* I am no more than a playboy. Is that what I am called here, in America? A gigolo?"

Emilie brushed her face against his. "Yes. But I don't care. We are who we are, Juan Manuel."

"I do not know … And, and what is that to mean, Emilie?" Juan Manuel asked, stuttering. "W-what you just tell me?"

Emilie took a satisfying swallow, so it seemed. "We'll find our way together." Pause. "You have come this far already so you can be with me. Across the Atlantic."

"Of course, Emilie."

"It is a price you have already paid. Me taking you away from Paris. Your home. Your work."

"My art, Emilie," Juan Manuel said, grabbing his heart dramatically.

She took his hand, placing it in hers. "Your beautiful hands, Juan Manuel."

Juan Manuel was a talented but struggling artist. He'd shown Emilie his artwork, and she thought him a great artist in keeping with Madrid's (Juan Manuel's birthplace) tradition of a city of great art, and great artists. He'd been studying art and selling it in Paris for six years, according to him.

"I must always admire them, Emilie." Juan Manuel's eyes were fixated on his hands too. "They make the art. Like a dancer her feet. They are my talent like my heart. They feel and love the art together. And the eyes, they see the beauty of everything. They are what make Juan Manuel Pagan. This body I own on this earth."

"The body I want!"

"But it is I who want you—"

"It will be our first fuck in America!"

"Yes, *qui*, the first fuck as you say, but not—"

"The last!"

Up off the couch, Juan Manuel was already undressing Emilie as she groped his penis.

"Oh yes, Juan Manuel! Yes!"

Her vagina, covered by the thick red bush of hair, was so wet she thought she was bleeding, having her monthly menstruation, but she wanted him, her Spanish lover, the man whose trip across the Atlantic she'd paid for, whose new clothes she'd bought, whose suite at the Martinique Hotel she'd paid for.

They hadn't gotten to the bedroom suite, that gaudy room, but were down on the floor, Emilie, her eyes blinking madly, screaming.

"Fuck me, Juan Manuel! Fuck me, fuck me!"

"I fuck you, Emilie! I fuck, fuck you!"

And Juan Manuel was doing this with all his might, with each inch of his hard prick, while his beautiful silky black hair sweat, some of it sweeping over his dark eyes as his body strained and jerked to contain the scum that was sure to come, but not before Emilie had her orgasm, was totally satisfied by him, her Spanish lover who had just crossed the Atlantic Ocean to be with her in America.

Chapter 5

Eva was on 125th Street in Harlem.

She'd gotten to Harlem by subway. It was a Saturday, her day off from Masthead Publications. Today would be a busy one. She was carrying an armful of groceries. She was being extremely careful with them, but there were so many Negroes crammed on 125th Street, not bumping into someone was more of a necessity than a feat.

For a community of mostly poor black folk, the Negroes in Harlem knew how to "style" themselves in a way—to Eva's way of thinking—that tipped over into exoticism. Clothes and fashion were like a tonic that temporarily cured the aches and pains of these people's day. There were hungry, starving children in this village of Harlem, but all was forgotten when a new pair of shoes or tie or blouse was bought by hard-earned money, admired, teased over, bought, and hunger was someone else's problem, not the person standing in front of the mirror who only saw what they wanted to see reflect back to them.

Eva had gotten over to 130th Street between Lenox and Seventh Avenue. She visited Harlem once a month. It was always on a Saturday, as routine. She'd spend three hours in Harlem, no more.

Trash cans bordered the stoop of the tenement located in the middle of the block. She looked up to the fourth floor. The tenement had lost most of its youthful color yet stood in the ground tenaciously rooted. A cold blast of a winter wind cut across Eva's face. Eva wore a brand-new beaver-striped hat.

When Eva shut the building's front door, it's when she felt immediate relief. The chill was still in her, but she removed her leather gloves after putting the bag of groceries down on the vestibule's cracked floor. Eva gathered her emotions and tried to separate (as always) who she was from where she was, this extreme dichotomy in her life she could do nothing about, for she was a loyal daughter to her mother, someone who loved her but had not moved on, forward, but still lived responsibly and within her small, meager means.

Eva was on the fourth floor of the walk-up apartment building. After tapping on the door, she waited for her mother to open the neglected door whose doorknob had rusted, not to the point of disgust, but to the point of a landlord's needed attention.

"Eva, darling."

"Mother."

Lilly Durant was creamy complexioned like Eva with straight black hair, and a fifty-two-year-old face that had not tired of its beauty.

"Come in, Eva. You're punctual, as usual."

Eva was in the apartment's compact living room with Lilly Durant, there being no vestibule or hallway, just the accessibility of a living room with decent-looking furniture that mixed and matched. Even if it was early afternoon, two lamps burned in the room. A shaded floor lamp and a porcelain table lamp. A slightly raised window produced fresh air.

"Groceries for me, Eva?" Lilly Durant said as Eva handed her the bag of groceries.

"For you and only you, Mother."

"Let's get into the kitchen."

Eva laughed.

The living room was wallpapered, but the kitchen wall was painted a dark chocolate.

Eva took to a chair as Lilly began putting away the foodstuffs. She knew her mother would rather do this without her help. She was an independent woman, proud, outspoken, and kind. She was a woman who could be anything she wanted to be, but her background had led her to Harlem, to domestic work.

"There," Lilly Durant said, wiping her hands clean.

The kitchen was tiny, but the table with the two chairs was adequate for comfortable sitting.

Eva had removed her coat in the living room.

"You are still with Maxwell De Wolfe?" Lilly asked without any warning.

"Yes, I am, Mother."

Lilly looked away from her, recoiled, and then looked back at her. "I am your only real social contact that has any meaning ... am I right, Eva?"

"Yes, Mother."

Lilly wore a purple blouse and granny shoes and looked more pious, at times, than beautiful when she spoke to Eva in this manner and tone of voice. "It's all you want out of life?"

"For now, Mother, yes, it is."

Lilly took Eva's hand. "I am judging you because I am your mother. The last six months of knowing of this sexual arrangement you have with this wealthy man has not been easy on me, Eva. There are many urgent concerns and worries in my heart."

Eva had not told Lilly the truth about her relationship with De Wolfe, chopping off a total of two years from it.

"I didn't want to worry you, Mother. That's all. I set out to be an actress," Eva said, her dark eyes near tears, "not a showgirl."

"I know, just like I thought your father would take care of me, not abandon you and Dorrell."

Dorrell Phillip Durant was Eva's older brother by two years. He and Eva were the only children from Lilly's failed marriage to Renaldo Edward Durant.

"You were disappointed by my choice at the time."

"Old men enjoy young ladies who frolic on stage half naked," Lilly said bluntly, her head wagging. "Who show off their young, desirable bodies. Something you've had since your youth."

It was an everyday modesty Eva had to subscribe to when young, but as a teenager her mother had seen her nude firsthand, the blossoming of sudden womanhood.

"You've never mentioned his age, Eva, but you don't have to."

"I don't know his age, Mother. Mr. De Wolfe has not told—"

"You mean 'Max,' don't you?" Lilly said, with a sharp tongue.

"I, yes, I do call him 'Max.' Yes, Mother."

"Someone as wealthy as him wants you to call him 'Max.'" Pause. "Bring himself down to your level, as if extending some charity to you," Lilly said with sarcasm and an arrogant brush of her hand across the tiny table's surface.

"They look at life that way. I know them since I work for them. There are always two sides of them. Maxwell De Wolfe's no different."

Pause.

"There's no God in his world, is there, Eva—only himself, is—"

"Must we, Mother, today," Eva said, irritated, "continue with this?"

"Simply put, I want more for you, Eva," Lilly said, taking hold of Eva's hand with a true desperation. "You are lonely. Alone. There, there is no substitute, Eva, for a real life."

"I am nothing of the sort, k-kind," Eva said, yanking her hand out of Lilly's. "You don't live my life, Mother, only I do."

"You have been educated. I saw to that despite—"

"Don't talk to me about education, when you're talking about my life, Mother. Condemning it. Insulting what has been my choice of how I am living it."

Lilly began rocking in the squeaky chair with her arms locked hard to her chest.

"Why do you do that!"

And Lilly stopped rocking, for she knew to what Eva had referred. "I am lonely, alone too. As you are. But I am fifty-two, not twenty-four. Not in the prime of my life. I have lived life. The bitterness of it, and its sweetness.

"But you, Eva. My darling Eva," Lilly said, looking up to Eva, who stood over her in the small kitchen, "have barely lived, yet are living someone else's life, not your own, but Maxwell De Wolfe's."

"I'm leaving, Mother," Eva said, taking a few steps backward. "I'm not staying my usual time with … What is normal for … between us."

"Then go, Eva, go. How can I stop you."

"You can't."

"And why would I want to. You don't live here anymore. Under my roof. Neither do you or your brother anymore. You live elsewhere, Eva. Belong to another world that doesn't want you."

EVA WAS IN THE BACKSEAT of the car, and today's brief confrontation with her mother continued to echo back to her. She was in a taxi, dependable, reliable. De Wolfe hired the White Dot taxicab service to drive her to any of their prearranged rendezvous outside of the Ballad building. This was one of those nights. A Saturday night when the snow had just begun to blow around in the wind that had carved its way through Manhattan.

She was in a fur and jewels and wanted to feel special but didn't. Her mother had set up shop in her head, and she would open and close her eyes and still see her, engage her mother's place in her life; and the many mirrors on the wall in her bedroom didn't lie to her either, this life she was living that didn't belong to her but De Wolfe, that her mother explained to her in plain but brutal language.

She was already visualizing this night out with De Wolfe. Of her participation in it in the speakeasy, the Ragtime, where the taxi was driving her off to. Tonight she and De Wolfe would sit at a nightclub table with a candle glowing in a glass in a dark room in a private setting (for they were not to be seen by anyone) and listen to live music come out of the adjacent room, and she'd drink the best of the Ragtime's wines and De Wolfe its best gins, and after he went to the bathroom, the night at the Ragtime would end for them. De Wolfe would leave the Ragtime in his Packard and she in a taxi. And if De Wolfe was up for sex, they'd rendezvous back at the Ballad building.

What she felt right now was not normal but crazy. Not someone who had space in her life, but margins. Her mother, in one afternoon, had taken whatever joy she thought she had out of her life, had driven an iron spike in it.

She wanted to talk to herself like she did back in her place, but there was the question of discretion, the taxicab driver in the car, who wouldn't let her be alone when she, ironically, most needed it. But now she was beginning to produce a formula, an outline in her mind to present to De Wolfe, to bring to some kind of justification for him to act on it if only he would.

But how much should she push him, Eva thought, to do something he'd not suggested of extending to her before? But Eva knew what so many rich men like him do for their mistresses, their women in waiting to heal their countless stresses and aches of the days and nights that they spend waiting on them. How they must routinely bring their bodies to their bed for their source of rejuvenation. The power of the boardroom to the bedroom.

It was their job.

SMOKE PASTED THE ROOM'S AIR. It wasn't just De Wolfe's smoke, but a combination of his and the other private rooms set in the back of the Ragtime's main room.

The Ragtime was one of many illegally operated speakeasies in New York City (the Limelight included). Prohibition had produced corruption (police payoffs), enabling rich men (De Wolfe) to indulge in illegal drinking without the penalty of the law. The "moralist" crusaders of the '20s had half won the long, contentious battle of forever ridding America's great thirst for alcohol and its purported ruination of American society. Society's will and government's will had collided head-on to hammer out America's future ethos.

De Wolfe twirled the fat cigar between his fingertips and then looked at Eva for what was probably the fiftieth time with an admiration that practically bordered on conceit that this woman, who was seated at the nightclub table with him, belonged exclusively to him.

The glow on her face from the orangey candlelight's flame unsettled him, again.

"You look ravishing this evening, Eva. But"—he'd noticed some apparent edginess about her tonight—"there's been worry on that pretty face of yours tonight," he said, touching her skin. "Or am I pretending to see something I shouldn't?"

She still hadn't figured out how she was going to tell De Wolfe what had been weighting down her mind since her Harlem visit.

"No, you're not, Max."

De Wolfe withdrew his hand. "Then …"

Eva had not had a moment in her life like this with De Wolfe, where she would express her feelings with deliberateness, calculation, for she must not act with force or demand, not with him.

"I am not unhappy, Max. I—"

"But to even use the word 'unhappy' in the context of being happy or not, Eva, in a sentence, you're still creating a contrast. An opposite condition that—"

"Max," Eva said, bowing her head, "it's not something I'm doing consciously, deliberately?" She'd said it, anxiously.

"No, of course you aren't, Eva. No, you're not."

"It, well, it just came out that way."

She wanted to control her caution but was doing a terrible job of it, she thought.

"Would you want to begin, try again?" De Wolfe asked, extinguishing the cigar in the ashtray.

"Yes."

He looked at her now as a daughter, not his mistress. He saw her youth, the inexperience that had not yet ripened into experience, that her character was sadly lacking. This was what happens in these kinds of situations, De Wolfe wisely thought, when a man of his age is fascinated by young women, which he, unashamedly, was. These are the awkward moments that crop up, where the older man must guide youth in a way that does not upset the proverbial applecart: make things worse, not better.

"Then ..."

Her lips trembled. "I was thinking of us, M-Max."

"That's always a good thing to know." De Wolfe laughed.

"But more in a way of what we do together s-socially."

"Do, socially?"

"Do ... or, or don't do, Max."

De Wolfe scratched his beard. "Now I'm confused, Eva, with the direction this conversation's taking on. Damn if I'm not."

"I love this place, the Ragtime," she gushed, "w-when we meet here. Y-you and I. I-I just love it!"

"Yes," De Wolfe said guardedly, "and, and so do I, Eva. Hell, when we step out the shadows, you mean." He laughed.

Eva's body looked as if it were about to shrink.

"And, and ..."

"I appreciate everything you do for me. Keep doing for me, Max. I-I am not ungrateful. I'm not!"

De Wolfe saw tears in her eyes.

"Hell, whoever said you were, E—"

"But I want to travel, Max. T—"

"Travel!"

"Yes!"

"You mean, with me!"

"Yes, Max, with you. You!" Tears streaked down Eva's cheeks.

De Wolfe looked around the room to see if there was anyone (possibly their personal waiter) looking on, even if he and Eva were the only ones in the room, the dark having muted the candlelight's orangey glow, making it pleasing only for the appetite of lovers and their privacy.

"I … I am speechless … Beyond words. Am quite …"

Eva was wiping her nose with a handkerchief.

"You are my mistress, Eva, not my damned wife," De Wolfe said in a scolding voice. "You do not make demands on me that not even my wife, Alexandra De Wolfe, can make."

Eva was dabbing her eyes and, when through, sniffed and then said. "W-what do I mean to you, Max!"

It was as if De Wolfe had been shot out of his suit of skin. "Mean to me—I love you!" He snatched her hand. "Love you!"

Her head dropped, and inwardly, she laughed subtly to herself.

"I, you, you want to travel abroad with me, then? Y-you and I?"

"I … only if—"

"Say it. Then say it!"

"Yes, yes, I do!"

His hand was hot, it's what Eva felt from it. "Men like you, who are in relationships like ours, Max—"

"Yes, I know their habits, dalliances, Eva, these men. T-their whims as well as you," De Wolfe said with some trepidation. "What men like me do. They travel abroad with their mistresses on holiday. Fun. Relaxation. Europe. Damnit. T-take the transatlantic route."

De Wolfe reached for the stubbed, extinguished cigar in the ashtray as if he were reaching for a life raft. The expression that slipped over his face was contemplative.

"Rarely have Mrs. De Wolfe and I traveled aboard." De Wolfe sighed. "Hell, way back in the past." Pause. "It's Emilie who, for many years, has been my steady, excellent companion on such trips. Has taken on Mrs. De Wolfe's role, splendidly. My daughter Emilie.

"Germany, Italy, England, France. Belgium. She has provided me great comfort during those trips abroad. Great relief too."

"I-I don't know that world, Max."

De Wolfe grimaced. His insides churned. He didn't know this feeling, to subject himself to someone he called his mistress for over two years now. Who had not asked for much since he'd given her so much, taken care of her every need, whim, but this was entirely different, had struck a tender chord in him he neither could dismiss nor ridicule.

"How much thought have you given—"

"Little, very, very little, Max."

De Wolfe was tickled pink by Eva's uncomplicated, simple response.

"Then it's more of an impulsive idea, cooked up on your part, Eva? Something loosely thought out, but, but strongly felt."

"Yes."

"Like a strong, unabated urge of some kind—can I say that?"

She shook her head. "I don't know, Max. Honestly, I don't." Pause.

"Then done!"

"Done!"

"Yes, you've convinced me." De Wolfe smiled indulgently. "You are in love, Eva. That's when someone like you, a tender-hearted young girl such as you takes flight. Fall into this pitfall. T-this romance for the moment. Its spontaneity and total joy. It has an unstoppable, unbendable will to it. Appeal.

"A-a rapture someone like me, an older man of my age and clear bearing can only provide. Not a young man of youth and vigor but who stumbles about in the world lost. Hell no. But me, Eva: someone of experience, ambition, and power. Who has made the world for you not empty but exciting. Not a goddamned dustbin, but thrilling beyond all walls, all horizons of imagination.

"Maxwell De Wolfe, Eva!" De Wolfe said brassily. "De Wolfe!"

Eva touched the rhinestone earring in her earlobe as if to make contact with something, a reality, not a fantasy De Wolfe had just danced around. De Wolfe had extolled false emotions, his, not hers. Her mother, this afternoon in Harlem, scared her. She showed her the other side of the coin, of just how much control Maxwell De Wolfe had over her. Tonight, she was reacting to it in what, she'd assessed, was the only courageous way available.

She'd wanted De Wolfe to hear her out, to listen to an idea she had, came up with in hoping to mitigate his power, where she didn't feel limited, small, and useless, at least for one night in De Wolfe's presence. But he had taken things and twisted them to his advantage anyway by putting love first and her second.

De Wolfe had won, again.

DE WOLFE LOOKED INTO THE bathroom mirror in the mansion, grinning into it, obsessively.

"Eva, she had me going there for a while. I actually thought she might be becoming restless … Hmmm …"

De Wolfe had chosen not to go back to Eva's place. De Wolfe & Fitch, it wasn't open for business on Saturday, but it did not stop him nor Cyrille Fitch from being in the office for most of the day, poring over reports.

Fitch had just as much energy as him. At times he felt he was in direct competition with him, and he thought it healthy to have this quiet competition between two such competitively friendly men.

"That goddamned Fitch!"

How could he stop thinking of Eva and her happiness? How could he? It meant everything to him, and he was going to make certain he'd never take it for granted.

De Wolfe turned away from the mirror and sat down on a lovely Chinese stool by the bathroom door. "You don't make a mistake with a woman like Eva Durant, no matter her youth."

De Wolfe paused after he'd yawned wide and long. "Damn if …" It was Emilie this time. Emilie had shot through his brain.

"She's at Rosalind Le Grand's place. How many nights has it been since she's come off that damned Parisian trip with her? Damned many!"

She ran her life her way, independent of her parents. Neither he nor Alexandra had a say in it since Emilie was a De Wolfe and had unlimited access to any and everything she wanted without her creating a stir mostly because she'd been trained in the ways of the rich, but also because of the smart way she conducted her affairs: calm, cool, and confident.

"Hell, if my daughter were a male, not a female, she'd be running my damned business. Even at her young, tender age, goddamnit!"

De Wolfe really believed this. There were telling signs that she had all the necessary assets in her to do just that.

"But women don't belong in business. The workplace. Mix in men's affairs. Not a goddamned one of them. Never. Just like they shouldn't have the damned vote. Have any such responsibility. It gets me steamed. They're too emotional. Fragilely constructed. Even Emilie. It's their particular undoing. Achilles' heel. Inferiority." Pause.

"Women should live a nun's life, but with sex!" De Wolfe chuckled.

These days, Emilie was in and out of the house. She was like a ghost. And he himself didn't want to be terribly emotional regarding these occurrences, but her being in the house at night did matter a lot to him.

"Alexandra, it's dinner at the dining room table then her room. Emilie, at least … This is temporary, I know. There's some fascination with Rosalind for now. Just give it time. Things will iron themselves out, return to normal. As of course they should."

De Wolfe stood then paused.

Just like with Eva, he thought. Maybe there was a restlessness creeping into her. He would look into a European trip for them to take together. It just wouldn't be soon. De Wolfe & Fitch was about to open up a long, extensive, important series of acquisitions. This was to be a grueling, demanding period for him and Fitch and the staff. Making money meant making more, not less. His father had taught him this sage axiom even if Florentz Klaus De Wolfe had not always lived up to it simply because of his romantic infidelities that he let limit his esteem for his company.

"My father was not a fool, but business cannot be defined by your latest mistress. I deal in acquiring new businesses, not new mistresses. I don't mix up the two diverse, disparate entities. Never."

De Wolfe walked out of the en suite, a bathroom of eye-catching Moroccan tile, and into his lavish bedroom that two ten-by-twenty-foot marble-topped fireplaces kept warm and toasty.

"Hell, you'll get your European trip, Eva. Europe will still be there for us in the spring. In the offering, my dear Eva."

De Wolfe undid his white silk robe to prepare himself for bed at this late hour.

"And as for you, Emilie, my darling daughter, there is no need for me to interfere in your comings and goings. You are young and frisky, like a colt. Rosalind, I don't know her like I don't know those other chums of yours. Only that they're rich, gossipy, and extravagantly spoiled, like you." De Wolfe laughed. "How wonderfully they thrive."

JUAN MANUEL WAS FOLDING THE tripod's legs.

"I am finished, Emilie."

Emilie was about to assume a different pose, but stopped.

"There is nothing more for me to do, *mon cheri*."

"Oh, I'm so excited by the idea, Juan Manuel. And you did take so many pictures of me. At so many different angles."

The photographs, all of them, were taken in the bedroom. All head shots of Emilie.

"I have so much to work with," Juan Manuel said, putting the Kodak camera on a nearby table. "I am so pleased by it."

When she got to him, she draped herself over him and kissed his lips gently.

"You are such a great lover and artist, Juan Manuel."

He kissed Emilie's neck, and she swooned.

"You, Emilie, your face, will be beautiful to paint."

This was what was happening between them: Juan Manuel taking photographs of Emilie for he could paint her, put her homely face on canvas, and then give it to her as a gift, or as Juan Manuel put it, "My heart, it will be in your eyes, Emilie. You will see so much of me in the paint. This thing I do. The struggle I find."

Emilie twirled.

"Why ... I did expect you to"—Emilie smiled mischievously—"photograph me in the nude, Juan Manuel, since it is my body you love so much."

Juan Manuel smiled and ran his hand through his silky black hair. "No, non, Emilie. I am a modest man. I do not paint lust. And that what be in my heart as I paint you. My ... my—"

"Loins?"

"Yes. *Qui.* You will not continue to seduce me while I paint you from the picture. No, Emilie, I will not torture that part of me with such abandon. Some fire I must dampen."

"Oh"—Emilie swooned again—"your language, Juan Manuel. When you speak it ..."

"It is poor, so poor, little of something, I know, Emilie," Juan Emanuel said, his eyes falling from hers.

"No"—she was now running her hand through his hair—"it is beautiful language. Seductive language. It makes my cunt wet and run with a fever. You do seduce me, Juan Manuel. Every word you speak. Every gesture that you make.

"I am yours, Juan Manuel. Every inch of me is yours."

HE SUCKED HER LEFT BREAST, and then his tongue licked her flesh up to the edge of her neck. She held on to his penis as he did this.

They'd made love and were still in bed. This bed that was so big and soft and comfortable and generous in the Martinique Hotel.

Emilie's eyes shut, for she was thinking of the pain tomorrow would bring for her: Juan Manuel's leaving her for his return to Paris.

She jerked his penis and then laughed. "I'm sorry, Juan Manuel."

"Ouch," he said playfully.

She looked into his eyes. "Why must you leave, Juan Manuel?"

"You know why, Emilie. It is how we plan. One week with you."

"It's not fair!" Emilie said, pouting.

Juan Manuel kissed her hand. "You must not protest when we are so happy. It is gloom that make the day go badly." He kissed her forehead. "This is not war."

Emilie shot straight up. "War? What—"

"I am sorry I am so serious. I am sorry, Emilie."

"It's just that I don't know how war, why it was inserted—"

"When we are talking about romance?"

"Yes, Juan Manuel."

"I have scars, Emilie. It is … World War I. I see this horror through my own eyes. The people of France, we feel this every day in us. The war we fight. The horror we see when the war, the Germans come to take away our land. What is our properties."

And it is when Emilie came to understand what it was Juan Manuel was, psychologically, addressing.

"It is still there, even if we speak of romance." Pause. "You do not know war, your country. This beast of a thing. *Qui.*"

Emilie was in a quandary, for Juan Manuel was right, and maybe if she were a Frenchwoman, she would fully grasp what had just occurred to her out of the blue, Juan Manuel, his brooding, his pitch of voice that fell flat and into a cadence of sadness, but she was not a Frenchwoman, she should not feel guilty for not knowing war or its effect on its victims.

"Emilie, where do you go?"

She'd gotten out of the bed.

"To the bathroom, Juan Manuel. I don't feel so good. My stomach."

"Yes, go," Juan Manuel said, waving his hand in disgust at her, burying his head under the sheet. "This always is the easy way out."

Emilie's eyes blinked rapidly.

She didn't want to fight with him; that would be the easy thing to do. Fight with him over something she didn't understand. Something that seemed, for now, bigger than her. That had, suddenly, come crashing down on her with all its force and pent-up anger.

When she returned to the bedroom, Juan Manuel's head was still beneath the sheet. Emilie stood near the bed's headboard. "I am sorry, Juan Manuel."

Juan Manuel's head popped up out of the sheet. "No, it is me who is sorry, Emilie."

"No, it is me, Juan Manuel!" Emilie said, flinging her body on top of Juan Manuel who took her into his arms.

"I am complicated, Emilie. I am not just this Spanish man who land in France. Pretty and neat. Who come there as an artist to learn the art. The craft of something."

Emilie was spraying Juan Manuel's face with kisses. "Yes, yes, Juan Manuel. Yes, yes."

"There is more to me. More than you see." His eyes squeezed shut. "I cannot tell you everything, Emilie. But all of it is true."

Emilie kissed Juan Manuel's bare chest and then felt a rush of confusion overcome her. For what Juan Manuel said, in his heartfelt way, sounded more like a riddle than anything she could identify. More like it should be studied by a psychiatrist, someone who examines the mind to unlock individual secrets that it harbors and wants to release but can't.

"I-I understand, Juan Manuel."

"Do ... do you, Emilie? Do you?"

EMILIE WAS STILL IN JUAN Manuel's muscular arms after they'd made love a second time. They'd fallen asleep together, but now Emilie was awake. She was thinking through what had happened before she and Juan Manuel had turned to sex.

She was rich. She had paid Juan Manuel's ship fare from Paris, paid for his stay in the Martinique Hotel, had bought him clothes, and had paid for his return fare for tomorrow's planned departure. She was the one in control of everything, what seemed his life based on these small facts. But now it seemed he was in control of her mind now that he'd spoken of his past scars and what appeared to have psychological depth.

She was not used to someone having an upper hand over her as she listened to Juan Manuel breathe in the bed. Today he'd added a new layer to their relationship that, up till today, had been all fun and sex and silliness. There was more to Juan Manuel the struggling Parisian artist than what she first thought. Maybe this was good, she thought. She prided herself on her intelligence, her education, and her ability to take a clear-eyed view of most situations.

Did she really want her relationship with Juan Manuel to be just all fun, sex, and silliness? She shut her blinking eyes. She felt he'd turned the tables on her because maybe he would be even more exciting this way, as a person full of complication, of suspense and mystery and peril; someone she could dig her mind into psychologically and free him of his burden and he would one day view her as heroic, blessed with a gift that extended beyond sex and frivolity.

Yes! Yes! Emilie declared to herself in the bedroom's quiet, where only Juan Manuel's light breathing could be heard but was not disturbing to her ears. She loved everything about him and would work through whatever it was that haunted him, that a war lay bare at his feet, at his soul, that she as an American had no personal experience with.

She couldn't wait for him to wake. For Juan Manuel to laugh. For them to make love again to top off the day.

Wake up, Juan Manuel. Wake up!

Chapter 6

Juan Manuel, from the ship's deck, was waving madly at Emilie. Emilie, her eyelids rapidly blinking, was throwing kisses at him. It was nine o'clock on a cold, blustery November morning. A day with a dull, bloodless gray sky.

Emilie was in the backseat of the canary-yellow Packard. She felt dizzy headed heading back to the house. Her spirits felt dead as if the day had already crushed her like a giant ant. Awakening in bed with Juan Manuel in the Martinique Hotel this morning and knowing that she would be seeing him off at the pier, her body drooped as if it were in a state of collapse. Juan Manuel had to help her dress this morning in the Martinique. Her arms had been like lead, her legs too.

Emilie was sitting in a tense position in the car, her knees pressed together, her hands clasped, airtight. She was mortified by what was to come next, that her life had just been shattered by Juan Manuel's planned departure. Her blood felt like it was bubbling up in her veins. Her head had no positive, assertive thoughts.

She wanted to say something to her chauffeur, Xavier, talk to someone, but felt that she couldn't move her lips, that they were prisoner to today's events too. What was her life before Juan Manuel showed up? Emilie thought. How did she spend her days? This thought frightened her, would knock her on her back if not for the car seat positioned against her back. When she saw Juan Manuel board the ship, she wanted to run onto the gangplank, race off to Paris with him. She would have if her parents knew he existed. She would have if she had confessed to them that she had found an artist in Paris whom she was in love with, and him in love with her.

And it wasn't so much her mother, Alexandra De Wolfe, but her father, Maxwell De Wolfe. She loved her father. Such a selfish, thoughtless act by her would hurt her father, not her mother. Maxwell De Wolfe would suffer a blow. Alexandra De Wolfe's life would keep to its steady grind, its bland, visible deterioration.

"EMILIE, SHE HAS NOT COME down to eat."

They'd finished their meal. Now talk could strike up between them.

Alexandra looked across the dining room table at the empty side chair.

"I wonder why," De Wolfe said, frowning.

Alexandra stretched her right arm out, mindlessly.

"Do you think maybe I should go to her room?"

Alexandra's head shifted slightly to her left with a particular aggravation. "Do as you please, Maxwell."

"As I please—yes, as I please."

De Wolfe sat at the table temporarily immobile.

Alexandra had no opinion on the matter. She was not involved in her daughter's life and expected it to stay that way. Emilie was raised by nannies, not by her. They were the ones who changed her diapers, when, as a baby, she had cried. They were the ones who nursed her. They were the ones who played games with her when she needed to be amused. They were the ones who scheduled Emilie's day around hers (around the clock) so that her daughter never got in her way.

She was her daughter for biological reasons only. Not in the true, practical sense of the word. Not interactively or—

"Damnit, Alexandra, I'm going up to Emilie's room to see what the hell's wrong with her," De Wolfe said, springing out of the chair.

Alexandra snapped out of her contemplations. She looked at De Wolfe as he walked away. "Go ahead," she said under her breath. "You are her father, Maxwell."

REACHING EMILIE'S BEDROOM DOOR, DE Wolfe slowed down. He wasn't in a temper, but a father under duress who had to have answers for his daughter if he was to help clear up her problem. For he suspected something had gone badly for her. It was two days ago that she'd brought her melancholy into the house. But this evening, he would be there for her, the child he loved.

"Emilie …"

"I'm in bed, Father."

"You've dismissed Carla for the night?"

"Yes."

De Wolfe was about to open the door when, suddenly, it opened.

Emilie was in a slip, robe, and slippers. Emilie and De Wolfe hugged.

"You did not eat dinner with your mother and me tonight, Emilie," De Wolfe said. They walked over to two side chairs and sat. He held her hand.

"I will eat later, Father, since that's no trouble."

"Oh, no such thing. You eat anytime you wish, Emilie, in this house."

He squeezed her hand. "Now what's the worry? The burden you're carrying on your shoulders alone, these days, young lady?"

"I-I've lied to you, Father."

"Lied … to me?"

"Yes." Now Emilie was pressing De Wolfe's hand.

"How?"

"I met a man in Paris during my trip there with Rosalind. He came back to the States with me. He was here for a week. But he's returned to Paris."

"Emilie … Em …" De Wolfe was at a loss for words.

"It's where I was at night, with him. At the Martinique Hotel."

"Slow down, Emilie, my god. Heavens. Hell … slow down, will you."

"I can't, Father. It must barrel out of me like a waterfall, like it is barreling inside of me. Two days ago he returned to Paris. He is a businessman, Father. I will not tell you who he is, his surname for fear you will want to ruthlessly investigate him when all I want to do is love him!"

"You, damnit, Emilie, you are asking too much from me. Too much from your father!"

"Then I am sorry."

De Wolfe's head slumped. "Hell, you are breaking my heart."

"I am in love. Mine is already broken."

"I've never gotten involved in any of your romances," De Wolfe said.

"There haven't been many, Father. To speak of."

De Wolfe gazed out into space: he didn't mind the lies, they were a part of the fabric of how he lived, the whole scheme of the world and how it operated. But now there was a big story before him, he, emotionally, must prepare himself for.

"Please, you must tell me more, Emilie."

"More," Emilie said haltingly. "There is more, Father. He is a businessman like I said. Not as rich as us, a De Wolfe, but—"

"He is married."

"Yes."

"The rascal." Pause. "With children?"

"Yes. But they are grown."

"What you mean is he's an older man!"

"Yes."

De Wolfe was in a panic. Was this Frenchman him! he thought. His counterpart!

"You will not continue to see—"

"I what!"

"Emilie—"

"This is my life as it is yours, Father. He will be back to the Martinique in three weeks' time. I will be there waiting for him. With no hesitation. I run my life like you run yours."

"Yes, yes, Emilie, but—"

"I will love him as long as he loves me."

De Wolfe began gasping for air. His lungs burned.

"He has separated himself from his family. There is a divorce—"

"They all say that! He's lying to you! The lout ... Frenchman's lying to you!"

"There are divorce papers pending."

"Liar! He's a liar, this Frenchman! A big, fat liar!"

"You cheat on Mother. You lie too. But he's not you, he loves me. Paul Tristan loves me!"

"You are naïve. Foolish."

"I am heartbroken. The time between now and then. It's why I'm melancholy, Father. I love Paul Tristan too much."

De Wolfe stood and then began pacing the floor as if clubfooted. His hand, he slapped it to his forehead. "You must learn then. Yes, damnit, Emilie, you must learn then without my interference, of how these nasty little transgressions work. Break us.

"No, no, I will not interfere in any of this. Intervene. I will just be here for you when this new world of yours cracks open, crumbles around you. I will be here for you as I am now in your bedroom. I will let you see what men like me, Maxwell De Wolfe, do, are capable of doing to young women like you.

"But I love my daughter. It has been the one true, consistent value of my marriage to your mother. That I have you, Emilie, as a daughter in this wretched, piss-hole world."

EMILIE LET THE DARK CREEP over her fluttering eyelids. Her confession to her father had ended. He had left the bedroom. She had space open to her to think, think, think.

"I lie so well. It came with much ease for me—didn't it. I felt trapped like an animal, but I had to confess something. I had to tell someone about Juan Manuel even if it was through Paul Tristan, a fantasized character. Yes, yes. H-how clever, clever of me."

She didn't want to talk to Rosalind Le Grand about Juan Manuel because Rosalind already knew too much about him from the Paris trip. She was not as mature as her. She'd not fallen in love. Rosalind never talked of getting much out of a relationship, only the things that are flighty and cheap and between the sheets, but not the things that keep a woman who's in love awake at night and feel the sweet delights of a tortured heart.

"Ha. Father, I knew it would be easy with him if I told him something, anything to ease his worries. He loves me, yes, but he is first and foremost a businessman who worships money.

"And then there's his mistress and his home life. How much time does he have in the day." Emilie laughed. "On his calendar. Not much."

All he came into the room for were answers, not to fix anything. If that was his goal, as a child he would have been more strict with her. Not let her taste the freedoms that gave her rights she, at her age, was unwilling to relinquish.

"Paul Tristan, you are a businessman, not an artist. You pay your own way in the world, not me. But still, my father does not approve of you as he does not approve of himself.

"It's amusing how I stopped him in his tracks, when he saw he was Paul Tristan, this rich, wealthy Frenchman I imagined. Yes, a mirror image of Maxwell De Wolfe."

Emilie took the pillow and hugged it to her chest and thought of Juan Manuel who was with her just two days ago before sailing back to Paris for three weeks without her.

DE WOLFE BANGED THE DESK with his fist.

"Paul, Paul, Paul Tristan!"

All he was doing was visualizing this Frenchman named Paul Tristan, and he looked like him, De Wolfe thought, someone short, pudgy, with a heavy dark beard, and the same moral compass as him.

"I do give a damn about Emilie and Eva, but this Frenchman, Paul Tristan, doesn't give a damn about anyone!"

He knew what Emilie was to him (especially a Parisian), a rich American tramp, whore, hump no matter her wealth. He gave up the fight before it was thoroughly fought. He had to: he realized he wouldn't win. Emilie would pursue this new adventure, and for the first time in their relationship, she would run back to him for solace.

"It will be my opportunity to prove to her just how much I love her, after the rich Frenchman fucks her, is done with her, and then breaks her tender heart. Drops my daughter on my doorstep."

All he should really be thinking about tonight was tomorrow, the new acquisition of De Wolfe & Fitch that would make the financial market's head spin. The firm, by this time tomorrow, will be the toast of New York City and the New York Stock Exchange, De Wolfe thought.

His life was running smoothly. He'd gotten to the bottom of Eva's problem and, this evening, to Emilie's. For a while, at least, he anticipated nothing but smooth sailing ahead.

"I have surpassed my father as a businessman by leaps and bounds. His shadow is far behind me now. Florentz Klaus De Wolfe was never a match for me. My power is unstoppable."

De Wolfe sat back in the chair and folded his arms over his chest, smiling. He'd been in competition with his father from the day he had assumed the firm.

"Florentz De Wolfe created the blueprint, but I, Alexander Wolfe, have made it all work."

TWO WEEKS LATER.

Eva was in Harlem and couldn't be more happy. She passed stores in Harlem preparing for Christmas with their festive festoons. She had a gift for her mother that had nothing to do with the holidays. She found it amazing that she never got out of breath climbing the four flights up to her mother's walk-up apartment. She considered herself in good shape even if she was no longer a showgirl who relied on a dance regimen to keep her body toned.

She loved her mother more than anything or anyone in the world, and Eva was going to tell her that today during her Saturday visit. This was the main ambition of today's visit with her mother, to reconcile what had happened two weeks ago Saturday, when she bolted out of the apartment in a bad temper.

After standing in front of her mother's door for a few seconds, Eva knocked.

"Eva."

"Mother."

Lilly Durant was all smiles, and she hugged Eva. Eva shut her eyes, and the good feeling that oozed through her made her feel childlike, a child who, growing up, loved her mother more than anything or anyone in the world; the same sentiment she carried with her today.

"I hope—"

Lilly drew back her head. "I love you, Eva."

"Not as much as I love you, Mother."

"I knew you wouldn't disappoint me today. I expected to see you." Pause.

"Here, Mother."

"Oh, Eva, you didn't have to."

Lilly took the small, pretty wrapped package. "Thank you, darling."

Eva covered her mouth before giggling. "You may open it."

"Why not!"

They walked over to a small couch that had a lovely glass face coffee table facing it.

Eva began unwrapping the package, and her heart began to swell just by looking at her mother's high level of anticipation to discover just what it was she was unwrapping.

"It's ..."

"I'll put them on for you, Mother."

"The most gorgeous string of pearls, Eva!"

"There," Eva said, "don't you look gorgeous!"

Lilly ran over to the small Victorian-styled mirror on the living room wall.

"I do look gorgeous!"

Eva hugged her from behind.

"I'll find somewhere to wear them, Eva"—Lilly smiled—"even if it's around the house."

And with this pause between them, Eva's nose sniffed the air.

"Yes, apple pie, darling. Is in the oven as we speak!"

"Mother, you *did* know I'd come today."

"The umbilical cord, Eva, has never been cut."

Eva loved her mother's Dutch apple pie, its flaky crust, the sweetness of the Granny apples. Her mother baking it in brown parchment paper.

"Mother, I learned a lot from my last visit with you."

Lilly didn't expect anything less from Eva: that the subject of her last visit would surface, for neither of them ran from obstacles, in this instance, Maxwell De Wolfe.

They drifted back to the worn couch together.

"I'm a kept woman, granted, Mother. But I do have some rights. I made it clear to Max that night. I, uh, acted on it, Mother," Eva said bravely. "There will be a change, one that is about me, my feelings for a change."

"I'm so happy to hear that."

"I had to give it a lot of thought. I wanted to. I think that was the most important thing. Progress. That I was forced to think about my life with him more carefully. More judiciously."

EVA HAD A SLIVER OF pie on her fork. It would be her last bite. She was savoring it, so she shut her eyes to further enjoy the anticipated pleasure.

Lilly had wrapped two slices of the Dutch apple for Eva to take with her.

"Eva, there's something I must show you. Two days ago it, uh, came in the mail."

Lilly left the kitchen.

Eva sat at the kitchen table dumbfounded, unable to make heads or tails of what just transpired between her and her mother. After swallowing the last slice of pie, she stood and then walked over to the low sink and washed off the plate, fork, and glass (she'd had milk with the pie).

Eva turned her head when Lilly got back into the kitchen and sat down. Lilly's back was to Eva, and Eva looked at this solid but slender-framed woman as if she saw some sense of despair in her. She rushed to her.

When Eva got to the kitchen table, Lilly drew the envelope out of her deep-pocketed apron.

"Here, Eva, it's from your brother. Dorrell. It arrived two days ago."

Eva registered shock.

Lilly's hand was shaking when she handed it to Eva.

Eva pulled the letter out of the envelope. She stood to read it.

December 2

Dear Mother,

This is the second of such letters I have posted to you since my incarceration. The first coming once I arrived to this primitive facility called Sing Sing, and now. How I loathe this prison. The savagery I have endured on a daily, unrelenting basis, I could write a book about. The warden and his trained dogs. Prison guards. Animals, the lot of them!

But I have cheerful news for you to entertain: I will be released from this sin-riddled hellhole of vile men and their sociopath vices in a matter of just two weeks! This, needless to say, tickles my fancy to no end. Needless to say, I have served my time and will reintegrate myself back into society as a new man, a new citizen of the world who has learned that crime does not pay, not even at the thin margins of the letter of the law for the mild crime I committed against society.

I was never a criminal but was treated as one. I was in the company of murderers, of violent, hard-hearted men who, if ever were to be returned to society, would continue their heinous, murderous ways to the fear and detriment of a peaceful, decent population.

But don't worry about me, I will find my way once I am released. I will seek more fertile fields. I will not become a millstone in any way to you. I will not return to hearth and home until I have proven fully that this new man I will become is worthy of crossing your doorstep minus a hat in his hand and of no hope in his heart.

I expect better days ahead. I will keep in touch.

With the sincerest of love to you as always, your loving son,

Dorrell

Eva sat, and her head felt heavy.

"He could have been such a brilliant person. My son."

"Full of words and deeds, Mother. But with little else to show for it."

Eva folded the letter and returned it to the envelope. She let it stay on top of the tiny kitchen table. She looked back down at the envelope.

"He takes no responsibility whatsoever for the crime, does he?" Lilly asked. "In the letter."

"No, Mother. Dorrell still dismisses it. Even if it sent him away to prison for six years. His head's still above the crowd. He's still unfazed, untouched by what he did. Still thinks he's superior to everyone."

"After a while, I tried not to remind myself of where Dorrell was. My son's reality, Eva. Practically blocking it out of my mind on many a day. It was my coping mechanism."

"Who wouldn't," Eva said sympathetically.

Lilly took the letter off the table and slipped it back into the apron's pocket.

"But I am a mother, Eva. Full of heartache for her child. For Dorrell. He has a prison record now. There's no easy way out for him."

"Then …"

"Yes, one day. One day he'll be back. It won't take long, will it?"

"Oh, Mother …"

They were holding each other.

They did none of this when Dorrell was sentenced, for neither was in the courtroom. Lilly, because her employer wouldn't give her the day. Eva, because she and Dorrell were never close, and she felt no need to be in court for his sentencing. Lilly had wanted her to go, to represent the Durant family, but Eva refused.

"I want Dorrell to be happy," Lilly wept.

Hearing Lilly's remark made it hard for Eva to swallow. But she was holding a mother who had two children who weren't happy, who had disappointed her more than they'd pleased her, but she still held out optimism that one day both she and Dorrell could reach that place.

"Me too, Mother. I want him to be happy too."

"It's all I pray for, Eva."

EVA HADN'T LEFT HARLEM.

It had gotten dark out on the streets, but the Saturday hustle and bustle continued, the approaching holidays adding its luster to a community that could use every last ounce of it. She laughed at the idea of buying De Wolfe a Christmas present. This Christmas was to mark their second Christmas together. But De Wolfe had a low opinion of Christmas, that he didn't believe in such sentimental hogwash—so buying him a Christmas present, for her, was nothing more than a pipe dream.

Eva looked at a small group of colored boys with Santa Claus smiles framing their faces. They knew poverty, Eva thought, but at their age, they had not yet understood its deeper meaning. At one time she knew it too but had not understood it. But when it began to appear that there was to be no way out for her, economically speaking, along came De Wolfe, and she leaped at the opportunity to live the lifestyle she now led. Where the rules of the game were clearly drawn, where there was no misunderstanding—especially not by her.

And now in two weeks Dorrell would be released from Sing Sing. Eva pressed the sheltering woolen scarf to her neck. She was happy for him, but it came with the pain of knowing her mother was back to living with a certain fear inside her of *that* eventual day Dorrell would show up on her doorstep with his hat in his hand. She had no idea of how Dorrell was coming out of his prison experience, of how much of a millstone he'd be on her mother. He'd bent her before, but would he somewhere down the road break her?

Oh no! Oh no! Eva shrieked.

She felt she was going to faint on 130th Street. She put her back against a tree. Now she was thinking of how she must look to passersby, her skin as white as a sheet. But she did feel unsteadied by Dorrell, her older brother by two years, and her mother.

Of just what their past might foretell.

Chapter 7

The naughty note had been placed on the queen-size bed, and it told Juan Manuel in what direction to steer himself.

The bathroom was foggy, for Emilie had started showering the instant she heard Juan Manuel enter the suite she'd paid for since his departure for Paris to guarantee its long-term securement.

The steamy bathroom's silver gray trimmed door was open, and Juan Manuel could see the red bush of pubic hair covering Emilie's vagina, and he began stripping his clothes off until he was naked.

She screamed out of lust and joy when she saw him, his erection, as he pulled back the glass door, and she yanked the tall Frenchman's stiff penis, and he groped her, and their bodies twisted together in the shower.

"Oh, hump me, Juan Manuel! Hump me … Pl-please … pleeeease …"

And Emilie felt her three-week lust, the three weeks that had passed as he guided his stiff cock into her hot box, and she screamed again and again as the pulse of his penis, and the raining down of the shower's warm water on her skin, tingled her into a state of delirium and faintness of head.

"I want to suck it too! I w-want to suck y-your cock too, Juan Manuel, after you fuck me, J-Juan Manuel!"

THEY WERE CURLED UP IN bed, their hair wet as cat's fur. They'd toweled, but their hair was still tousled and wet. They'd been talking about what they had done in the shower like two young lovers who were in no way ashamed of their passion or greed.

"When I lick your cunt, Emilie," Juan Manuel said, looking under the sheet at Emilie's red patch of hair, "it is sweet to my tongue. Very sweet, Emilie. The juice."

"Oh … Juan Manuel!"

"I am in heaven at the time."

"I've never known this kind of lovemaking, Juan Manuel. With the others, it was so pedestrian. So—"

"Be gentle with me, my English. I do not know this word 'pedestrian,' Emilie. It—"

"Ordinary, Juan Manuel. Something that is—"

"*Non*, but we, we are extraordinary together, *mon cheri*."

She began kissing him.

"Be careful, I am soon to recover my strength. My urge—"

"To fuck me, Juan Manuel!"

"*Qui*, to fuck you, Emilie!"

When Juan Manuel looked into Emilie's homely face, he'd always think of her body. The beauty of its sculptured parts: legs, breasts, and her full rump, and its infinite capacity for arousal. In fact, Juan Manuel's eyes saw beauty in most things but could not lie about all things, not Emilie and her manifest, disadvantaged face he thought in his native language, Spanish.

Her tongue went into his mouth, spinning his saliva on the tip of her tongue. Then she laid her head back down on his chest and held his limp penis in her hand.

"I will suck your cock soon, Juan Manuel. Very soon."

"Soon, yes, soon. Very soon, Emilie."

Pause.

"I thought, thought, that …"

He knew what she was thinking. "The painting?"

"Yes, Juan Manuel."

"No," he said unapologetically. "The painting is not finished. It will be too soon. The painting do you no justice, Emilie. Love rushes at you, but not when you paint. The heart beats, *qui*, but the brush can move but so fast."

She laughed and then said, "But I am disappointed, no matter your silly excuse."

"No, no, it is not excuse," Juan Manuel protested. "It is the truth. You will not find fault in my art when it speaks to me this way."

Emilie saw the earnestness in Juan Manuel's dark eyes. "You, art, I have studied it, Juan Manuel," Emilie said, letting go of his penis. "I should know better. I know it has taken the great masters—"

"El Greco, Goya, Velázquez—"

"Yes, yes, Juan Manuel, I know of them. Who they are in the art world."

"It is not for us to decide, know when the painting is finished, it is the painting. It *must* be."

"Yes, yes, I agree, Juan Manuel. It makes such perfect sense," Emilie said, her eyelids rapidly blinking.

"It is why, the next trip I come to America, it will be ready. I am sure of it. This is the feeling that overcome me. My spirit. The sense the painting is making to me. It is telling me, Emilie."

DE WOLFE WAS PUTTING HIS socks back on.

"Emilie is seeing him again, Eva, the Frenchman. He's back. She hasn't been in the house the past two nights. Paul Tristan."

De Wolfe (a few days ago) had told Eva about Paul Tristan. Eva, like De Wolfe, had not approved of what Emilie was doing, seeing this older French businessman who had children but had told Emilie of pending divorce papers, but she liked his name: Paul Tristan.

"Of course Mrs. De Wolfe doesn't know about the affair."

"Of course," Eva said. She was under the comforter, naked. De Wolfe had come from a drinking hole and straight to her for sex in the Ballad Street setup.

When De Wolfe put his socks back on, it meant no more sex for him and Eva for the night. He didn't like sleeping barefoot. It was a strange habit of his he couldn't give any accounting for, so he accepted it as something normal, since he was Maxwell De Wolfe.

He lay back near Eva's knees. "How much longer is this damned charade going to continue, Eva, before this fucking Frenchman breaks my daughter's heart!"

Eva looked at him and saw a man who was truly concerned about his daughter and her welfare. This was proving one thing to her: that De Wolfe loved Emilie De Wolfe. He had brought his home life to the bedroom, and while not expecting it, she felt more than comfortable with it. She was having her family problems, ones she couldn't discuss with De Wolfe, but at least she could be helpful to him with his.

"D-do you think he …"

"Might love her!"

"Yes, Max. He's back in America from France, isn't he? A rich Frenchman who must—"

"She's ugly, for god's sake, Eva. Like her mother. She has a lisp, and her eyes flutter fitfully like, like goddamn bird wings. What man can love my daughter but me, Eva. Or … a man with a voracious cock!"

"I'm sorry, Max."

De Wolfe lifted his head, glanced into Eva's eyes, and then patted her thigh. "Eva, you're only trying to help, I know, but you've never seen Emilie." He laid his head back down. "You're the most beautiful woman I've ever seen, have known, Eva. You'd stand out in a sea of beautiful women. Emilie, she's the opposite, total opposite of you.

"She and her mother. Their other common trait is red hair. Bright red hair." Pause. "But Emilie, now, she is imposingly shapely. Ha" De Wolfe laughed. "She could even give you a run for your money.

"She does fill out a bathing suit quite divinely. So …"

"That does have its advantages, Max." Eva laughed.

"Damned right!" And then it was as if De Wolfe had assessed what Eva had just said.

"That damned French pig!"

"You mean—"

"Sex, sex, of course it's nothing but goddamned sex for him!"

She saw De Wolfe was genuinely upset with this Frenchman. And then as if her brain were tumbling, turning over and over as if dice, she thought of them, how they began. Wasn't their beginning the same, not lust on her part but on his. Her knowing the advantage, at the time, was all hers, her beauty, her womanly wiles. How the game is played in the hotly contested world of showgirls and older men and the burlesque of pretense and posturing and bidding, of which girl is prettier or more seductive or erotic in the sharp glare of stage lights and afterward off stage where they are wooed and bedded.

"He will ruin her, this pig, Eva. But I will be there for her, not my goddamned wife. She is made of salt, of low temperature. Her passion as dead as a goddamned doornail. Hell!"

It was a torrent of words flying out of his mouth, out of his heart, of frustration and a life that was foul and putrid, one, temporarily, Eva thought, De Wolfe had lost control of. This man who had so much but did not want this problem for his daughter. But somehow realized that he must wait it out. That Emilie De Wolfe, this young lady, was at her womanly best, like her, like all women who trade away their principles for temporal things. For men and sex.

"Yes, I will wait," De Wolfe said, his eyes turning red. "Emilie is not to blame. She is blameless in this open act of deception by this devil, P-Paul Tristan."

DE WOLFE WAS IN HIS office. Literally, he could tear his hair out a chunk at a time. Or, maybe, after today, watch it turn gray like a man made of stone. But he was sweating at the temples, for he was having a difficult time with a magically gifted chemist the company of De Wolfe & Fitch was funding for an invention that—if completed—would revolutionize the plastics industry, and the company would bathe in a boatload of money as a consequence.

But Enrico Falco was a kooky, reclusive genius, one whose home was in the laboratory, not in the world of common sense or mutual cooperation with a corporation that was putting its foot, figuratively, on top of his neck (De Wolfe admitted), but it was for Falco and his invention's own good. De Wolfe had been shepherding him through the thickets as William Hearst had Thomas Edison—and look what Edison had done for Hearst's wealth! De Wolfe thought over and again in trying to maintain his patience with the young, unproven inventor while, at the same time, push him as hard as he could toward the final product reaching a broad marketplace.

And then there was Emilie. She'd not been home for five straight days. How he missed her in the house! Alexandra, in a cold, faraway voice, had made her lone inquiry regarding the matter last night at the dinner table. "Maxwell, is Emilie traveling abroad on another trip and neglected to tell us?" And he kept his head down while he fumed, but he replied, "No, I know where Emilie is. She's perfectly fine." But below his calm exterior was this tornado that was about to erupt, that wanted to roar and upend the situation he was in: a daughter who was fucking Paul Tristan and a wife accepting the slimmest explanation of his as truth.

De Wolfe looked up and the Battersby wall clock he bought in London four years ago, it ticking away, ticking another day off the calendar in his office, reminding him of how days march on in to night, and his endless search for peace and serenity that was becoming more and more elusive.

"Oh well … Shit … shit …"

IT WAS MUCH LATER WHEN **Marilyn Ochs**, De Wolfe's secretary, entered De Wolfe's office. She was a short, stocky woman who wore round-wire thin glasses and her hair in a intensely rolled bun. She looked quite imposing despite her small stature.

"Mr. De Wolfe, it's your daughter, sir."

"The phone …?"

"Yes, it rang only seconds ago."

"I …" Pause. "Thank you, Ms. Ochs."

De Wolfe snatched the phone on his desk.

"Emilie!"

"Father!"

"I know where you've been the past—"

"With Paul Tristan!"

"You foolish girl!"

"I will not argue with you, Father. But you and I will talk tonight, Father. Tonight!"

"Yes, I think it's high time … is vital we talk," De Wolfe said reasonably.

"It will be well after Mother's in bed. In my bedroom."

"Why not mine, Emilie?" De Wolfe laughed, as if he were competing with her. "Choose mine for our tête-à-tête."

"At eleven thirty we shall talk."

"So you're finally coming home. I missed you."

"Good day, Father."

"Good—"

Emilie had hung up the phone, and De Wolfe was looking at it with a streak of red in his eyes.

TONIGHT WAS THE NIGHT FOR **De Wolfe** to be with Eva, but he would explain his absence to her. This would be nothing new for her. This was the freedom he maintained over the years with his mistresses:

the capability to maneuver as he saw fit without communication or apology to any of them. Only Eva was the exception, for he'd discuss what it was Emilie had planned out so exotically for them, the meeting of the minds as it were, to take place in her bedroom as if she had an upper hand in this war of nerves he had such vast experience with on an everyday basis, being the owner of De Wolfe & Fitch.

De Wolfe was in his bedroom. He'd just glanced at his timepiece. He did not expect Emilie to make herself heard when entering the house, the floor's carpet thick, the room doors on the floor, when opened or closed, quiet, if courteously executed.

"Eleven twenty-seven," De Wolfe said.

On his way home from the office, he tried to find this situation with Emilie amusing, since his day had been full of blustering and bullying, most of it aimed at Enrico Falco, someone who used few words but even over the phone sulked, besides his general behavior toward him being arrogant as hell, De Wolfe thought. He had it out with the Italian and then handed him over to Fitch who finished him off. But amusing, no, he couldn't put what he was to do with Emilie in that neat context, since five days out of the house with Paul Tristan spelled trouble no matter how sure he was of himself.

It was eleven thirty.

De Wolfe opened Emilie's bedroom door, and there she was, this daughter it felt like he'd not seen forever sitting in the setting he was accustomed to. A slip of light fell over her face. A face that was expressionless and pale.

"Emilie."

Emilie stood. Her arms reached out for De Wolfe.

When De Wolfe reached her, she kissed his cheek. "Father," Emilie said it in what was a weary voice. "Let's sit."

And so they sat.

"You're still dressed. Haven't changed for the night."

Emilie was in a long, flowing black dress and a white high-collared blouse. Earrings and a bracelet were the only two articles of jewelry she wore.

"I'm not staying, Father. Paul Tristan is waiting for me back at the Martinique."

De Wolfe's blood had begun to boil.

"Your lover."

"It's why we're here, Father."

"You asked for this meeting, not me. You scheduled it."

"But you wanted it as badly, didn't you?" Emilie said, staring De Wolfe in the eye, suddenly, not blinking.

"I was to exercise patience with you, Emilie. It was my—"

"Philosophy toward me."

"But it's running thin."

"I'm going to marry Paul Tristan."

"Marry him!" De Wolfe said, leaping out of the chair with the cane.

"I'll propose to him tonight. It's all planned. It's why I'm being fair with you, Father, by giving you fair warning of my intentions. What they are!"

"What the hell's gotten into you!" De Wolfe had stabbed the floor with the cane.

"Paul Tristan's divorce is final. It's been done," Emilie said, wiping her hands clean. "Paul Tristan will no longer be my lover but my husband."

"You-you've gone mad, mad, impossibly, out-outrageously mad! Insane!"

"Nothing of the kind." Emilie smiled. "Not in the least, Father."

"Damn, you're sinking me into the goddamned floor with this defiance of yours."

"I will move to Paris, immediately. Stay in a hotel until Paul Tristan and I purchase a chateau. Something that won't take long."

"The Frenchman said that!"

"No, me, Father, me. It will be my life that I seek. I control. My taste in things and moments. Of how I live."

De Wolfe sat back down and bent over, his head in his hands. He began knocking his forehead with his fists as if he were going insane with pain.

But Emilie maintained her faraway, distant gaze; how a child looks when lost or a twenty-three-year-old when their fantasy has become their reality and nothing more substantive can destroy or replace it.

De Wolfe raised his head and looked over at her. "Where do we go from here, Emilie? H-how can I stop you?"

"But why would you want to stop me, Father? I'm happy."

"T-this Frenchman?"

"You will call him by his name, proper name, Father, or this conversation between us will end now. Immediately."

De Wolfe's eyes shut. "Paul Tristan. Paul Tristan. Paul Tristan."

"Yes, yes, yes ..."

She's making me a part of her madness, De Wolfe thought. *The Frenchman has fucked her to the point a sickness is in her. It's in her blood and brain.*

"Can I meet him, this ... uh, Paul Tristan, darling?"

Emilie's eyes stopped blinking, since she'd shut them, but her body was tense.

"He knows of you, Father. Your great success. He is afraid of you. That he might come off inferior, without talent, and then regret the meeting."

What, De Wolfe thought, *my ways are known in Paris too? They've circled the continent?*

"I will be there as your father, Emilie," De Wolfe said, reaching for her hand, taking it. "Not as a businessman. The owner of a multimillion-dollar corporation, of De Wolfe & Fitch."

"It will not matter to Paul Tristan," Emilie said, her eyes still shut. "He will not let it matter. You do not begin or end in Paul Tristan's eyes, Father. You are one: seamless. There's no businessman or father separated out in this."

De Wolfe grabbed his aching heart. He leaned back in the chair with all the weight in him, his legs felt weak and useless.

Emilie heard him breathing hard but felt no reason to care. All she cared about right now was returning to Juan Manuel, to the Martinique Hotel. This was an interruption she had not planned this morning when she awoke. But spending part of the morning with Juan Manuel, her thinking became bigger and bigger until she thought of marrying him, of sailing off to Paris to marry him and them purchasing a chateau there, of Juan Manuel and his art, of her and Juan Manuel's babies and the nannies and everyday help.

Emilie stood.

She would propose to Juan Manuel as soon as Xavier drove her back to the Martinique Hotel in the yellow Packard. She had told Juan Manuel she must see her father. Juan Manuel had not bothered to inquire why. Being an artist, he was a person of little demands. He had lived a carefree life, a bohemian life. The war had arisen again, this the second time between them, but did not linger like before, only to the point of Juan Manuel recounting it.

"I'm leaving, Father. I'm going back to the hotel to be with Paul Tristan."

De Wolfe looked up at Emilie. "And there's nothing I can do for you, Emilie? N-no more than this?"

"Nothing."

"To stop this?"

She walked over to him, stooped over, and kissed his sweated forehead.

"I love you, Father."

WHEN DE WOLFE WALKED OUT of Emilie's room, he was an empty man: torched by sadness. But what he really wanted to do was assume his power and then exert it, awaken Fagan, and then order him to drive off to the Martinique and coerce his daughter to come back home with him to the De Wolfe residence. He'd knock Paul Tristan on his ass. And if his actions created a wild, violent scene in the Martinique's hotel room with the Frenchman, then so be it!

But in walking back to his bedroom, he began to feel powerless. As if the world had caught up to him and he was only one man in a universe of many. He stopped at his bedroom door and thought of what his name and reputation had done to this Frenchman who was leading Emilie, his daughter, down this dark, despicable path. A path he was all too familiar with.

"Ha. This Frenchman must travel in good company if he knows of my ways as Emilie so eloquently stated. Enough that it frightens the poor man to death. Put me at an immediate advantage, and him, a disadvantage.

"Maybe one day Paul Tristan and I will find common ground. If it is true he is divorced from his wife. If it is true he marries Emilie and he becomes my son-in-law. If all of it is true and possible."

And then the mystery of Paul Tristan will end, will be put to bed, and there would be flesh and bones. He would know just what kind of businessman the Frenchman was. How wealthy he was and what enterprises that maybe could help him expand his company more on the continent. Thus, create even a wider net of wealth for him.

"This might not be a bad thing after all," De Wolfe said, opening his bedroom door at eleven forty-seven. "What Emilie has gotten herself into with the fucking Frenchman."

"WAKE UP, JUAN MANUEL! WAKE up, I'm back from my father's!"

"Em ... Emilie, qui, qui ..."

Juan Manuel was drowsy; he'd wanted to be awake when Emilie got back, but between reading a book and being bored, he'd, unintentionally, fallen asleep.

"I spoke to him."

"You don't tell me where you go when you leave." He belched and then pardoned himself. "So I do not know," he said, brushing back his silky black hair.

"No"—Emilie laughed—"you wouldn't."

"So tell me, what you speak of? But before that, Emilie, you never speak of your mother."

Emilie began unbuttoning the sable's fat buttons with Juan Manuel's aid. He was in long johns.

"I will not bore you with her, Juan Manuel." She picked up the book Juan Manuel had been reading that was at the foot of the bed and opened it. "She's as blank as this page."

"I will not laugh with you, Emilie."

"Why, Juan Manuel—when it is amusing?"

"It is not good—it is all I know to say."

"Your mother—"

"She die. I lose her when an infant. Disease. Famine. So they tell me. I was no more than one. It is a bad story for you."

"Oh, I love you, Juan Manuel, I love you!"

"But why, Emilie, why?"

"There's so much I don't know about you. So much you have yet to tell me, that's why. It's what makes this, what we have, so exciting, thrilling, Juan Manuel!"

Juan Manuel's forehead wrinkled. "Sadness too?"

Emilie kissed his red lips. "You'll be happy with me, Juan Manuel."

"Yes, I am, Emilie."

Emilie slung her arm around his neck. "But not for just tonight, but always."

Juan Manuel released her waist, and Emilie took immediate note of it.

"What are you saying behind the words, Emilie? Or what you doing? These words you use with politeness but chase after more than what they say?"

"You are so smart, Juan Manuel. Clever." She took his hand and kissed it. "Will you marry me?"

Juan Manuel looked away from her, out into the bedroom, and then back into her eyes. "This is what you ask your father to do? Go to him for? This thing you ask?"

"No, not exactly. I told him I *will* marry you. I was not seeking his permission."

Juan Manuel's smooth, even expression hadn't changed. "You finally tell him. You are brave enough to tell this rich man of me tonight?"

"Yes, Juan Manuel."

"What he say, Emilie? What?"

"He was shocked."

"And that I am an artist, Emilie? What, a beggar."

"Yes."

"He is ang-angry … then upset with me?"

"It wouldn't matter to him if you were a wealthy businessman like him, Juan Manuel. You are a Frenchman. On the continent. Who has deflowered his daughter even if my father knows I am not a virgin. But to him, it is the highest form of debauchery. A man like my father. He submits it no other scrutiny."

Juan Manuel did not understand everything Emilie had said, but enough to know the old French word "desbaucher" and that he was guilty.

"But we must wait with this idea!"

"Wait! But I can't!"

"I don't know the word 'marry' for me now, Emilie."

She was breathing so hard it was as if her face had turned blue.

"Water, Emilie, I get you a glass of water!"

Juan Manuel ran off.

But Emilie wasn't thinking of water, only what Juan Manuel had said or not said. He didn't flat out say no but sounded like it. He was hedging, unsure of himself. She must convince him differently!

Juan Manuel came back into the bedroom with the glass of water and reached out to hand it to Emilie, but Emilie, instead, slapped it out of his hand, and the glass hit the floor, the water splashing.

"How dare you!"

Juan Manuel was stunned as he looked at Emilie and then the glass on the rug.

"I just proposed to you, and you cannot give me a yes or no!"

"I ..."

"How dare you!"

She buried her head in the pillow and began crying, her long black skirt flowing over the bed. Her tears, Juan Manuel could practically hear. His sensitive artist's soul responding.

He got to the bed, got on top of it, and on his knees crawled toward her, and then took her into his arms. "I am sorry, Emilie." Pause. "You are not responsible. Not you." His voice was strong, resonant.

Emilie was sobbing, using the sheet as a handkerchief to dab her eyes. Her red hair was bright and alive, as if the pain of this overwhelming love she had for Juan Manuel had scorched it.

"T-then who, who is, J-Juan Manuel?"

"Events. Many others. That make up the day, Emilie. Dead or alive. That fall on my shoulder. Make this for me."

Emilie was more lost, more confused. She turned to him, looking into his eyes, this beautiful man she loved and who made her feel there were no boundaries to love, but an endless stream of dreams.

"They live inside me, Emilie, after the lovemaking. After the paintings. These things that make no sense to me, but I know them. And them me. We have same memories."

He turned himself away from Emilie as if ashamed by what he'd said, the clumsy English, the attempt to make what was real to him sound simple, not complicated, but feeling all too inadequate just the same.

Emilie kissed his smooth back. "You must not feel this way, Juan Manuel."

"But I do," Juan Manuel whispered softly. "There is no end to this pain in me."

All Emilie knew was she loved him, and if she had to nurse him back to good health, repair him to somewhere she hoped with all her heart and soul Juan Manuel wanted to attain, she would.

"Juan Manuel, don't you understand, I will take care of you. I will shelter you. Your art, this gift you possess in your hands and heart," she said as softly as Juan Manuel had spoken before. "I have money. I have the support that will protect you, Juan Manuel, from the world. From this nasty, degenerate, repulsive place."

Slowly, Juan Manuel turned to Emilie.

"I will birth your children. They will live well. We will have a happy family, Juan Manuel. Don't you see, this is all I want?"

Juan Manuel kissed her blinking eyes. "Yes."

Emilie took a deep breath. He laid his head down on top her plump bosom.

WHEN JUAN MANUEL WOKE, SO did Emilie.

They'd dozed off arm in arm over three hours ago. It was midmorning.

She kissed the top of his head.

"What's wrong, Juan Manuel?"

"Before, we settle nothing, Emilie. After we make love tonight."

Emilie kissed his shoulder. "You're right, Juan Manuel."

"I wish to marry you, but we must wait, Emilie."

She was anxious, but she must not let it show. Maybe it was time for her to grow up, she'd thought before falling asleep in Juan Manuel's arms after they'd made love. Her life was full of possessions, of obtaining the things she wanted because of her father's immense wealth. A room full of toys when young, the yachts and cars and trips abroad as a teenager and adult. She always yearned her father's love, and that she had secured too. Her life was a series of obsessing and then owning; and currently it was Juan Manuel, someone who was offering resistance to a new obsession, him, and he now had become an object to own even if emotionally, she loved him with a fevered heart.

"But how long, Juan Manuel?" And then Emilie grabbed his hand and let him touch her heart. "I can be as romantic ... dramatic as you, Juan Manuel. My heart," Emilie said, uneasily, "feel my heart, how it aches when you touch it."

"Yes, it ache like mine," Juan Manuel said, pressing his hand to Emilie's heart. "It is no different in temperature."

"But ..."

"I cannot think here, Emilie. In this foreign country, this America for now. My head ..." Juan Manuel grabbed it. "I must be in Paris."

"But why!"

"I don't know why, but it is true. Just for three weeks, Emilie, no more. And then I return a—"

"Back and forth, back and forth. It must not be Paris then New York, Paris then—"

"But the next time I come, I will marry you! Meet your father! This I promise!"

"I ... I ..."

"Do you not trust me? Do you not?"

Because of the dark, the bedroom, and the hotel room's drapes shut, Emilie could not see Juan Manuel's dark eyes, but Juan Manuel's voice sounded as desperate as her, and Emilie realized there was now this silent horror in her, of losing Juan Manuel, something she'd not felt or cared about with any man before him.

"The portrait. I will come back from Paris with the painting, Emilie," Juan Manuel said, "of you, Emilie. Your face, your smile, your soul painted on canvas for us. All this for you, Emilie."

THIS AFTERNOON DE WOLFE HAD gotten the call. *Now what?* he'd asked before picking up the phone when Marilyn Ochs told him who it was: Emilie. But when he did speak to Emilie, he said nothing but listened to Emilie's instructions. It's why he was parked outside the Martinique Hotel. The car in front of his was Emilie's. The second he arrived, Xavier had gotten out of the car. De Wolfe didn't bother to acknowledge him, for he knew Xavier's mission.

"Fagan, I'm sure Ms. Emilie will be down any minute." De Wolfe braced himself with the cane. "You might as well let me out of this goddamned car while I've got breath still left in me."

"Now, Mr. De Wolfe, it can't be that bad, sir?"

"Hell, you want to bet!"

Fagan opened the car door for him, and De Wolfe stepped out of the Packard.

Fagan stood behind him and then smoothed out the back of De Wolfe's long black cashmere coat. De Wolfe leaned into the cane and then looked up at the hotel's glittering marquee.

"Martinique Hotel," De Wolfe said with great disgust.

"Fagan, here she comes, Ms. Emilie." De Wolfe saw her through the glass enclosure, she and Xavier, who was carrying her bags.

"Good evening, Fagan. See you in the morning."

"Good evening, Mr. De Wolfe. Yes, sir."

When Fagan got back in the Packard, he swung around Emilie's Packard, there being enough room in the hotel's ample driveway.

"Father!"

"Emilie!"

They stood there in the cold like two ice-stiff statues in a park of pigeons.

Xavier opened the car's back door with Emilie entering the car first and then De Wolfe.

Xavier put Emilie's bags in the car's trunk. When Xavier got back in the car, he didn't have to be instructed to do what he quickly executed: shut the glass partition.

It was six ten.

Emilie was looking out of the car's side window.

"It's over then, this affair between you and Paul Tristan? This great, topical romance of yours," De Wolfe said sarcastically; something it seemed he couldn't wait to say was hot on the tip of his tongue. "He's left you? Your marriage proposal to him fell as fast and flat as a damned lead balloon. The Frenchman's jilted you, has he!"

"Ha." Emilie laughed soulfully. "It's what you think, Father? Your self-indulgent story? Rant? Lie to yourself?"

"It's what I know, Emilie. He never had any intention of marrying you in the first place. But don't worry, my darling," De Wolfe said, pushing his cane away from him and then patting Emilie's hand. "I'm here for you, your father."

She laughed again. "My hero, Father. Medals and all on your big, hairy chest, is that it, Father?"

"I will still earn your respect—if nothing else. You called me here to—"

"Paul Tristan has not left me, Father, he's left the States but will return, like before, to me."

"The rat!"

"See," Emilie said capriciously, "you have misread Paul Tristan's intentions once again. Someone you don't know."

"And I suppose you do," De Wolfe said, grabbing his cane, "after these brief sexual encounters you've had with him in the Martinique."

The car was moving through the busy Manhattan cobbled streets and gas lights.

"We're getting nowhere with this, Father."

"Yes, I am tired of this inconvenience. Discussing someone who is a phantom to me but has stolen my daughter's foolish heart."

"Don't say that!"

"The hell I won't!"

"It's, because it's not true, Father. His mother, it's his mother this time."

"What will it be the next time!" Pause. "She's ill, I suppose, in bad health, the old—"

"No, Paul Tristan respects her. He comes from the old school, Father. Paul Tristan ..." Emilie stopped. She yanked a handkerchief out her pocketbook and began crying liberally in to it. "It-it's with respect, respect. How Paul T-Tristan treats her."

De Wolfe felt badly. He wanted this Frenchman out of his daughter's life so badly that he himself was out of balance, teetering.

She was young, foolish, yes, but he must not let the Frenchman, Paul Tristan, drive a wedge between them.

"Don't, Emilie, let me."

Emilie handed De Wolfe the handkerchief.

"That's all, Father. It is because of his mother. He has no father, just her. She raised him to be wealthy, with ambition and fortitude, Father. She understands the divorce but worries about me, of course."

"Yes, yes, a parent is still a parent at any age, Emilie. No matter. Something you'll find out, dear, soon enough," De Wolfe said magnanimously. "When my grandchildren are born."

"She's worried if, that I am worthy of—"

"Worthy of her son!"

"Yes, of Paul—"

De Wolfe was hot under the collar by the implication. "He is the one in question, under surveillance. A microscope. He hasn't explained to her you're the father of Maxwell De Wolfe, an American scion, one of the wealthiest, most powerful men in the—"

"He will, Father. Paul Tristan will. He has felt embarrassed by the affair so soon after the divorce. His family put in a bad way."

"Then the Frenchman has scruples, does he? Isn't that something. Now that's something new, damnit."

Emilie smiled charmingly. "I just caught his fancy, Father."

De Wolfe patted her hand, again. "That you did, Emilie. That you did."

"And he does admire you—"

"Even if I intimidate him. He is frightened of me. My power and wealth."

"Yes, but one day he shall overcome that fear, Father, he said."

"Yes, one day, Emilie." De Wolfe smiled. "If and when the time comes, Emilie. Paul Tristan meeting someone like me. A De Wolfe."

"WELCOME HOME, EMILIE." THOSE WERE the first few words issued by Alexandra De Wolfe at the long dining room table after she and De Wolfe and Emilie had partaken of dinner.

"Thank you, Mother. Now you must pardon me," Emilie said, getting up out of her chair. "I must go up to my room."

"Of course, Emilie," De Wolfe said, putting his napkin down on the table.

Alexandra's eyes trailed Emilie, and when she was far enough away for Emilie not to hear her, she said, "You are smitten with her once more, Maxwell?"

"What do you mean by that!"

"I am not blind even if you would wish me. But I'm not. I know when it is business that makes you sulk and when it is Emilie. I can distinguish between the two, Maxwell. You are a different person when your loneliness permeates the house."

EMILIE HAD DISMISSED HER MAID, Carla.

She sat at the vanity table, looking into the handsome mirror, and then away from it, being seduced by a boredom she'd felt for the past two days since Juan Manuel sailed for France.

She stood. "I feel useless, without purpose."

She couldn't leave from the Martinique Hotel, not until she began to feel the world was crumbling around her. She was sleeping in the same bed she and Juan Manuel had made love in, dreaming those thoughts over and again as if they could spring out of the ether and Juan Manuel would be there, in broad daylight fucking her until she climaxed, her throat rippling, and the magnificent orgasm shrilled.

At times she clutched the sheets as if having an orgasm; told the hotel's maid not to change them. And when she issued this command to her, she knew she had crossed over the line of sanity into insanity.

And now the new lie she told her father tonight. The new pretense to protect Juan Manuel. Now a mother was involved, another fictional character connected to the fallible plot to deceive.

"Oh, what a damned liar I am!"

And it was all because of a Frenchman she met in a humble bookstore in Paris. A man who looked at her and saw in her what she saw in him when two eyes meet and silence ends the brief, lovely encounter with a single conclusion.

She fell on top of the bed. "How does this end?"

Emilie began thinking of the portrait. When they parted at the pier, Juan Manuel reminded her of the portrait he was painting of her as if he had to. As if there was some lingering doubt from her there would be no painting, but there wasn't.

The only thing she thought of was him returning to her three weeks hence. Hoping his trip to Paris got him there safely, but knowing even while standing on the long, slender wooden pier that morning that she would return to the hotel room she'd deposited monetary payment for for another month of securement and spend her time in the room as though Juan Manuel was there with her. Lie in their bed and suffer. Make her unbearable torture force her back to her father's house, back to what her mother understood about her life with her father: what loneliness feels like inside a thirty-two-room mansion, in its four beautiful, well-structured walls of rich stone.

Chapter 8

Eva had just left her mother's apartment. She'd just come off the stoop and was walking briskly down the brick steps.

Across the block, standing on a stoop, were two brothers, ages twelve and ten.

"She is beautiful, ain't she, Lemuel?" the ten-year-old said.

"You can say that again!"

Both were bundled up, dressing more warmly than what was called for, the temperature ranging between thirty-four and thirty-six degrees and no wind. Not like it'd been a few days ago in Harlem, when the temperature dipped to eight degrees with headwinds.

"I wonder ..." Lemuel rumbled down the tenement's steps and across the street.

"Hey, miss, miss, me and my brother is new to the neighborhood. Is you white!"

Eva stopped in her tracks and spotted the other brother join him on the sidewalk, lurking behind him.

"Lemuel, why'd you say that to the lady for. Fool!"

"Shut up, Oscar!"

"I seen that other woman in there. The old one. She white too?"

Eva just stared at him.

"He ... sorry, miss," Oscar said. "He's ten. So don't know no better. But we ain't used to living around whites and all. Not the neighborhood we come from."

Eva simply shook her head in disgust and then started walking down the sidewalk, again.

"Didn't know whites lived around coloreds, that's all, ma'am. Not in no Harlem, miss." Pause. "But you still is pretty, miss. Still is."

When Eva got a good distance away from the boys, she laughed to herself. Yes, there're whites in Harlem, who, because of economics, are stuck here. Whites who could tell those two boys a thing or two about poverty. Those boys had a lot of catching up to do, for sure, Eva thought. But there were other things on her mind.

Today her mother had told her about her brother, Dorrell. She'd gotten another letter from him a week after the first one arrived. He'd asked her to send one hundred and twenty-five dollars to Sing Sing prison before his release. When Lilly told Eva she had, she was horrified.

"Why'd you do it, Mother? Why!"

"I know it's a lot of money, Eva, but—"

And Lilly went on to explain to Eva why she had done what she did, and even though she did understand she didn't want to, she realized the wheels were beginning to turn again, that Dorrell Durant was back in her mother's life to stay this time, not unless he committed another crime that sent him back to Sing Sing prison.

And then there was De Wolfe and his daughter, Emilie. It was as if she (the mistress) had become a part of the De Wolfe family. It had begun to feel uncomfortable for her, having all of this firsthand information from a man she didn't love but respected. This was not what she had bargained for if there was such a thing in being a kept woman. In being out of sight of the public, shrouded and kept a deep, dark secret.

But more and more information was being fed to her in greater detail. And she was becoming emotionally entrapped in it in ways she had not expected. De Wolfe, this powerful man, was now saddled down by something that he felt had gotten out of hand, yet he saw some future stake in it for himself if Paul Tristan, the French businessman, was sincere with Emilie. The linkage of fortune, if, in fact, Paul Tristan had such wealth. But De Wolfe kept waffling back and forth, at one point hopeful, and then dark spirited about Emilie's chances with the Frenchman. Sometimes seemingly desiring her opinion, input, and other times wrestling with it only to brusquely dismiss what she said as if she were a child whose thoughts had no grounding or significance. It was hurtful to her, like a cold slap across the face she must accept from De Wolfe, once more, pointing out the unevenness of their relationship.

The subway station wasn't far off, but she didn't feel in the mood for returning to Ballad Street. It seemed she needed the fresh, cold air, to take it in and make her head feel lighter. She didn't grow up on 130th Street. This block she was walking. Those two boys wouldn't know her even if they weren't "new" but "old" to the block. She grew up in Newark, New Jersey, but her mother moved to Harlem because of two things: better job opportunities (domestic work) and her.

When Eva reached 125th Street, there were more shops. Street activity was at its peak. She walked into Amos's coffee shop, and there was the usual loud talk and the standard remark from Amos, but always done in good taste and with a bright lightbulb smile on his ordinary face.

"Hey, white girl. How you been?"

"Fine, sir."

Amos Walcott was a dark-skinned Jamaican man in his sixties with a huge knot on his forehead. He worked the counter in the small clean shop with rows of pictures of Harlem life on its green-painted walls, about twenty in total.

"Your nose look red, mon, but you, now you still look pretty as hell, girl!"

"Thank you."

"The usual?"

"Yes, please," Eva said, sitting on the stool at the counter. There were a few men in the shop but no women. All the men stared at her, being that she was white, this oddity sitting at the counter, but not for long: loud talk soon resumed.

"There you are … Coffee black as me, mon. But got it a little cream to lighten it," Amos said, handing the jar of cream to Eva. Eva took the jar and thanked him and then poured sugar out of a tall sugar shaker and into the white porcelain cup.

She paid Amos the two cents.

As Eva sipped the hot coffee, she began to feel better, less uptight and anxious. She shut her eyes, smelled the brew, and wondered about tonight with De Wolfe, of just how big her role had become. Thinking of De Wolfe's troubles in ways that weren't depressing her, but were making her see how small her life was. And it wasn't De Wolfe's fault but her own, for she'd chosen this status for herself, not Maxwell De Wolfe and his money.

A STRONG GUST OF WIND kicked up off the sidewalk that caused Eva to hold on to her hat until the wind died down. She returned to holding on to De Wolfe's arm as they walked down by the East River.

"Eva, I picked a hell of a time for a walk with you!"

The shock was still in her, for De Wolfe and she emerged from the Ballad Street building at eleven thirty-seven and took to the east side where it was desolate. But it was still a daring move on De Wolfe's part to suggest they take a walk together. Neither felt in fear of anything: of being seen or, worse, mugged.

"Eva, I'm counting down the days, goddamnit, as well as Emilie for Paul Tristan to sail in from France!"

Eva recognized this was why they were walking these desolate lower Manhattan streets at this hour of the night. It had to be connected to De Wolfe's troubles with Emilie, and like her, this afternoon in Harlem, the cold air being a source of comfort and sustenance for De Wolfe.

"Of course, Max," Eva said timidly.

"The days are building, and with them, this thing that has to happen for Emilie's sake." De Wolfe's voice sounded like what he looked like with the cane, his hobbled walk, the pain he obstinately refused to give in to unless it reduced him.

"She isn't herself, Eva," De Wolfe said, passing by a paint-chipped lamppost, "but who would expect her to when all she wants is to marry the Frenchman. To live in Paris and bear his goddamned children. Who wouldn't be. Her dream of dreams."

"I want it too, for it so much to happen too, Max. The resolution of—"

"His mother, hell, she controls nothing. Absolutely nothing. That old Frenchwoman. If he's in love with my daughter, the mother controls nothing." Pause. "Like I control nothing. She will marry the Frenchman above any objection I pose. My protestations.

"This is the feckless run of my power over her. I don't like this," De Wolfe said, shaking his head in the black top hat. "I don't like the way this smells. I smell a goddamned rat. It's what I smell."

"Neither, neither do I, Max. I have tried to be optimistic—"

"That damned word again! Don't use it in my company ever again, Eva! Don't fucking use it!"

De Wolfe stopped in his tracks. "Let's head back to the building."

Unfortunately, she'd been counting down the days too for Paul Tristan's arrival from France. Tension was building to a point where there were too many people involved, a crowded field.

"I don't see a soft landing ahead. I just don't, Eva. It doesn't seem anywhere in the cards."

And suddenly, Eva felt strange walking out in public (even if it was on a dark, desolate street on the east side of Manhattan after eleven o'clock) with De Wolfe. This older man with the cane who had a daughter who was rich and complicated, who could do whatever the hell she chose to do as long as it was lawful, she didn't kill anyone or steal from anyone, engage herself in any criminal activity, and even then, who knew what strings De Wolfe could pull.

And yet she must show sympathy for her, a spoiled, bratty, hysterical woman who'd fallen in love with a Frenchman, someone who had money and must have a mistress stashed away like her somewhere in Paris. Who was at his beck and call. Who would still remain in the shadows even if he lived up to his solemn promise of marrying Emilie De Wolfe. The rich Frenchman affording her that kind of life like De Wolfe had afforded Alexandra De Wolfe, Eva thought.

They were nearing the Ballad building with the single lamp light above the metal front door casting its dim light down on it. Silence between De Wolfe and Eva had pursued for a couple of blocks.

Eva's hand dropped down into her small purse for the building's key.

De Wolfe halted her hand and then smiled salaciously.

"I need a good fuck, Eva. A good fuck from you tonight, okay!"

THE CHANEL PERFUME DRIFTED LIGHTLY in the Packard's cabin. The Chanel was discreetly applied on Emilie's neck and wrist, a neck Juan Manuel's teeth would bite into and mark her skin red.

Emilie had ached all last night, her vagina throbbing, her joy mixed with her salty tears of yearning, of wanting to be in Juan Manuel's arms despite all of what was to come next for them when her father found out (her confession) Paul Tristan was Juan Manuel, not a capitalist, but an artist. This striking revelation she'd deliver to her father tomorrow. Tonight, she was to be with Juan Manuel. They would make love, and then she would tell him the secret her heart held. The good news she had for him, that would pleasantly surprise him.

She had no fear of her father's reprimand, his razor tongue. She was strong enough to stand up against him no matter how badly he spoke of Juan Manuel, degraded and humiliated him for his low social status and moral turpitude. She'd already crossed that psychological bridge. Her father bullied men but was no match for her. She was a woman who was mightier, more powerful than him. For she loved Juan Manuel. Whereas her father loved her.

"Here we are, Ms. De Wolfe."

"Yes, yes, we are, Xavier." Pause. "But if you will, pull the car off to the side of the Martinique's driveway. I'd like to think. There's plenty of time, still."

And then quickly, Emilie changed her mind.

"No, never mind, Xavier, you may do what is appropriate." Then. "Oh, you, do follow my original instruction."

The car sat at the side of the driveway. Emilie was examining her ring finger and saying to herself, *You won't be naked long.* She would buy her own wedding ring and, of course, Juan Manuel's. Emilie shut her eyes, and that was enough to spring today's reality thrillingly back to her.

"I'm ready, Xavier."

The door opened, and Emilie was helped out of the car. Xavier disappeared, having gone to the trunk for the luggage.

When Emilie stepped into the suite, she burst out crying. It was the emotional strain she'd been under for the past three weeks of waiting for Juan Manuel. She'd turned on the room's lights and stood back to look around this sumptuous suite that would always be hers and Juan Manuel's. This place where heaven met earth on equal terms, since this room was her heaven on earth.

"How childish all of this feels to me. The excitement I have for Juan Manuel!"

She stole a glance at her watch. If all went as planned, Juan Manuel would arrive to the Martinique by seven thirty. It was six forty. She would not pull the stunt she pulled on him before, leaving a note in the living room while she showered in the bathroom and waited for him to come to her to fuck her in the steamy shower.

"No, I don't care where we fuck!" Emilie shrieked. "I don't!"

She was wearing a tight woolen checkered skirt, something that clung to her hips. She touched the silk blouse and held on to her breasts. She felt Juan Manuel's tongue on them and then lost it, seeking the divan to sit on. She kept her back straight to retain some level of energy before Juan Manuel came through the door, not in any way waste it.

She knew that these empty minutes waiting for Juan Manuel would be hard on her. It was worse than three weeks ago. Everything was worse than three weeks ago. Her father marking the time with her. She saw it in his eyes, the way he dreaded this day.

"But now it's here, Father, for Juan Manuel and me. You can't change anything. My fate. He'll be here with the painting he promised me. My portrait. You can't send him away. He's committed no crime. Has done nothing wrong.

"He only loves me. Oh, how Juan Manuel loves me."

This little talk of hers relaxed her. She glanced at her watch again. It was seven forty-five; she only had forty-five more minutes before Juan Manuel came through the bedroom door.

Emilie had been to the bathroom. She had to pee. She was nervous again. The door to the suite, it should open at any second. She stood by the door in anticipation of Juan Manuel.

Knock.

But why, Juan Manuel! Why must you knock!

"Yes, yes …"

"Ms. De Wolfe, I, it's Billy, the bellhop, ma'am. I was told to bring—"

Billy was looking at Emilie.

"I'm sorry, ma'am, but I was told to deliver this to your room."

"My room!"

"Yes, yes, M-Ms. De Wolfe."

"Then bring it in!"

"Yes, yes, ma'am."

Emilie knew what it was at first glance. The large, thickly wrapped package she was staring at.

"And, and this, ma'am."

"A letter!"

"Will, will that be all, Ms. De Wolfe?"

"A letter!"

"Ms. De Wolfe, ma'am, w-will that be—"

"Yes, yes!"

Slam.

This didn't feel right. "Juan Manuel, Juan Manuel, is this a prank, a stunt like ... something I would pull on—"

Nothing felt right to Emilie. Emilie thought she knew his personality. He was playful but in a serious way, not like this. This ... He would want to be with her for the unveiling of her portrait. Juan Manuel would want to celebrate the moment with her, his art, his talent. See her exhilaration himself.

He wouldn't do anything like—

"The letter!" It was in her hand. Emilie examined it and saw it was mailed without a return address.

Emilie collapsed to the floor. Juan Emanuel's painting, Billy (the bellhop) had put against the wall.

Emilie had not let go of the letter; it was as if it were attached to her hand, or more like nailed to it.

"No, Juan Manuel, no, you can't do this to me!"

Slowly, stiffly, without any overt emotion, Emilie used her sharp fingernail to open the envelope, and surprisingly, it was opened with little difficulty. Tears that clouded her eyes were cleared, and Emilie breathed with a bitterness that continued to shorten her breath, as if the air out of her mouth were spurts of sickly sound.

"I love you, Juan Manuel. I love you. I will always love you, Juan Manuel."

> Dear Emilie,
>
> I write you in your English, not my French. I can have someone write this letter better for me but donot. I know you read the French well for I see you remember, Emilie. I write you at bad time because I am not there with you. I am not coming back.

"You pig! You fucking pig, Juan Manuel!"

> It is not you but me who is wrong. I talk of the war but donot tell you everything I know. Now I do. Now

you will know everything there is, Emilie. All shape me to become this man. I look for no mercy. The life I give myself come from many things I run from but cannot hide.

I love other woman. She is not young like you but very old. I will not tell you the age. We donot have sex. She let me have sex with young woman like you. All she want from me is tell her I love her. I love her, Emilie. It is easy to say for me. I love her.

The war is when she find me. I am without food. Am without the shelter. I fight the war for France but am left with nothing. She see me in the streets of Paris. I am to hungry to beg. Limp like a starve dog. She tell me it is my eyes she cannot forget so come back to where I am and make me hers. It donot happen right away. I donot always know what she want but then it become what I want. I donot know if she is a mother. I donot know but I love her like she is the lover.

We donot have sex but she let me have it for she know I will all ways come back to her. She say she not in jepordy and for you it is the same. She know of the time I spend with you in the America. Of the painting I paint of you. It is what she know because I tell her everything.

She is not happy I break young woman hearts. I am not either. But I am young and want sex. I fuck you, Emilie. I fuck you. It is what I do. But you are the first one I paint of the woman I fuck. It come from the heart and I know not why. The war teach you so much you forget. It is the cruel animal that make no sence to those men who fight it. Who are hollow like the dead.

Your fathers money will not find me. Donot come back to the Paris to look for me. Le Figaro bookstore it was a mistake. I donot go back there any more. This very old woman is rich. She hide me as she please. I follow only her.

I will find other woman. Young like you. There are so many in the Paris. You will not be the last. The old woman know this. The hand she feed. The place she stand.

I will keep to the paint. Be the great artist. How you find me when you come to the Paris.

Au voir mon cheri Emilie,

Juan Manuel

PS Juan Manuel Pagan is not my name it is different.

Emilie fainted.

EMILIE WAS DAZED WHEN SHE awoke.

She was on the rug, and her head, having processed so much, was in a silent state of shock. She wiped at her mouth, for she'd slobbered and the saliva had hardened, caking her lips.

Her face felt swollen.

She opened her eyes and saw the heavily wrapped painting near her head. "Juan Manuel ... The letter ..."

Juan Manuel's letter was to her right. "What did it say? What?"

Emilie picked up the letter. She was lying on her back, holding Juan Manuel's letter with both hands; it was mere inches from her eyes.

Emilie was weak.

She patted her face to feel if it was swollen. She angled her head to her right and looked at the wrapped painting again. She took her fingernails, for she was within arm's length of the painting, and began scratching at it with them but was too faint; she stopped.

"Juan Manuel ... I"—she patted her stomach—"but I have a surprise for you, I have ... The baby, Juan Manuel. The baby. I'm carrying your baby, Juan Manuel. Don't you know that? Don't you know that? Your baby, Juan Manuel."

It was the good news she was to tell Juan Manuel after their lovemaking, the sex, the reestablishment of who and what they were to each other, that she was carrying his baby, that she had missed her period, was close to two months pregnant, something her doctor recently confirmed.

Emilie shut her eyes, and her thoughts drifted off as if they'd become detached from her.

"Paul Tristan ..." she murmured. "Paul Tristan ..."

Her body stiffened and then totally relaxed again. "Did your mother, s-she has approved of me, hasn't she? I-I am worthy of you. I am—I know I am, Paul Tristan," Emilie said calmly. "You would not do this to me, Paul Tristan. Not you, Paul Tristan. No, not you."

The thought of Paul Tristan, the wealthy Frenchman who had divorced his wife for her, who would arrive soon from Paris to tell her the good news, of their impending marriage, that things had gone well in France for them with his mother.

"You are such a good man, Paul Tristan. Such a noble ..."

Emilie opened her eyes and realized she was still down on top of the floor. She struggled to her feet.

"A painting of me! I don't want to see it! I don't want to see it, Juan Manuel!"

Emilie scooped up the letter and then, with all the strength left in her, ripped Juan Manuel's letter in half.

She screamed.

Emilie ran into a room with a desk and pulled out its middle drawer, for she knew there were two pairs of scissors in it, small and large pairs (she'd used the smaller scissor before).

She snatched the large pair of scissors out of the drawer.

"I'll kill it—I'll kill this monster, Juan Manuel! You put inside me! My belly! Your baby!"

Emilie ran into the bathroom and faced the mirror.

"You monster!"

She stopped, stepped away from the mirror, and dragged herself over to the toilet seat and sat. She was trembling.

Juan Manuel loved an old woman, Emilie thought. *An old woman, not me.* A woman of Paris. A woman of Europe's war. A woman who let Juan Manuel live a life of desire, lust, and a freedom that always brought him back to her.

"I am nothing, Juan Manuel Pagan. Y-you have made me nothing in your eyes. I will be unhappy the rest of my life. At twenty-three, I will have found my only true love. Suffer you, Juan Manuel, forever. Until I die. There will never be any other man for me but you … you, Juan Manuel …"

She was what she had imagined, concocted, this man, Paul Tristan, whom she could never love or him love her. Another wealthy man like her father. Another wealthy man with a mistress and who would not love her not like a Juan Manuel even with all his flaws.

"It will be my dreadful life," Emilie said, puzzling up her homely face. "I will marry a man who thinks only of money, of position and his scale of power. He will measure himself against the world and always come up short, won't he? A Paul Tristan.

"And each day I will wait for him in a room. In a big room in a mansion. A …"

Emilie began to cry, the scissors fell out her hand, and then she lay down on the bathroom's tile floor.

"I will kill myself and this monster inside me. The baby must die with me. The baby. Juan Manuel's baby. Father, you will know what happened to me. My humiliation. My shame. My grief. Why I killed myself. C-committed suicide. You will piece everything together. My story, Father.

"None of this will be a secret to you. This life I live. What I was seeking but could never find. No matter how wild or unpredictable,

Father, it is what I wanted more than anything from Juan Manuel. Anything, Father. Anything."

Emilie grabbed the scissors.

"I will become my mother if I don't die. If I live. If I don't kill myself. I will become my mother, cold and … living life joyously. I will …"

She looked at the large scissors' blades. "Now. Now!"

Emilie raised her arm.

She stabbed the sharp scissors into her stomach, and blood gushed out of her belly.

Chapter 9

The detective in charge of the murder physically resembled Fagan Dooley. He had a walrus mustache and a pudgy, ruddy face and was short like Fagan.

De Wolfe had entered the living room in a panic.

Two days had passed since Emilie's suicide. She was found this morning by the Martinique Hotel's staff.

Detective Delaney O'Brien knew who De Wolfe was from pictures of him in the tabloids, so he didn't have to identify him; but he would still know him anyway, as a twenty-seven-year veteran of the police force, as a father of a daughter who had successfully taken her life by suicide.

"Mr. De Wolfe, I'm Detective Delaney O'Brien."

"Where is she—where's my daughter, Detective O'Brien!"

"In the bathroom, sir." O'Brien's finger pointed to the hallway, and De Wolfe could see from where he stood the bathroom's open door.

"Can …"

"By all means, Mr. De Wolfe. We haven't moved your daughter's body. But there's a sheet covering her, of course. And"—O'Brien paused—"the smell, sir. Your daughter's been lying there for … We won't know how long, many hours, sir, until the autopsy's conducted. But I'm sure it's been a while."

O'Brien took another look at this man who was shorter than him, whose eyes were ruby red and looked as if they'd bled from the instant he got the news of his daughter's suicide till now.

"Come with me, Mr. De Wolfe, sir. I have to supervise your movements. You mustn't touch her, sir, or anything in the room. I'll pull the sheet back and all. At least you can identify Ms. De Wolfe." Then O'Brien grabbed De Wolfe's trembling hand.

"I understand your grief, Mr. De Wolfe."

Police personnel were in the living room chatting.

O'Brien led the way.

When De Wolfe saw the white sheet covering Emilie, he began to whimper profusely. The first breath through his nose was a foul one. Quickly he began breathing through his mouth.

O'Brien knelt over the sheet and then looked up at De Wolfe, who was about three feet off his left shoulder.

"Prepare yourself, Mr. De Wolfe. Take a deep breath. It's my advice to you, sir. When it comes to something like this. Of this sad occurrence, sir."

O'Brien pulled back the sheet, and what De Wolfe saw was the scissor sticking out of Emilie's stomach and her dried blood on the front of her blue dress and the sickish, pale look on her face. The look of death he knew he'd never forget for a lifetime.

De Wolfe grabbed his stomach and then puked.

"Where is she, Helga? Mrs. De Wolfe?"

"In her bedroom, Mr. De Wolfe."

Fagan had already taken the elevator back down to the mansion's underground garage.

Helga, the tall, sturdy, beautiful, and blue-eyed blonde German maid had De Wolfe's items of clothing and made her way off to the hall's coat closet.

De Wolfe turned his attention to the grand staircase. He kept walking with the cane until he got to it and then ascended the stairs laboriously.

Fagan was back, and De Wolfe, from high, looked down at him. Fagan began climbing the staircase with him, for he was on a mission De Wolfe had assigned him.

De Wolfe walked down the second floor's hallway and then turned back to Fagan.

"Put it on the bed, Fagan."

"Yes, Mr. De Wolfe."

"I'm heading to my study." Pause. "I'll see you in the morning."

"Yes, Mr. De Wolfe."

De Wolfe turned left as Fagan proceeded forward and toward De Wolfe's bedroom.

"I must do something. I am not dead. My mind is not dead. I must deal with reality, at least for now. I must protect Emilie. My daughter …"

Emotionally, he was about to break down, but caught himself, understanding what his mission was, what was vital in order to make what he had constructed in the car on his way home work.

"I love you, my darling Emilie."

De Wolfe got to the study door, opened it, and then closed it.

Minutes later, De Wolfe came out of the office. He was rocky. He was carrying an envelope.

He was at Alexandra's door.

"Alexandra, I'm back."

The door opened.

"Thank you, Elsa."

Elsa's wrinkled face was steeped in grave pain.

She stepped out of the room, shutting the door behind her.

"Everything's done, Maxwell? Emilie's body's in the city morgue?"

Alexandra sat in a chair near the window with the floor-length drapes shut; this was an ordinary evening for her. The room was faint of light.

"Yes, everything's done. Everything."

De Wolfe couldn't wait to get to her, his hand pressing down on top of the tapered cane's handle with extreme force. For him to get this thing over with!

Alexandra's eyes had no sign of pain or worry or any confirmation that Emilie had died.

"Why did she take her life?" Alexandra asked, her thin, swanlike neck turning to De Wolfe in a way to suggest a minimum of inquiry and interest.

"She was in love with a wealthy man, Paul Tristan. A businessman. A Frenchman," De Wolfe said, leaning on the short cane.

"Married?"

"Yes."

"And he promised what for her?"

"He wrote her a letter. Would you like to—"

She waved her hand out in front of her objectionably when she saw the white envelope centered in De Wolfe's hand.

"No. I will not read the sordid thing. The sexual affair she brought into your life, not mine."

"No, Alexandra, not yours. Of course not."

"I knew there was something going on in her life, some awkward activity, circumstance of an odd nature," Alexandra said, turning her head quickly from De Wolfe. "Her many absences, disappearances from the house. But knew you knew why, Maxwell. That nothing escapes your eye, your cunning. That you were more than aware of her carnal conduct.

"And now she is dead."

"Yes, Alexandra: our daughter, Emilie, is dead."

"Are you leaving the room?"

"Yes," De Wolfe said, continuing to move toward the door.

"You will arrange the funeral, Maxwell? Everything that's called for, appropriate? The formality?"

"Yes, everything, Alexandra. Everything. You won't have to concern yourself with anything. Obligation. Just be there at the funeral. Emilie's mother."

"She was having sex, lots of it I would imagine, presume, with the Frenchman? It's why I used the word 'carnal,' I suppose."

De Wolfe shut the bedroom door and then began making his way to his bedroom.

When he got into the room, he headed for the small desk and then sat.

"Goddamnit!"

His pudgy hands ripped the envelope to shreds.

"I knew Alexandra wouldn't read it! Not a lick of it!"

He'd read Juan Manuel's letter. Detective O'Brien handed it to him and told him it was his to keep.

"Emilie ripped the goddamned thing in half. In, in fucking half, didn't she!"

And he wanted to do the same after reading it, but instead, he had stuck it in his pocket. He reached down inside his pocket and felt it.

De Wolfe laughed.

And as if he had planned it this way, he took hold of his silver-plated lighter and, with a devil's glint in his eyes, began burning Juan Manuel's letter in the ashtray until it turned black, smoky, and smelly.

"You fucking Spanish bastard."

De Wolfe had quickly constructed the story of Juan Manuel being an artist, not a businessman, that Paul Tristan was a figment of Emilie's imagination. A person who did not exist but was created by Emilie to appease him, lead him down a false, blind trail.

"But it was you, Juan Manuel. You scum. You bag of Spanish scum who fucked my daughter. Stole her heart. And then jilted her, you sick, sick bastard. YOU SICK, SPANISH BASTARD!"

But it wasn't about money for Juan Manuel; he had the old Frenchwoman to supply that for him, De Wolfe thought. An old Frenchwoman who had set aside worldly woes, transactions, for she could use her feeble mind and her money to trap Juan Manuel in her sick, demented world to make him happy and remorseless. Who, together, had formed this strange, powerful alliance.

No, it was about Juan Manuel's lust, his prurience.

De Wolfe shut his eyes.

"His lust, my lust … Man's lust … Eva … Eva … Damnit …"

It was the weakness in all men, big or small, rich or poor. It was the evil in all men, but he had no mercy for this bastard, the Frenchman, Juan Manuel.

"French, Spanish, you FUCK!"

De Wolfe grabbed the cane and then rose to his feet. "No, Alexandra wouldn't read a letter from Emilie's lover, Paul Tristan. She wouldn't even sniff at it. It was too far below her. Too trite and pitiful. It shortened inquiry of him. Me dealing with her. This soulless, impotent woman I married!"

He was over at the bed where the wrapped picture was. He saw the torn paper, what Emilie had tried to do but had failed miserably in her meager attempt.

"Emilie could do only so much in, in her sad, gloomy condition," De Wolfe said, tears stinging his eyes. "She won't even cry. The mother of my child won't even cry for her daughter. Her daughter's death!"

The picture was wrapped in heavy brown paper and expertly tied by strong string.

De Wolfe began untying the string, sobbing, a mess of tears, staining the brown paper.

"You did this, Juan Manuel. You."

Emilie's portrait was framed.

"It is framed, a wooden—"

And De Wolfe was looking at a 20" x 26" portrait Juan Manuel painted of Emilie.

"You made her beautiful. You made Emilie beautiful, you fuck!"

He couldn't love her; no man could love her but him, her father, not her lover, her seducer, someone who fucked her. Juan Manuel saw who he wanted to see, how he wanted Emilie to look. Like Emilie saw who she wanted to see, who she wanted Juan Manuel to be, someone to love her. But Juan Manuel, the Frenchman, De Wolfe thought, put his fantasy, the lie to himself on canvas, Emilie's was in her mind, her soul, her heart; all the timid, vulnerable places that conspire for a person to go crazy, to commit suicide and hate a world where ugliness and beauty compete against each other with open, ageless contempt.

"WHAT DO THEY WANT FROM me?" Alexandra had woken out of her sleep, removing her blinders. She had asked the question as if she were asking it to the blackened room, not her heart.

"De Wolfe and Emilie kept me out of their lives. They rejected me. I had no choice but to hate my daughter as I hated my mother. I hold no responsibility for that!"

Alexandra covered her mouth, for it was the first time she'd made such a confession and it was because of Emilie's death. She was lying flat on her back but then rolled onto her side, something completely uncharacteristic of her.

"Mother died an alcoholic, but I won't. De Wolfe will not drive me to that fatal end. No!" Alexandra said bitterly.

But everything must be connected to Emilie's death now, the impetus to spill her soul like she'd just done was because of Emilie. *I must delve more meticulously into my life than what I have in the past,* she thought.

"But there is no remedy for me, no hope. I have already recovered from Emilie's death. I have eased it from my consciousness. I did not form her, her personality, her character, her many characteristics. De Wolfe did."

And she found a Frenchman, a businessman like her father. And he made promises to her that he never meant to keep. *But De Wolfe has never made promises to me,* Alexandra thought. She was something his family, the De Wolfes, bought and her family, the Bauers, sold. She was but a piece of flesh.

"Emilie, she was the result of this ungodly creation. She stood no chance. No chance in hell. My goddamned daughter."

The sadness that would afflict Emilie's life began the day Emilie was born, Alexandra thought. She was high strung. Vain. And quite impressed with herself—wasn't she? She set herself forth on a path certain to fail. *My daughter died as she lived, recklessly, without regard for her mortality*, Alexandra thought.

She was hell-bent on one day destroying herself. These modern, wayward rich girls.

"I will die differently, but De Wolfe will not be the cause. He lives like Emilie lived, recklessly. I will outlive De Wolfe. I will bury him one day too. I will be the lone De Wolfe survivor.

"A De Wolfe will not bury me."

Alexandra had received great glee from saying that out into the room. She put her blinders back over her eyes in the blackened room.

EMILIE DE WOLFE'S FUNERAL WAS the talk of New York and its tabloids' headlines and sizzling society pages. Emilie De Wolfe wasn't just another eminent socialite who died, but one who had committed a violent, love-crazed death, one that had a titillating back story of a mysterious lover who, eventually, jilted her, leaving Emilie De Wolfe, the young, rich, future De Wolfe heiress of great fortune, no other option left but to kill herself in the ritzy Martinique Hotel with a pair of scissors as her weapon of choice.

This was what De Wolfe, the grieving father, had to contend with. He was able to control the flow of information disseminated by the police department (De Wolfe, over the years, a heavy donor), but the press De Wolfe could not rein in. De Wolfe had referenced them as "scavengers," "scum," "muckrakers," "the dregs of a civilized, democratic society," but nothing had blunted them from storming the "king's castle," for more and more fuel to toss on a burning house.

De Wolfe had issued a plea that if they were to continue their merciless campaign to hound, besiege, and badger the De Wolfe family, then go after him, not Mrs. De Wolfe; to lay off of her, a grieving mother who had lost her child under unfortunate circumstances that were beyond her control. A mother who was grieving and heartsick and was herself at death's door. A mother who loved her daughter and now begged for human succor from not just the local press but the world.

De Wolfe had made such a plea simply because he didn't want the press to in any way come in contact with Alexandra De Wolfe, snoop around, and potentially discover what kind of mother she *really* was, for the press to begin a series of new sensationalized stories for the satiated public to feed from with morbid curiosity and callous fixation, and its will and pitiless motivation to try to destroy the De Wolfe family.

All De Wolfe could reasonably hope for was after five days of a relentless, organized blitzkrieg of lunacy and perversion by a biased press, that it move on to juicer targets or that Emilie De Wolfe's suicide would run its course, die its own slow, natural death on the press's obituary page without as much as a whimper.

Chapter 10

EVA THREW THE *DAILY RECORD* to the floor in revulsion.

She bought the paper today off the corner newsstand to keep abreast of the Emilie De Wolfe case but now regretted it. This was the scenario for her, buy the newspaper, let it enrage her, and then throw it down somewhere in the bedroom after reading through it.

She and De Wolfe had not been in communication since Emilie De Wolfe's suicide. This Eva expected. De Wolfe's private life must be protected at all costs. She knew the press was camped outside Wolfe & Fitch on Broadway like a pack of wolves. The papers' photographs of De Wolfe were not ones she was accustomed to seeing. In those photos, De Wolfe was all smiles and charm, since, customarily, it signaled that De Wolfe had pulled off another financial coupe, and his grin or smile could plaster a billboard and make it sing.

But this was not the other Maxwell Engelbert De Wolfe who was being photographed now; this De Wolfe was an unappealing tycoon, who had either a scowl on his face or a bitterness that leaped off the page and into a person's heart a thousandfold. It was a De Wolfe who looked like he'd aged in his black top hat that couldn't hide a face that had added wrinkles, the agent of grief and its cruel entry into him, the pores of his skin that not even De Wolfe's black beard hid away.

The press, though, Eva thought, picking up the paper off the floor and then astutely studying it again, was dragging Emilie De

Wolfe through the muck and mire, making who Emilie was sound more like a slut than a socialite. It was like a steady drumbeat, a lynch mob that had collected, tracked its prey, cornered it, and hanged it by its neck in effigy—this rich girl.

Eva felt De Wolfe's pain. She did miss him since her life was so limited, so drenched in secrecy. Her publishing job didn't help, a publishing firm that loved stories, and the gossip among her mostly young, talkative coworkers was as bad as the press's. She had not engaged in their gab fests and, as always, kept strictly to herself, offering no opinion. She just kept her head down at her desk and simply pressed forward hoping the Emilie De Wolfe story would soon dissolve into oblivion.

She'd visited her mother the past Saturday in Harlem, and her mother had not heard from her brother, Dorrell. It seemed the money was holding up well for him, since it would be the only practical reason for Dorrell to contact Lilly. After all, it was a hundred and twenty-five dollars, a lot of money. She still wouldn't bank on Dorrell changing his ways, that prison had in any way rehabilitated him (not that prison was built with that mission in mind). But being someone as smart as Dorrell, maybe he would come away from the prison experience with a new perspective on life: *walk the straight and narrow.*

"How I wish for mother's sake, and the sake of our family."

She saw how the De Wolfe family was being treated, a family in the glare and heat of the media's light. How she felt for De Wolfe and his well-being. How she hoped he would be able to hold up under the assault, the torrent of opinion, and the besmirching of a daughter who thought she'd found love but probably felt in her heart she never would. They weren't all that different in age, Emilie twenty-three, her twenty-six—three years apart.

But when she found De Wolfe, she was not looking for love but stardom. To be someone in show business, the world of Hollywood and Broadway, the Great White Way. That was her sole ambition not until De Wolfe derailed it. It was just the struggle of a young girl to obtain that height of attention and adulation, for the world to bow at her feet to acclaim and claim her, to make her a household name and a worldwide sensation, to build herself into a stage star or silent screen star, or both.

She hadn't taken a shortcut toward fame since no longer was she balanced on that path. She was still with De Wolfe, waiting for his scandal to clear. For his private life not to be under heavy guard, duress, surveillance, not because of something he'd done but because of a tragedy, Emilie De Wolfe's death that affected others, his family and her.

But no one knew of her, only her. Eva Durant, Eva laughed.

"I'm the one who's going through a lot emotionally too, who's mixed up in this tragedy as well."

FAGAN OPENED THE PACKARD'S DOOR and then shut it. De Wolfe trailed him, and when he looked straight ahead at the Ballad building, he felt he'd been freed of an enormous burden.

De Wolfe handed Fagan the key to the door. They were inside the building facing the stairs, and De Wolfe, with the aid of his cane (more than ever), proceeded up the creak-filled stairs until he reached the second landing to join Fagan who had the slender key in hand. The door opened.

"Thank you, Fagan, and good night."

"Good night, Mr. De Wolfe."

De Wolfe, when Fagan turned to him, lightly patted his back.

EVA HEARD DE WOLFE IN the hallway, and her heart exploded.

She didn't know when it would happen, this nightmare would be lifted, but for the past three nights she'd been preparing for this moment. The Emilie De Wolfe story was finally ebbing away, drowning in its own, by now, ink, mundaneness, bland drumbeat, the story located on page 5 or 8, no longer front page in the dailies.

Eva bounded off the bed and toward the door to greet De Wolfe, because it meant the lonely hours had finally ended for her and that what was her normal life would return with a vigor; the end of this tragedy, of her personal nightmare.

She stood at the door and then flung it open.

"Max!"

"Eva! At last, Eva! At long last!"

Eva saw a man who was relaxed, as if all of life's whips and woe had suddenly melted away. She and De Wolfe kissed and hugged but nothing more physical. When De Wolfe stepped into the bedroom, he looked around it like a stranger, like a man who had returned home from a long, arduous journey and soon, joyfully, began to unwind in its comforts.

THEY HAD WOUND UP IN bed, him in his underwear, she still in her negligee, panties, and bra. She lit a cigar for him, and De Wolfe rested back against the headboard with the ashtray sitting on top of his plump belly. Once De Wolfe took his first puff from the cigar, he appeared relieved.

De Wolfe took Eva's hand. "I've ... those bastards ... I've been humbled, Eva." Eva felt the pressure De Wolfe's hand had applied to hers. "It has taken something like this to humble me."

"H-how, Max?"

"How ... hell ... how ... There are things mightier than me out there, Eva. That's how."

"The press?"

"Yes, yes, I did use the obnoxious word 'bastards,' didn't I. They can make out of you what they will. It's been my grim lesson from all of this. It's what's rocked me most the past two weeks of this fucking travesty, Eva. They paint your life the way they please. See it.

"And I could sue all of those bastards for slander, all of them, and it still would not end. Mean a damned thing to them. It's an endless trail. A—"

"The stories they've written have repulsed me, Max!"

"I didn't read them, but they were highlighted for me by my people. I don't even know many of those faceless bastards, cowards, who turned Emilie's life inside out like a goddamned pocket full of dirty, filthy lint!"

Tears sat in De Wolfe's swelling eyes. "Every night I cry for my daughter, for Emilie, Eva. Every goddamned night of the week!"

Eva took the ashtray away from De Wolfe and hugged him.

"And you, I missed you with all my heart, Eva. Not the sex," he said, looking up at her. "Who the hell cares ... It was the companionship, the warmth of your breasts, the kindness that's in your heart, Eva." Pause.

"Alexandra De Wolfe might as well be a shadow in the house these days, haunting it, Eva. It seems to be her sole purpose. To haunt the mansion I live in hell ... hell ..."

How awful that sounded, Eva thought. But she'd not judge Alexandra De Wolfe, she knew enough about her life with De Wolfe and Emilie De Wolfe to know that she (an intimate stranger) should not judge a woman whose spirit had been broken by many potent events, who slept with her husband and heard him just use the word "companionship" to her in describing their illicit relationship, not "whore."

"Was there not one time in her goddamned miserable life she loved Emilie? My daughter. Was there not one part of herself she found attractive or could give particular attention to as merit? Things between us are far worse, not better. Emilie's death has ...

"I lied to Alexandra."

"Lied?"

"Emilie, the Frenchman's name was Juan Manuel, an artist with talent, but otherwise, useless."

"Juan Manuel, but I thought—"

"Paul Tristan does not exist. My daughter created her lover for her own device and deceit. Her own little game of subterfuge to appease me."

"I don't understand, Max. What do you mean?"

"Paul Tristan was to give the relationship a degree of repute, standing. He was fashioned as a wealthy businessman, when all along Emilie was fucking a young French artist who, through luck, or fate, if you will, was pulled off the streets of Paris after the war by an old, rich Frenchwoman who now keeps him and who he loves sentimentally, at least."

Eva's head was spinning. "Loves?"

"There's no sex between them in their strange alliance. Just the words of love from him for this batty woman who's given him the freedom he wants to seduce women, a world of them at his wont, then leave them. And if they commit suicide like Emilie, there's no blood on his hands!"

"How did you—"

"It was in a letter the fuck sent to Emilie. The detective handling the case turned it over to me at the Martinique. The suicide scene. No one else knows of it but me, him, and now you. There was a painting too of Emilie. The bastard painted her, but not Emilie, but someone else, not her, making his crime even more reprehensible."

"Then she was, was beautiful, Max, in the painting's rendition of her, is it fair to say?"

"Yes, indeed," De Wolfe said, crying again. "But not beautiful by your standards, Eva, but beautiful by … he disqualified the things that made my daughter physically ugly. That make my wife the same. That make any woman who is not beautiful ugly.

"He made her look … ordinary." De Wolfe cleared his throat. "I kept the illusion of Paul Tristan alive by—"

"Telling Mrs. De Wolfe that there was an actual Paul Tristan."

"Even made up a fake envelope for her with, supposedly, the letter sent from Paris to Emilie in it …"

"But …"

"Hell, Eva, hell, I knew she wouldn't read it, have nothing to do with it, and she didn't. She stuck her nose as high as you or me sniffing a pile of horseshit."

Eva looked across the room at the wall of various mirrors she looked into every day, often to kill her loneliness and see what De Wolfe and other men saw in her.

"And now for another truth no one knows of but me and Emilie's private physician: Emilie was pregnant by Juan Manuel. The fucking dago!"

"Pregnant!"

"He impregnated her. What added to her emotional imbalance. Emilie's fucking madness. She was to have the fuck's baby!"

"She ... she ..."

"Killed it! Killed it, Eva!"

Eva was mortified.

"But am I happy, ever happy the baby's dead, that Emilie murdered it, do you hear me, Eva! That I am not the grandfather of a spic, a mixed breed, that Emilie didn't allow it to enter the world. For if I knew this had happened between her and her spic lover, I would have killed the baby myself. Had it aborted. Killed anyway.

"I would not have allowed a spic baby to enter into the bloodlines of my family. De Wolfe family. Anyone that was connected to it!"

Eva had never heard De Wolfe spew such venom and racial hatred. She knew him to be a racist, but his rant involved the killing of a baby, a baby that was innocently conceived and horribly killed by a mother who chose death over life.

"I'm tired," De Wolfe finally said, wearily.

"I'm glad you're here, Max."

"It's been hard on you too, hasn't it? All of this?"

"Yes."

He kissed the side of her arm. "You have the Masthead job and me but very little else in your life, don't you, Eva?"

Whatever De Wolfe was after, Eva thought, she wouldn't go along with it. She wouldn't open her emotional self up to him, not when this was the beginning of the end of Emilie De Wolfe's hold over the press, over New York City, over office gossip; when life would return, somehow, back to normal, and Emilie De Wolfe's life would be remembered by brief occurrences, not by grief.

"I haven't forgotten our holiday in the spring, Max."

"Ha. Why, you haven't, have you, Eva!"

"In fact, I'm thinking about a wardrobe." Eva smiled prettily. "To wear on some faraway island, remote and strange."

De Wolfe laughed.

EVA WAS IN FROM HER job at Masthead Publications. She'd inserted the fat key into the lock and held the slender one in her hand and was about to climb the stairs to get to her living quarters but abruptly stopped to sit down on the stairs and stared out onto the drab vestibule.

She wasn't tired. Her job had not sapped her energy. Even her eyes held up under the strain of that of a proofreader, the sometimes-tedious job of finding a writer's mistakes that were at times funny and at other times unforgivable for the writer's blatant carelessness.

De Wolfe had been with her for four straight nights. He had not returned to the mansion, to Alexandra De Wolfe, but chose to spend his days with her. Tonight would be different. Last night he'd told her of his plan to return home. He appreciated the respite she provided him, but the time had come for him to face up to his "only reality."

When was it she was certain Alexandra De Wolfe knew of her?

"I've never asked myself that question. I wonder why."

Eva pondered while fidgeting with her pocketbook, thinking yet not thinking.

"Does it matter? She knows I exist. She likes it that I exist. That De Wolfe has me. In her world, it doesn't matter what rich women's husbands do. I provide Alexandra De Wolfe relief from De Wolfe."

She and De Wolfe had not had sex since Emilie's death. The four nights were spent with her holding De Wolfe's hand, of listening to his pain, his worry, and his self-doubts; the wanting of Emilie De Wolfe back, and then hoping she'd found peace in heaven. His emotions askew, all over the place.

De Wolfe had not touched a drop of liquor since her death, he told her. And said he was trying to become kinder, more charitable to people he was in daily contact with, mainly his staff at De Wolfe & Fitch. In recent heated negotiations, he was allowing Cyrille Fitch to take on an even bigger role in the firm's negotiations: stage the scene, and then the execution.

What she hoped for from De Wolfe now was that they'd go back to the old ways, the old schedule. De Wolfe being with her three days a week. She wanted to think that what'd happened the past four days was an aberration, but she couldn't be one hundred percent sure. The newspapers no longer ran the Emilie De Wolfe suicide, but De Wolfe's unmitigated grief was a sobering revelation to her. She'd thought he would have recovered by now, regained his footing and perspective on things, that the wound wouldn't extend this deep.

Eva stood on the creaky stairs leading up to her living quarters. "But it is."

Alexandra De Wolfe could basically ignore him if she chose to and it wouldn't affect the marriage. Alexandra De Wolfe could be a dark, feckless figure, but she couldn't: she was De Wolfe's mistress.

"Alexandra De Wolfe has this huge advantage over me."

Her job, Alexandra De Wolfe, a woman as rich as her, did not have to console her husband, to boost his ego, to make him feel like a superman in his universe of potent men and their war over money, to be the kingpin, to change the world in ugly ways, not beautiful, not how she wanted to through her artistry, through her stagecraft, the egalitarian act of giving, sharing from a stage with bright lights as its crown jewel, ennobling a humanity she'd, at one time, believed in, aspired to when youthful and one hundred percent involved.

It was February 2.

"Mercer Street's the next block, isn't it, Fagan?"

"Yes, it is, Mr. De Wolfe."

De Wolfe's sigh was like a cannon shot circling the globe.

Fagan didn't quite know how to feel, sorry for De Wolfe or not. He had been with the mistress he'd never seen, but his time with her was up. It was time for his real life to reemerge. De Wolfe was coming home to Mrs. De Wolfe and the mansion, not Ballad Street and the mistress.

The press had tried to get to him. They even offered him money under the table to spill the beans on De Wolfe. They were after the big exposé, the kind that pulls the sheet off a man, denudes him, exposes his balls. He barely knew Emilie De Wolfe but grieved for her only because she was young and because of the cards life dealt her.

But as far as Fagan was concerned, the De Wolfe family was not the story, especially not De Wolfe. He had a strong loyalty to the man. De Wolfe treated him well (in a way, they were a team), better than most people had. And he paid him well.

Fagan had no respect for the press. The whole lot could burn in hell as far as he was concerned, them and their lousy, two-bit money. De Wolfe's money was good enough for him!

"Fagan, you've been a good friend throughout my misery. This bad stretch of mine."

"Now, Mr. De Wolfe, you know that doesn't sit straight in this kind of arrangement between us, sir." Fagan laughed.

"No, but you have, Fagan. Hell, it's just, it's high time I told you. Hell, this hardship, I haven't been the easiest person to be around."

"A child, young lady like Ms. Emilie. I don't want to even think about losing one of my daughters, Mr. De Wolfe. Wouldn't be any good for my nerves. Nobody's nerves, sir."

"There've been times, Fagan, when I look at the whole goddamned world as a piss-hole." Pause. "But then the next day, or whatever the hell it is, I'm back in the office. Grinding it out. Back to being Maxwell De Wolfe. Back to buying happiness, Fagan, for myself. But the world still stinks like a mound of horse dung."

WHEN DE WOLFE FOLLOWED HELGA into the dining room and Alexandra wasn't present, De Wolfe asked, "Helga, where is Mrs. De Wolfe?"

Helga looked down at De Wolfe with a fretful face. "Mrs. De Wolfe no longer eats her meals at the dining room table, Mr. De Wolfe."

"She what! How the hell long has this been going on!"

Helga paused and then responded. "For the past three nights, sir."

Yvette, the chef's wife, stepped into the room.

De Wolfe headed for his chair and then sat.

FINISHING HIS MEAL, DE WOLFE'S dour mood hadn't changed. The pheasant soaked in wine did him no good, nor the charlotte russe. He'd been sitting at a dining room table where his was the lone body present. It was bad enough that he could never have Emilie at the table with him, but now it was Alexandra, a woman who was no real company at the table for him but at least a presence, at least an illusion of something stable, that kept order in the household, not this, this disorder that he heard loud and clear, that was unsettling and would have to be dealt with, further disrupting his life, its static condition.

Alexandra had tampered with a routine, an unwritten rule of the De Wolfe household, and she'd be dealt with by him.

TAP.

Elsa opened the bedroom door.

"Mr. De Wolfe."

"I am here to see Mrs. De Wolfe."

"Mrs. De Wolfe," Elsa said, pivoting herself, "Mr.—"

"You are dismissed, Elsa," Alexandra said.

When De Wolfe entered the room, Elsa shut the bedroom door behind her.

"I expected you," Alexandra said from the back recesses of the room. "I just had no idea when."

It was like he was following a trail of soft light until he got to her. She was sitting at her vanity table carefully powdering her cheeks.

"You know full well where I've been."

"Yes, Maxwell. That unmentionable place, with that unmentionable woman," she said, turning her face to him, putting down the powder puff.

"What the hell are you doing, embarrassing me. Insulting me in my own goddamned house!"

Alexandra stood and then took to a chair near her bed. "I did what I chose to do."

"Without my permission, something I would've rejected, never permit you to do," De Wolfe said, drawing nearer to her. "How dare you eat in this room!" De Wolfe said, stabbing the cane into the rug as if it were a weapon.

"I will not argue with you. Ha. You are grieving."

"You goddamned soulless bag of shit!"

"And who is to blame?" Alexandra said coolly. "Who is the culprit in this opera—plotted as it is—since you have such a great affection, passion for opera, Maxwell?"

This was far too shocking for him. De Wolfe had to collect himself; this was an evening of shock.

"I have sat in this room uncomplaining. I have met the standard of my bearing. I have accepted who I am and what I must daily endure as a result of it," Alexandra said as if lecturing De Wolfe on what it takes to be a wife of a wealthy man, under the weight of his thumb.

"I am not heroic, no, not that, Maxwell. I am how I've been shaped by generations of people like us. Just like you, Maxwell. But of course, you know this better than I."

"You are quite wicked, aren't you, Alexandra." De Wolfe smiled as cunningly as Alexandra was. "Beneath your reserve, that unruffled veneer you wear, you are quite the wicked one," De Wolfe said, leaning on his cane.

"Call me what you will, please, Maxwell. When has it ever mattered? Even a 'soulless bag of shit.' What does it matter to me, Maxwell?"

"Cry for her, why can't you cry for Emilie, goddamnit!"

"Emilie was never a problem between us. It's always been you, Maxwell. You, not Emilie."

"Cry for my daughter ..."

"I will not do something that is uncommon to me. Not even you can, in any way, force me. Not even you through brute force and threat."

De Wolfe glared at her. "You will stop this. This is the last night you'll eat in, here in this goddamned bedroom." Pause. "You will not disparage me in front of the staff. The people I pay to serve me. You will not further attack my dignity. Blight my name. The De Wolfe name."

"And what about mine? My dignity, my name? Ha." Alexandra arched back her head. "But why discuss it, Maxwell." Pause.

"Just remember who I am. A Bauer. A woman of great wealth, but money I do not have to touch because of you. It is not necessary for me to, Maxwell, but it is there. In wait. At my disposal at any moment … Time of my choosing."

What is this woman trying to do, De Wolfe thought, *match my power with hers? What kind of preposterous … insanity has gotten into her? Great wealth? Great wealth, when I have enormous wealth!*

"You're stuck here, just face up to it, the deplorable fact, Alexandra. You're stuck in mud, in the undertow of filth and rot and greed and past crimes. From now on and until eternity. You may dine wherever the hell you please in the mansion, wherever the hell it suits you. It will become routine among staff," De Wolfe said, walking away from her.

"Will fade into the day's landscape of daily activity, barely noticed … or regarded by anyone."

"I'M SORRY, SORRY, EVA!"

De Wolfe and Eva were looking down at a limp, impotent penis, De Wolfe's limp, impotent penis.

Both were nude, in the bed. They'd tried having sex after a month without it, but De Wolfe couldn't get a hard-on. A stiff prick.

"Don't worry, Max. It's all right."

"What the hell's wrong with me!" De Wolfe flung back the covers. "I know what, I know what!"

And Eva knew too, it was Emilie De Wolfe; this had all begun with her death, first De Wolfe's lack of interest in sex and now their attempt tonight collapsing, resulting in what they were looking at: a dead penis.

"Max, I have to go—"

"Not the bathroom, Eva!" De Wolfe said in a panic.

"Yes, I—"

"Because of me!"

"No, Max, of course not. Peeing was invented long before you came along," Eva laughed, hopping out of the bed. "I'm sure."

With Eva out of the room for no more than a second, De Wolfe took the large pillow and covered his face.

Eva had shut the bathroom door, and even if she had to pee, there was no reason for her to leave the room when she had; she could have waited. But she felt De Wolfe needed time with himself, and that she could extend to him this much of herself. He was fighting demons that he alone must wrestle. The situation called for privacy.

DE WOLFE REMOVED THE PILLOW from his face. "Am I Paul Tristan? Or am I Juan Manuel? Which one am I! The wealthy version of myself, or the goddamned cheap one. But does it matter: De Wolfe's the seducer of young girls."

De Wolfe grabbed his penis. "Dick! Prick! Peter! Cock!"

De Wolfe was living with this kind of unrelenting guilt because of Emilie. A young girl with little experience being misled by an older man.

"How am I any different with Eva? What I have done to young girls like my daughter?"

No matter that he'd been with Eva for over two years, she was still a young girl whom he had preyed on. She was a showgirl among all the others who were young and inexperienced in relation to vile, disgusting older men like him. They were lambs in the wilderness. Those girls stood no chance like Emilie stood no chance against Juan Manuel, this Frenchman with every tool of the trade: the innate guile to charm, persuade, and then seduce.

He had to stand in judgment of himself if no one else would, De Wolfe thought. Before Emilie had died, she'd tried. And with him and Alexandra no longer eating at the dining room table, that too was a judgment of him. But to him, they had not struck the necessary blow to hurt or cripple him or make him stand before the altar of moral judgment.

"But now the time has come—look at me, my cock. Look at me. It's betrayed me. Soft as cotton, a fucking cotton ball. It's judged me, my own penis stands in judgment of me. And this is my punishment!"

De Wolfe felt this horror grip him, this primitiveness, where every aspect of him and his power had not boiled down to money but sex. His power in the bed, between the sheets with a woman, someone red blooded with flesh and bone and desires, and lust …

"Lust, lust, lust!"

This is what killed Emilie. What he, Maxwell De Wolfe, carried more powerfully inside him than power: lust. The one thing Emilie couldn't control even if she called it love. In the end it was lust because it was so central, its demands, in killing her. She wanted Juan Manuel with all her heart and soul to fuck her, simply fuck her in the end— nothing more. Because if there was a *real* Paul Tristan and they had begun with this same appetite of lust, and she'd borne his children and tried to live a normal, decent life, and if, after years of marriage, she no longer lusted for him, the marriage would have failed.

"Emilie's life … it would fail. Fail. Fucking fail!"

Eva, washing her hands at the sink, felt she had given De Wolfe enough time to himself. She was worried about him but not anxious. She trusted his thinking. She admired his brilliance. It was Emilie at the root of his sudden impotence, after all, nothing more exotic or profound. De Wolfe's daughter's death.

Eva opened the bathroom door.

De Wolfe heard the crack of the door when it opened.

"Eva, Eva, let's try again, Eva! We must try to FUCK AGAIN!"

Chapter 11

Ninety percent of what Caesar Stark wore today, he'd stolen. From his newsboy cap to the Bulova watch, to the woolen argyle socks, to the shoes he wore. Caesar Stark was a petty thief. He'd served time in jail, but not in the "Big House." He was a fast talker with a light, wispy thin voice for someone who was built like an ox.

Caesar Stark stood on the corner of Ballad and Farragut Streets. Caesar looked like he was casing the area for a future heist. But in actual fact, he'd just been hired by the Amsterdam Moving Company a few buildings up from Farragut Street.

A March wind was knocking the stuffings out of the day.

Caesar ducked his head, pulled a pack of Pall Mall cigarettes out of the pack, covered the match with his fleshy hand, and then lit it and then let the howling wind do him the favor of blowing its flame out.

When he looked to his left, he saw someone he never expected to see in a million years round the corner.

"It can't be … Motherfucker …"

She didn't notice him, but Caesar was so startled he actually became tongue-tied.

"Eva, man, fucking Eva Durant!"

Eva was at least forty to fifty yards opposite him on the other side of Ballad Street.

Caesar still hadn't budged from the corner. "Man, she still looks pretty as Christmas. That gorgeous flame of a dame!"

He was going to yell at her, but something inside him cautioned him not to. Maybe it was him being a thief, on the wrong side of the law and not the right side for most of his life, that ditched the thought.

"Yeah, man, let me see what that living doll's up to. On this here side of town."

Caesar switched over into a mode he was good at when selling himself to a new employer as a solid, reliable worker. Someone who could be trusted and never got in trouble and would do the job better than any company hire it ever had before him. It's the malarkey he'd handed Amsterdam Moving Company a few minutes earlier.

Caesar stamped out the cigarette and then jogged but so far down Ballad Street until he was in lockstep with Eva. It put him at least thirty yards behind her. He still occupied the other side of the street.

He stopped when Eva stopped. Caesar crouched low enough so as not to be seen (there was no one on the block but him and Eva; it was deserted). "What the fuck she doing?"

Caesar saw Eva had pulled a key out her pocketbook. She didn't look around her physical environ but felt at home in it, he thought.

"She's what, fucking going in that fucking building! Eva!"

The day was fading, and there was no daylight, but dusk. And then, suddenly, Eva vanished.

"Is what I just saw a mirage or fucking what?" Caesar said, straightening himself.

For some reason he knew Eva wasn't going to exit the building, and if she did, would it matter? he thought. She was an old childhood chum. At one time he had a crush on her as wide as the moon. But who didn't in Newark in those days, the neighborhood they lived in. Who the hell in their right mind didn't!

But this was intriguing, more than intriguing, he thought. But just how much should he investigate the situation? Or should he just go up to the building, knock on the metal door, and end all this mystery, suspense, or …

"Let me …"

The light over the building's door popped on.

It froze Caesar. He remained where he was for a few seconds more but then decided to make his way down Ballad Street.

When he was opposite the building, he saw what he had observed from the distance, no windows on the building's first floor and no lights on the second, at least not any shining out the front of the building.

"Hmm …"

Caesar ran across the street, and from the left side of the building, he chose to take a tour around it since it was all open ground, nothing to fence in the building or in any way impede him. And when he got to the right side of the building, he looked up into two windows that had radiant light.

"So what's that all about? Work … she works here? Eva, man? I wonder, just wonder." Caesar removed his cap and scratched his head. "Live, she don't live in here," Caesar said, patting the cold brick. "No way. No fucking way, man."

Caesar kept looking up at the two windows, puzzled. He remained there for about another minute or so and then began walking away. When he got to the sidewalk, he began running up the street as if being chased. When back on the corner of Ballad and Farragut, where he'd started from, he looked back down the short cobbled street.

He lit up another Pall Mall. "I either got me something here, or it don't amount to a hill of beans. Shit." He took a puff on his cigarette. "Or a gold mine. A fucking pot of gold … don't ask me why I got that kind of creepy feeling going," he said, tugging down deftly on the tip of his snug-fitting cap.

"But I kind of feel it in my bones. Got a hunch that something is shaking. B-big could come outta this here situation for me."

It was the years of him being a thief that made him size up situations before he acted on them. Never mind it was Eva Durant, a girl so beautiful any poor sap would whistle at her even if she was holding on to another guy's arm and risked getting busted in the chops for his troubles.

"Oh, if she ain't a dish. A dame right out of this world!"

He smoked the cigarette hands free, since he'd dashed both hands inside his pockets, walking up Ballad Street at a slow clip.

"Dorrell," he said as the wind swirled the smoke, "gotta Sing Sing vacation, right? But heard he got out the can recently. Served his time. Free as a fucking bird of paradise."

At one time he and Dorrell Durant were close, but Dorrell was after much bigger jobs than him. As for himself, he liked nickel-and-diming the system, but not Dorrell. Dorrell was after the big heist, the big money that makes a name for hoods like them, earns them respect and admiration from the bottom up.

"A smart motherfucker. Don't know if he's worked a natural-born day in his fucking life, though!" Pause. "Boy like him is too smart sometimes. Think they can fuck over anything and get away with it spit clean."

Caesar just knew he broke his mother's heart, Lilly Durant's heart, when he started his life of crime. They started out at about the same time even if he was a year older than Dorrell.

"Dorrell …"

Caesar was still stuck on the corner, the wind whistling in his ears. "Wonder if he knows Eva, what she's up to, man?"

One thing Caesar knew, they weren't close. They just never got along, period. Eva, he remembered, was artsy. She liked cultural stuff. Something she talked about all the time.

"Spoke a different language than him. For sure. How girls do them, man." Caesar's shoulders dipped. "I know where he's staying. Sure as hell do!"

But first things first, Caesar thought. Since his company was right up the block, he was going to keep tabs on Eva. See just what she was up to down on Ballad Street.

"Find out shit on my own. Don't need fucking Dorrell's help."

He doubted if Dorrell knew anything, not the way they hit it off. And if he did know something, it was through his mother.

"I'm gonna keep an eye on you, Eva. Yours truly. See what the fuck you up to these days. See whether or not I struck fucking gold or fool's gold, sister!"

"I'VE FINALLY, AFTER ALL THESE months, Fagan, had a good day. A day I didn't expect ... To spend with only the intermittent interruptions of thoughts of Emilie. That is good, isn't it?"

"Yes it is, Mr. De Wolfe."

"I just hope it continues," De Wolfe sighed. "In fact, I was beginning to think such profound torture would never end. The mind, Fagan, is as devious and controlling as the heart."

Fagan nodded.

The car was two blocks from Ballad Street.

"I need her, Fagan. I need her."

Fagan wanted to turn his head to De Wolfe but was afraid to. It's the first time De Wolfe had mentioned who was inside the building on Ballad Street, hidden behind its brick and mortar, away from sight. The first time he'd dared to with him.

"You're the only person I can say this to."

Fagan, for the first time in his relationship with De Wolfe (chauffeur), felt De Wolfe had said too much. That abstraction was better than truth.

"It's good to sit back here for a minute, Fagan. To compose myself. Breathe, Fagan."

THIS WAS THE SECOND NIGHT that Caesar Stark hoped his luck would change. Yesterday he'd waited for Eva Durant to show up on Ballad Street, and she was on time, so he had her schedule down pat. Of course he hid himself, observing her from afar. Of course there was no problem, since he knew where she was headed.

Eva lived in the building. Eva did not work in it. Caesar stood out in the cold air until eleven o'clock last night. It's when the two lights on the second floor went out. He knew then something fishy was going on. He was curious whether or not Eva was living there with a man, but up till now there'd been no evidence to support that.

Caesar was to start his new job with Amsterdam Moving Company Monday. It was Friday. He had a lot of time on his hands, for he didn't have any plans of doing anything crooked for the present. No criminal schemes up his sleeve. But tonight he was hoping his prospects would change.

It was ten o'clock, and from where he stood on the other side of the street, in the dark, in an open dirt lot that was recessed, he saw what he hoped to see last night, a car with big, fat headlights rolling importantly down the one-way street.

"Shit, oh shit!" Caesar was excited. Instinctively, he crouched down, even if there was no need to.

The car was a black Packard, and immediately Caesar thought of money!

From where he stood, he could gain an excellent view of everything. He'd been smoking his Pall Mall but tossed it. His eyes were trained on the building with the dim light hanging over the door, but he would still be able to see the figure, the man in the rich man's car when he got out of the car well enough to form opinion.

The waiting was killing Caesar, even if a lot of time had not been eaten away, it just felt like it. Caesar had positioned himself more to the right of the lot, for he wanted the best view possible that he could obtain of the man who'd eventually emerge from the Packard.

"There he is, there the motherfucker is!"

Caesar had disregarded his chauffeur, for his eyes were trained on the man with the black top hat and the cane and the limp, and when the man turned his head, immediately, he knew who he was.

"Maxwell De Wolfe! Fucking Maxwell De Wolfe!"

For who in their right mind in New York City didn't know Maxwell De Wolfe? He could read. He read enough ink on De Wolfe, saw all the pictures of him and his daughter in the papers. Pictures of De Wolfe in the Packard. De Wolfe walking into the office of De Wolfe & Fitch; the biggest story hitting the city of New York in years.

"Eva's his babe! De Wolfe's fucking Eva! She's his fucking mistress!"

The scene continued to unfold before Caesar's eyes. Yes, something he couldn't believe was happening to him.

He saw De Wolfe and his chauffeur duck inside the building, and then about a minute later, the chauffeur emerged from the building.

"Damn, man, damn, this is fucking juicy."

He saw the chauffeur look around the area as if by habit and then get back into the car and then drive off.

"What have I stumbled onto?" Caesar asked, now out of the lot, but staying on that side of the street. "What, fucking what!"

Even if it was a chilly night, Caesar was burning like a candle. He would see what time the lights from the two windows would go off tonight, and if the Packard would return for De Wolfe, but he'd already scratched that alternative off the list.

"I know about them rich motherfuckers like De Wolfe. I know all about how they fucking live. De Wolfe's old lady don't care if she sees his old ass tonight or not. Them rich bitches don't care about shit.

"De Wolfe's docked here for the night. Ain't going nowhere. Eva, Eva, the most beautiful girl I ever seen, man. Fucking De Wolfe. Fucking one of the wealthiest men in the world, fucking ..."

Caesar stopped, for he had what he wanted, he thought. His gold mine! His pot of gold!

I⠀T WAS TWELVE FIFTEEN, AND Caesar was heading back to what he termed his "rat hole" in Harlem. He was walking back uptown. It was like he was being hit by one thunderbolt after the other. He still hadn't recovered from tonight's discovery. His primary thinking, currently, was focused on Dorrell Durant. He wondered if Dorrell knew about what was going on with Eva, or better still: Lilly Durant.

"Do I wanna fucking dig up Dorrell? Do I need him in on this scheme? Fucking scheme? 'Cause Dorrell ain't gonna care, give a never mind if it's his sister we gonna work on. There's big bucks in this shit here. Big dough, man."

He'd never deny Dorrell was way, way smarter than him even if he got caught doing his last heist that got him a seven-year stretch in Sing Sing.

"Who the fuck cares. What the fuck for. Everybody slips up once in a while in this fucking game. Ain't nobody's perfect. Ain't meant to be. Don't stop nobody from stealing, just 'cause them fucking coppers catch you. Nobody bats a thousand all the fucking time."

What was he trying to do, convince himself that he should involve Dorrell in on the caper? That Dorrell would come up with a better scheme, package—a better way to handle De Wolfe than him? But then there would be a two-way split, and it wasn't that he was greedy, he could use the kind of loot that'd come out of the deal, but Dorrell was always after big game, the big payoff.

Caesar lit a Pall Mall.

This would be a huge decision he'd have to make on his own. He and Dorrell had always gotten along when they were young, but they were grown now. Did Sing Sing harden him? Did Sing Sing make him a better criminal, a smarter one?

There was a lot for Caesar to contemplate. He didn't want to blow this thing with De Wolfe. After all, De Wolfe was one of the wealthiest men in the world, and maybe, after what he was about to pull off, it could make him the richest crook in the world.

LILLY WAS STANDING OVER AT the kitchen sink washing down string beans. She was about to transfer them into a small pot. She was preparing dinner for her and Eva. This was Eva's Saturday to visit. This was the one thing in her life she looked forward to. She was wearing the pearls Eva gave her a few months ago, even if she was in a plain dress. She stopped what she was doing.

"I'm so happy all of Maxwell De Wolfe's problems have faded from the public's eyes. I'm so happy for Eva."

She certainly suffered through that trying period as Eva's mother. To know that Eva had the kind of connection she had to De Wolfe, a father who'd lost his daughter to suicide, and how it was being reported in the papers he was handling it. Her Christian heart went out to De Wolfe, of course, but her main worry was Eva, how De Wolfe's profound depression could be affecting her.

It's why her visits to the apartment during that tumultuous period she'd keep her eyes on her, look for any signs of depression, even if Eva wouldn't share the loneliness of her life with her, that argument they had had before and now rejected, so, for them, it'd become off limits. They preferred, mutually, to steer clear of it.

Today, though, Lilly would bring something else up just as flammable: Dorrell.

"Maybe after dinner. After we've eaten," Lilly said. "I need a pleasant day. But I must not be a prisoner to my feelings," Lilly said cautiously. "Eva's presence is important to me today. More than ever."

Lilly and Eva had eaten dinner, and Eva had gone into the living room to wait for her. She was pinching the white doily pinned to the fat arm of the sagging sofa's cushion. For some reason, she didn't want the day to end. It'd been such a pleasant stay at the apartment. Childhood memories were raised between her and Lilly. A lot of laughter mixed between the good cheer each exuded. Lilly's memory was much the keener than hers (maybe she was born to be an actor, she'd thought at the time, not her!). Eva laughed ever so lightly. But it was good to know you were young at one time, even if it wasn't that long ago, only felt it.

This was proof of the selfless nature of her mother, Eva thought, glancing around the living room. *To live in Harlem, in this apartment. It was motivated by me, really, for her to be physically closer to me.* Newark was too far away for these kinds of convenient Saturday visits between them. Someone had to shorten the distance, and it was her mother who shouldered the task. She was the head of the Durant family, undoubtedly.

"Eva, I caught you doing that!"

"Caught me doing what?" Eva said, turning her head to her.

Eva had been pinching the couch's doily, something she'd do as a child.

"Look down at your—"

"Oh, you mean this!" Eva pinched the doily harder.

"Yes, that!" Pause. "My children!"

"Your—"

"Yes, children," Lilly said, sitting down next to Eva. "I have more than one child. Not just you, Eva."

"Must we, Mother?" Eva said snottily.

"I love him, Eva. No matter what Dorrell's done. At what stage he is in his life."

"Then you've heard from him?"

"No."

"No, and you won't. And you know why," Eva said angrily, "because he hasn't run through the money yet. The hundred and twenty-five dollars."

Lilly half smiled. "You're right."

"Otherwise, you won't see him."

"But I want to, Eva. I want to, with all my heart."

Eva, in her heart of hearts, wanted to empathize with Lilly, but they were talking about Dorrell, her brother, and when they talked about him, the memories from the past of him, ran far down inside her, opened up hurts that had not healed, nor did she want them to.

"I want him to be well, to be safe. He survived prison," Lilly said with tears in her eyes. "That's all I know, Eva. The extent of the experience. But I want to know more. I pray for him, Dorrell. I pray for my son."

Eva held Lilly.

"When I hear from him—"

"It'll be for more money, Mother. More of your money, not because he's your son, he wants to talk to his mother. It'll be because of him. It's always been because of him. He's always at the center of everything. The universe."

"But suppose it's because, when he calls, Dorrell calls, Eva, that he's back in prison?"

"You must stop this kind of thinking, Mother," Eva said, releasing Lilly, looking her dead in the eye. "It'll get you nowhere. Dorrell won't change, Mother, Dorrell—"

"But how do you know that! Can you say that!"

"I know because he doesn't want to. He thinks he's smarter than the world, so therefore, he can outsmart it. It doesn't matter how many times he fails at it, falls short. Don't you see, Mother, he'll keep trying. He won't stop. Not Dorrell. Not your son."

"Why, why!" Lilly shrieked.

Eva grabbed her.

"At times I thought I was in Sing Sing with him."

"I ... Why can't I feel like you?" Eva said, pressing Lilly's head to her breast.

"A parent, at least me, when Dorrell was born, saw his life differently, Eva. That's the difference between us . Through a much different lens. It's that simple."

And I suppose it is that simple, even when it comes to Dorrell, when a mother says it, Eva thought.

THE EMPTY LOT HAD PRACTICALLY become his refuge for this the third night of Caesar Stark waiting on Maxwell De Wolfe to reappear on Ballad Street.

Caesar's face was beginning to take on the appearance of a fiend's. A heroin user who sweated at the thought of De Wolfe (not heroin) and what he was doing in the Ballad building. Caesar's new job as a mover with the Amsterdam Moving Company, he ditched as of today. He didn't bother to report to the company just up the street. He didn't give a "flying fuck" about that job. He was on to bigger things. A bigger, better opportunity.

"De Wolfe's gonna show tonight. He's gotta. Eva's cunt's getting cold!"

But he wasn't cold. He hadn't been cold since the scheme he cooked up began rattling around in his brain; that made perfect sense to him. "I'm gonna be rich soon. Fucking rich. In the pink!"

In his "rat hole" was when Caesar cooked up what, tonight, would open the floodgates for the kind of moola he could only dream of, not ever really believe in.

"Yeah, De Wolfe, you gonna butter my bread. Or maybe I should say biscuits. 'Cause I'm gonna bring you to your fucking knees."

CAESAR JUMPED.

He saw the black Packard.

He was dressed in black, all black, gloves, hat, etc. And now was time for him to cover his face with the black mask. After Caesar executed that, his attention rebounded back to De Wolfe. Caesar edged more to the front rim of the lot.

"There he is, that—"

And then Caesar was stuck in place, unable to move his limbs as Fagan and De Wolfe got out of the car and began to go through their normal routine.

"De Wolfe! De Wolfe!"

But it was too late. De Wolfe was already in the building, and Fagan was back outside about to enter the car.

And Caesar did move but, by doing so, had dropped down on top of the lot's dirt and onto his knees. He ripped the black mask off his face. And with his eyes shut, he heard the car drive away from the building, but he didn't look at it. He just continued to hear the car in his ears in a muffled way that seemed more fantasy than real.

He dashed up Ballad Street as if his pants were on fire. He was on Farragut Street, huffing and puffing. Caesar was a ball of energy and nerves and bewilderment, and a stomach that ached near to the point of fear.

Caesar stopped and then leaned against a short building. He began pummeling his palm with his fist. "I couldn't do it, I couldn't do it, I couldn't fucking do it!"

He felt like a punk, a chump, someone who was not big enough for the job he'd had in mind. For his scheme was quite simple: he was to run across the street and yell out (at the top of his lungs) Eva's name and then, then—

And that's what scared him the most even when he'd consolidated the plan, the "then" part of it. What would happen then, next? That was the part of the plan that frightened him. And still pounding his palm, he began to think it wasn't well planned out. What would De Wolfe's chauffeur have done feeling he was physically threatening De Wolfe? Would he have had to kill the chauffeur?

And what about De Wolfe? He wouldn't be carrying the kind of loot he desired. De Wolfe would have to hand cash over to him for this kind of operation: blackmail.

"Man oh man oh man ..."

Caesar was beginning to see all the holes in his plan leaking out like a bag of water poked full of holes.

"I ain't shit!"

He was a big, tough guy who was crying like a baby, crying because he did not know how to go about separating De Wolfe from his money. Crying because he did not know how to blackmail De Wolfe in a way that he wouldn't get caught by the cops, making it easy pickings.

The night was dark, ten fifty-two.

Caesar Stark threw the black mask down into the gutter and knew he needed help: someone smarter than him. Much.

Chapter 12

"**D**orrell Durant? Boy hangs out at Lula's Lounge up in Harlem every night of the week since he been out the Yard. Giving them dames up there a fit—so I hear!" It's what Caesar was about to enter, Lula's Lounge, a lounge located in a run-down, beat-down-to-the-socks building that Lula Angel, a middle-aged torch singer, owned and operated after a short singing career overseas where she was hailed on the continent as a Negro singing sensation.

Caesar got the information regarding Dorrell Durant from a Bowery contact.

Lula's Lounge was a significant part of Harlem's night life. It was also known for cheap women with soulless eyes; for drunks who, at Lula's bar, cursed at the moon; and for fistfights that would start and stop, giving Lula no need to call the cops, the police precinct, a few blocks south of the sorry-looking lounge.

A much-used Brunswick pool table with solid rails and tapered legs and leather-made ball pockets was set off to the right of the bar. Dense smoke curled the billiard balls but did nothing to muffle the clicking of the cue ball when smashed against an 8 or 9 ball zooming for the side pocket.

It was ten thirty-six, and even in the dark, where Dorrell Durant sat in a booth, his skin glowed, and the dame he held, with her flashy pink dress and sexy eyes, looked into his eyes as if she'd just found a pot full of diamonds. She didn't look like the other dames in Lula's.

Maybe she was from somewhere else and didn't belong there. Maybe someplace south of Hoboken, New Jersey.

Dorrell, with his beautiful face, took one look at Caesar Stark and broke out laughing.

"My dear lady," Dorrell said, looking at the sexy woman squeezed up in his arms, "may I introduce to you a dear, dear old friend. Someone I grew up with in the charming bowels of Newark, New Jersey. Where con men breed like rats!"

"Dorrell!"

"Caesar!"

Dorrell Durant was on his feet hugging Caesar, the two men of equal height, standing over six foot tall, but Caesar was the much heavier of the two by at least thirty pounds.

"Now, may I ask you, Veronica, uh, I am correct, aren't I …? Veronica …?"

"Oh yes, you're right all—"

"To leave the table for a bit. The gentlemen and I have a great deal to talk about, I'm sure," Dorrell said, winking at the saucy dish, "don't we, Caesar? Unless, I'm sure, you wouldn't be in Lula's honoring me with your presence. Having hunt me down no better than a wild beast off its chain.

"But don't you dare go off too far now, uh, Veronica. I have future plans for you and me tonight."

"No, not at all. I'll be over there, in the other booth, Dorrell. Two booths over, okay!"

Veronica switched her way from the table, and the heat in her hips made Dorrell only imagine what she could do to a man in bed, given a chance.

"Sit down, Caesar. Sit down."

The hard round plastic table was small but able to accommodate two glasses filled to the brim with liquor.

"What are you drinking tonight, my good man? Drinks, all drinks are on me. My personal tab."

"Scotch, the best this joint's got!"

A glass of Reuben's Scotch was on top of the table along with Dorrell's glass of dark red wine. They'd been talking for a short spell. "Yeah, I know Wimpy Lewis. What well-bred gentleman residing in the Bowery doesn't."

"So he said you was on my side of town, up here."

"Yeah, I've been compensating for lost time."

"You mean, fucking all the ass you can get your fucking hands on!"

Dorrell ran his hands through his smooth black hair. "Caesar, my good man, it seems I'm going to have to wash your fucking mouth out with soap!"

Dorrell was in a blue flannel double-breasted suit with a white laundered handkerchief sticking out of the top pocket. His appearance was one of elegance, not that of a con man who took enormous pride in his trade of bait and switch.

"A dog's life doesn't even compare to Sing Sing. How those fucking degenerate guards treated me!"

"It's why they ain't sending me up there! No way. Not my fucking—"

"Caesar, what is it that you wish to discuss, besides rekindling our old childhood acquaintanceship this evening?"

Caesar smiled, for he couldn't wait to see the look that was sure to blow up on Dorrell Durant's mug once he got the news why he was in Lula's Lounge.

"I have a big job, major job for you, Dorrell."

"For me, you … A big … major job for me?" Dorrell said derisively and then looked at Caesar as if he were looking at a piece of chewing gum stuck to the bottom of his shoe.

"Yeah, fucking me, Dorrell. Fucking me, motherfucker!"

"Look, Caesar, I call a spade a spade, you know that. We're from Elmwood Avenue, but that's where our commonality begins and ends. You're a petty crook—"

"Who ain't been locked up in no upstate penitentiary, motherfucker."

"Because you're on the low end of the scale when it comes to crime, not the high end, Caesar. It's really that simple," Dorrell said. "Now, isn't it?"

"Right. You right."

"I would have gotten away with that damned gallery heist," Dorrell said, reflecting on his remark that intensified his dark eyes, "if not for that fucking cowardly pig, Prigg!"

Dorrell was hired by Richard Prigg III to steal a valuable one-million-dollar painting out of a reputable New York City art gallery. It was a night job. A job that required daring. Dorrell climbed like a cat burglar, through the gallery's second-story window, successfully cut the picture out its frame, and then handed it over to Prigg in a false bottom trunk. Prigg paid Dorrell two hundred dollars for the job.

Only, Prigg got squeamish when trying to smuggle the picture out of the country before boarding the ship, on his way overseas to jolly old England to sell the painting through a bustling black market. The customs agent inspecting the luggage suspected something fishy was going on and at Prigg's trial said Prigg's eyes bounced around in his head like Ping-Pong balls, and his forehead had sweat up a storm. So with the discovery of the million-dollar painting in the false bottom of Prigg's trunk, Prigg ratted out Dorrell Durant.

The failed heist received a measure of publication in the New York City dailies for a day or two, Richard Prigg III, that is, not Dorrell Durant.

"You can call me the fuck you want," Caesar said, a scowl crisscrossing his face, "but I got something hot for us."

Dorrell's hands tensed. But what he really wanted to do was laugh in Caesar Stark's face, but Caesar was a rough-and-tumble customer, someone who'd crack open a man's skull just for the hell of it.

"How much you make off that art heist that got you in the slammer, huh, Dorrell?"

"Enough …"

"Well, it ain't even gonna touch what I got lined up for us."

"Us? You haven't told me anything yet, Caesar—nothing that's even sparking my interest or curiosity. And now we're partners in crime?"

"There's someone you and me know, Dorrell ..." Caesar said tantalizingly. "Real fucking close to. 'Specially you."

"Me?"

"Yeah, you."

Suddenly, Dorrell felt uneasy in regard to what Caesar said. He was living off the hundred and twenty-five dollars his mother sent him before his release from Sing Sing. He didn't even know if he was ready, mentally, to return to a life of crime, even if he was prudent and practical enough to understand that eventually he would have to take back to that path of least resistance, after first satisfying his thirst for freedom, and when his mother's money dried up.

"Then spit it out, Caesar. Let me hear what kind of high-end heist you're talking about. Got in mind to whet my fucking fancy and talents."

"You know of Maxwell De Wolfe? The one who was hogging them headlines recently with that suicide fucking broad, fucking crazy daughter of his, don't you?"

"Of course, Caesar," Dorrell said, his finger nudging the empty wineglass away from him. "The dailies beat the hell out of De Wolfe and his daughter, Emilie De Wolfe. Dragged her through the mud and then took after De Wolfe, hoping to break him—those heartless fuckers!"

"Yeah. Not that I kept up with them stories every day in them newspapers," Caesar said, scratching his ear. "Just—"

"So what do you have to do with Maxwell De Wolfe? T-that wealthy white man?" Dorrell asked, like he'd just grabbed Caesar by his coat collar and was shaking him like a rag doll.

"Not me but you, fucking you, Dorrell."

"Look, you see that lovely dame sitting two booths over waiting on me? What, Veronica ... right? Well, she's got the same thing on her mind that I have on mine. So say what you've got to say, Caesar, or—"

"De Wolfe's fucking Eva. Eva's passing for white!"

What Caesar said shocked Dorrell Durant down to his foundation. His eyes hadn't moved but stared straight ahead at Caesar as if they'd turned to ice.

"She's his fucking mistress, Dorrell. Fucking mistress, man. Living downtown on Ballad Street. Passing for white. A colored girl passing for white, white, man, white!"

Dorrell bent over. He held on to the table for support. "I'm going to puke. I-I 'm going to puke, puke my fucking guts out!"

"Not on me you ain't!" Caesar said, scurrying out of the booth. "Fuck no!"

Caesar looked on as Dorrell grappled with himself.

"Man …"

"Yeah, I know, Dorrell!"

Dorrell's face was red, but for now there was no sign of him throwing up.

"Sit, Caesar. Sit. I-I don't, no, no longer feel under siege, a-attack. I—sit, man."

"I don't know how long this shit's been going on between them two, Dorrell, but that motherfucker De Wolfe set her up on Ballad Street." Pause. "Know where it is?"

"Yeah, yeah, lower Manhattan."

"It's a sweet setup. Staying in a fucking building by herself. All alone. De Wolfe—"

Dorrell was gathering himself. "De Wolfe can drop by whenever he pleases, but on a strict schedule."

"You fucking still smart as hell, Dorrell. Uh-huh. Figure it all the fuck out quick as hell. Prison ain't did nothing to your brain I can tell. It's why I want you in on this here with me."

"Dorrell, Dorrell!"

"Do me a favor, Caesar, shut that broad up. Tell her, whatever her name is, I said, to get lost!"

"My pleasure!"

Dorrell, at the table alone, figured he had to clear his head. This was totally unexpected: his sister Eva passing for white. He heard a ruckus in Lula's, but couldn't care less.

Caesar got back to the booth.

"You heard her, Dorrell, heard the—"

"Yeah," Dorrell said sullenly. "I don't need a broad right now. I need more facts from you, Caesar."

"Got plenty of them." Pause. "I want to blackmail De Wolfe, but don't know how, Dorrell. Don't got a clue. Nothing, man."

"I do. It'll be easy, man. Real easy."

"Was gonna bum rush De Wolfe the other night. Put on a mask and was dressed all in black, and—"

"Blackmail's a sophisticated crime," Dorrell said, looking intensely into Caesar's eyes. "Not street crime executed by hacks. It has to be well planned out. The bait is the lure."

"T-the bait?" Caesar asked, confused.

"Eva. My sister."

"Oh, right, right, Eva."

"Her value to De Wolfe will make whatever demands we make easy."

"So what you mean by that, Dorrell?"

"She's colored. He won't go to the police. If it's exposed that he's been sleeping with a colored girl, it'll be the greatest scandal since, since"—Dorrell laughed wickedly—"Emilie De Wolfe's suicide. Now that's funny, ain't it, Caesar. Funny as shit!"

"That white rich bitch! Ha!"

"The police, they won't even be an afterthought to De Wolfe. Notifying them. He'll concede to our demands and—"

"When do you want us to get together to put this shit—"

"We'll work it out. But we mustn't be seen together, Caesar, after tonight. Not out in public. Not in any of my or your usual hangouts." Dorrell smiled. "But we'll work all of that out, the details, the kinks. You see: you never know who's watching.

"You should never let your ego overwhelm your better judgment. Good old-fashioned common sense. The Prigg heist taught me that lesson, Caesar. And the six years I served in Sing Sing prison."

THERE WOULD BE NO SUBWAY train to take Dorrell back down to the Bowery tonight, back to his seedy, dumpy hotel room. He was walking the streets of New York for a reason, to free every drop of thought and emotion pent up in him. The world had just offered him a golden opportunity, yet he was devastated by what Eva, his sister, was doing: passing for white.

His and Eva's skin coloring was identical, yet he never in his life had any notion of passing himself off as white in the white man's world or desiring to be white and not colored. If he'd chosen to pass as white, he'd be as successful as any white man alive, Dorrell thought. Even Maxwell De Wolfe.

"Why, fucking why, Eva!"

He didn't need the Sing Sing experience to remind him of race relations in America, as to where he fit in. It was just the daily pounding, grind of being black. The daily dedication to it, of being looked down on, of not being able to rise above a racial identification connoting inferiority and shabbiness. The hopelessness of Harlem, this jungle he was walking through tonight, that was crying out its poverty in forced silence. He belonged to a downtrodden class of people, despised and discarded, and then quarantined.

But maybe I was born to be a crook, Dorrell thought. That even if he were white or had crossed over the color line to pass for white, he'd still wind up a con artist, would still operate outside the law, on the criminal side of the social divide. He loved living on the edge, the nearest thing to a fall. This trait persisted in him since small. His mother, she detected it too.

But even if he was a crook, he never forgot who he was: a Negro. That was one thing he took pride in, being a colored man. As a child, all he did was read books. Religiously his mother got hold of books for him and Eva from the local library. And although they were white stories he read, white men who composed and operated the world, he lived on Elmwood Avenue among his colored brethren. And although the colored race languished in mostly bitterness and dejection and sorrow, he witnessed their struggle to do right under the rule of prejudice and doors that closed in their faces, and he empathized with them, the underdog, not the top dog.

He, by no means, had not recovered from what Eva was doing with Maxwell De Wolfe. How she had stooped so low. It had to do with her ambition, Dorrell thought. She was college educated; he was not, yet he was smarter than her by a wide margin. He read and absorbed and could move in and out of different worlds with little complication or discomfit.

But she had taken on the white world as an imposter, of someone who didn't belong, but who had rejected her race, her color. He was a felon, a convict, but she, in his mind, had committed the bigger crime: that of passing for white.

"What exactly is De Wolfe doing to serve her ambition? Where is she headed with De Wolfe, being his fucking mistress?"

She wanted to be an actress, it's all she spoke of when young. Never was she talked out of it by their mother, for Lilly Durant believed in great accomplishment too. It's how he failed his mother, but once he got over the hurt and heartache he gave her, since it was still his life he had to live, no matter how tattered or of no value it was perceived by his mother, he could not change the caliber or quality of his being.

"Mother knows of De Wolfe. There's no secret there. So how has she accepted it? Managed this disgrace? How has Eva brought De Wolfe into her life without mother's reprimand and grave disappoint in her?"

Soon, very soon he would be in Harlem to visit his mother, Lilly Durant. They will discuss Eva at length before he destroys her life with De Wolfe, for that's what he will do with hatred and contempt toward De Wolfe and his white world, and years of sibling dislike of Eva, his sister, for rejecting her black world, Dorrell thought.

DORRELL HAD TOLD CAESAR WHEN they met earlier today in midtown Manhattan, among a sea of white faces who wouldn't know or remember them from Adam, or for that matter, in any way take significant notice of them, that they were to be on a fast track with the De Wolfe operation.

Of course Dorrell was the brains of the operation (even if there was to be no brawn) but didn't want Caesar to think that he was no longer a vital part of the decision-making process, that he was being cut completely out of it. He must keep Caesar happy, pacify him, continue to remind him that he was the one who spotted Eva, knew the action to take, but not the right course of action to pull this big money caper off. Otherwise, down the road, there could be trouble from him.

"Don't worry, Dorrell, De Wolfe's on his way. This is his day, man. Coming for the cunt. Eva's juicy cunt!"

And even though Dorrell was hell-bent on wrecking Eva and De Wolfe, for his sister to be degraded by Caesar Stark, his crude comments, angered him.

"Just keep your mind on one thing, Caesar, and that's De Wolfe and his money!"

"Who, what you in charge of what I gotta say!"

"No, but ..."

"Then don't cross that fucking line with me, Dorrell. De Wolfe or no De Wolfe. I'm a man, man, and I say what I wanna. So keep that shit straight!"

They were in the empty lot on Ballad Street, across from 10 Ballad Street. They'd been in the lot for no more than ten minutes.

Caesar, by now, felt comfortable there'd be no one traveling the block and assured Dorrell, earlier today in midtown Manhattan, of the same. Of course Dorrell wanted to see for himself just how the "pigeon" (De Wolfe) functioned in this environment. Caesar had told him the routine, but Dorrell, being a thorough, detailed person, wanted to witness it for himself.

It was mid-March, and though there was a wind, it wasn't clocking a high speed.

"So what I tell you, Dorrell. Quiet as hell down here this time of night. As a clam."

It was seven five.

"Yeah, haven't spotted a living soul yet," Dorrell said it politely, but his insides were still scalding hot from Caesar's tasteless remark regarding Eva and De Wolfe. He really wanted to defend Eva, but how could he?

"And you ain't gonna see nobody. P-promise you that. I know my shit. You smart, man, but I ain't no dummy neither!"

The guy's starting to get on my fucking nerves! Dorrell thought. *This afternoon. Now. And I don't like it when that happens. My thoughts lead me into dangerous fucking places. Evil things I don't want to think about. Conjure up.*

And it was a little over a half hour later when De Wolfe's black Packard rolled down Ballad Street.

"De Wolfe. The old fucker's here!"

"Yes, so I see"—Dorrell smiled—"so I see, Caesar."

"Now watch and see what happens," Caesar said, snatching Dorrell's arm and prompting him forward, practically putting him on the edge of the lot. "Don't worry, they ain't gonna see nothing. Been doing their shit for so long, if they saw somebody out on the street, think it was a ghost."

All Dorrell wanted to see was this routine between the chauffeur and De Wolfe. And then it began between them, and Dorrell and Caesar stood on the front rim of the lot silently as both watched.

The chauffeur came out of the building, got in the Packard, and then drove down the block.

"See, Dorrell," Caesar said, bubbling, "just like I told you before, wasn't it? Ain't nothing different from what I said."

"No."

Dorrell began to think, to bounce thoughts around in his head.

"The chauffeur's the key to all of this."

Caesar tugged on his cap. "How come? What for?"

"You'll see what I'm getting at after I explain it on our—"

"Yeah, let's get the fuck outta here. Wonder if De Wolfe fucked Eva by now. Probably just good for one fuck a night no way." Caesar laughed loudly. "Old fucking ass."

And that bad, violent sensation washed over Dorrell again, the kind he tried to suppress, but at times it was the only thing that actually relieved him.

DE WOLFE'S SEX LIFE WAS in ruins. Two nights ago he got a hard-on, but it came and went. He began humping Eva, but within no more than a minute, he climaxed, and a small quantity of scum dribbled out his penis.

Am I being cursed? Am I!

His power was being depleted by a sex act, never mind him not being able to satisfy Eva. He would have thought by now that he would have recovered from Emilie. *Do I have to see a psychiatrist?* he thought. *A quack! Lie on a fucking couch!*

Even the view of Manhattan from the backseat of the Packard this morning did him no good. The skyscrapers and the majesty of the city seemed to be mocking him this morning, his power.

But now, in the house, Alexandra had fought through her bitter emotions, of fighting him and defying him, and was now back to her sedate, docile ways, back to eating at the dining room table with him. It'd happened a week and a half ago and had not changed. This, at least, for him, showed some overt sign of his recovered power within the mansion.

"I feel like a beaten man, though," De Wolfe said, staring at Fagan's bowler. He felt like crying. He had with Eva, cried his eyes out. She had been particularly patient with him, such a value to him and his psychological health when he was with her. But when he was away from her, the nights he wasn't at 10 Ballad Street were the most dreadful, the most deafening when he attempted rationalizing, reasoning with himself, that De Wolfe & Fitch was enough power for him, enough of who Maxwell De Wolfe was.

"I'm so happy the press has taken its poisoned pen and pointed it elsewhere, Fagan. Those rotten, spineless, craven despoilers of decency," De Wolfe said no more than a half block from De Wolfe & Fitch at 11 Broadway. "I can still see them, though, that army of ragtags camped out in front of De Wolfe & Fitch, out to ruin my name. Thus, me."

Fagan hadn't heard this rant from De Wolfe in some time. At one time, during his embattled relationship with the press, it's all he heard. And sometimes he would add his own venom, chip in with what those ragtags could do: GO FUCK THEMSELVES UP THE ASS!

"I would not wish that on anyone. Not a solitary soul. Not even my most vile, hated enemy, Fagan."

"I agree, Mr. De Wolfe. One hundred percent. There were nights when I couldn't sleep myself, sir. Many of them, to be honest with you, Mr. De Wolfe."

But as for his life, De Wolfe thought, he had transitioned from one crisis to another. There wasn't the glare of cheap story making or lightbulbs from cameras flashing garishly in his eyes, but the private life of his sexual life, its functionality for him at the age of fifty-seven. He wanted to hold his penis right now, just to know he had one, that he hadn't lost it in this jungle of thought ensnaring him, making him wish his life would snap back to normal, back to what it was, for he could at least breathe again, at least enjoy his wealth and privilege, all the things he'd built to the ripened height of perfection.

THE WHITE MAN WAS THIN, scrawny-looking, but neatly attired, smart-looking, clean shaven, and had a thin part in the middle of a clumpy shock of brown hair. Edward Winston Henson looked bookish and at one time was a successful New York trial lawyer, but two lousy marriages and booze landed him on the Bowery where he'd been for six years of his forty-eight years, still boozed up and ambitionless. But on this day Dorrell had sobered him and cleaned him up, and he was the old Edward Winston Henson with a slew of law degrees tacked to his law office's wall.

But it was the dollar Dorrell offered Henson to do this job that took him off of skid row for one day and put him back in a suit of respectability.

Henson knew he had but two minutes to pull off what he had been paid to do for Dorrell Durant, so Henson passed the pearl black Packard in front of the De Wolfe & Fitch building once to gain his bearing and then swung back around, walked out in the street, and approached the car from the rear. He tapped on the car's glistening side window.

Fagan looked to his right and then rolled down the window. "What is it that you want, sir?"

"I am carrying an envelope for Mr. De Wolfe that he and he alone must possess. This is no trifle matter, sir, but one of stern bearing," Henson said in a deep, grave voice.

"Who in god's name are you!"

"Take the envelope, sir. If not, you may regret your choice once Mr. De Wolfe's made aware of this innocuous advance from me and your curt dismissal of it."

Stunned, Fagan had no idea of what to do: step out of the car and cuff the skinny stranger by the neck or go along with something he might just "regret" not doing, as the stranger had soberly suggested.

"Take it!"

"Yes, of course. Of course. Let me have it!"

"Mr. De Wolfe will know what to do with it," Edward Henson said, now walking away from the car. "Today, you have done Mr. De Wolfe a great service, my dear fellow."

Henson suddenly vanished into an ocean of white faces traveling Broadway's downtown corridor.

Fagan was sweating, looking down at the white envelope that had only De Wolfe's name on it, and then out the front windshield of the car wondering what effect the contents of the envelope would have on De Wolfe once it was opened and read.

And then De Wolfe appeared, exiting the grand building and proceeding down its broad, extensive front steps.

Immediately, Fagan attended to him, but his hand trembled when he opened the door. "G-good e-evening, Mr., Mr. De Wolfe."

"Good evening, Fagan."

It was five thirty.

Fagan, when he got to the driver's side, felt his knees buckle. He seemed to be holding on to the car door for dear life. He opened the car door, and there it was again, the white envelope on the car seat staring up at him with a serpent's eye, this thing that had a slimy tongue and no heart, was cold as hell.

Now, should I, now? I have to. I can't start the car and then hand it to De Wolfe!

Fagan looked back at De Wolfe, and it seemed De Wolfe was in deep thought, the kind Fagan had seen so often over the years, that had a steel-like focus and determination. But it had to be done!

"Mr. De Wolfe ... s-sir ..."

"Yes, Fagan?"

"A man, a man ..."

"Yes, yes ...?"

"He approached the car. A, a stranger to me, sir. And handed me this!"

"An envelope, Fagan!" De Wolfe took it and studied it for no more than a second. Then he said, "But why!"

DE WOLFE WAS SITTING WITH Alexandra tonight at the dining room table, and they'd eaten their pleasant meal, but all the while, his mind was on the envelope the stranger handed to Fagan this afternoon and what its possible contents contained. After he'd asked Fagan, "But why!" Fagan groped for accurate words but then got to the gist of the stranger's remarks. The trip to the house was blanketed in silence, and an awkwardness between De Wolfe and Fagan ensued and then prevailed as the minutes ticked by and his mind became more and more pinned to the letter, what it might mean, for it had begun to feel as if there was something precarious about it, a time bomb of some nature set to blow up in his face. It's why he couldn't wait for the dinner to end at the dining room table and for him to retire to his bedroom and, under the luminous lamp on his desk, read his future.

Alexandra had finished eating.

"The pheasant was divine, Maxwell. Will Jules ever disappoint us?"

De Wolfe put down his glass of Bauer's wine. "No, Alexandra, it is out of the question."

"And just to think, the Belgrade's tried, at one time, to steal him away from us."

"Over my dead body!"

"It is such competition, holding on to someone like Jules. A chef of his rank."

"Like an Olympic event, Alexandra. The competitive sport of polo."

"Yes."

Standing, De Wolfe wobbled. "I must go to my room, Alexandra. I must take a nap. The day has been long for me. I think I'm turning old."

Alexandra dabbed the napkin with her mouth. "Good night."

"Yes, good night."

Alexandra sat at the dining room table and gazed out into space. She was glad she had returned to the dining room to eat with De Wolfe once more. De Wolfe's mistress was still locked in his vise; she was still there to service him sexually and make him feel omnipotent. But she did have a place in his life, of affording him the respectability a man like De Wolfe not only wants but also craves.

She was eating under the beauty of lights, the beauty of a room she helped design and lend it its refinement. And she was refined. She was noble where she sat in the dining room, a part of the room's magnificence and grace and attractiveness. This was her nightly gift to herself, without flaw, without interference, without any insinuation of competition.

WHEN DE WOLFE SAT DOWN with the envelope he had taken out of his hip pocket, he felt much heavier than what, on the scale, he actually was.

"Whoever the fuck you are, now, now you will have my counsel!" De Wolfe said, turning on the lamp's light. "You fuck, you fuck. You fucking slimeball!"

He felt threatened from the moment Fagan handed him the letter till now. And with his heart beating like a wild stallion's, he wanted to tear the person who wrote the letter he was pulling out of the envelope with a twitching hand, into shreds, bits and pieces, tatters.

"You are having your day with me, whoever you are. But mine will come, you rat you. I surely will win in the end," De Wolfe said, anticipating the danger to come.

De Wolfe slipped on his glasses. "Now to read your filthy words that spew from your filthy, sewerage of a mind!"

> March 17, 1924
>
> Dear Mr. De Wolfe,
>
> You are being watched. We are three in number. We are three con men. As for me, I have served time in Sing Sing Prison among the dregs of society: murderers, thieves; exporters of what condition humanity can breed in its most perverse forms of greed and purchase.
>
> But I digress, sir.
>
> We are aware of your arrangement with Miss Eva Durant.

"Eva! You, you, who the hell are you!"

> Have you recovered from your shock? Then let us proceed. Our first demand is: you are not to, under any circumstance, contact Miss Durant regarding our knowledge of you and her. She, also, is being watched.
>
> The second demand is: we will mail a letter to your office in the name of Franklin De Witt (a fictitious name to be sure, of course). It will contain further information pertaining to this most pertinent matter.
>
> But during the interim, just for you to know, Ms. Eva Durant is withholding a deep, dark secret from you,

sir. One that if revealed, will create the nature of scandal (if not supersede it) of your daughter Emilie in the tabloids. Except the power of this scandal will, personally, sink you like the Titanic, defame your name for life.

We harbor no fear that police will in any way be remotely involved in the commission of our crime against you.

Finally, I have no respect for the craven press either, their daily libelous antics and hunger to hurt (the bumbling fools!), but they are guided by the little people of a democratic convention who hate rich men like you, but wish they too were rich, could sit in the seats of power, and mock poverty by thumbing their noses at it.

PS. And lest I forget, in three days time, when the letter from Franklin De Witt is received by your office, you, sir, will walk out your office building, and before entering your Packard, will flash a newspaper signaling that you have received the letter, and the next day, at six o'clock, I shall be in touch with you by phone to continue our discussion regarding this urgent matter.

Sincerely yours,

Anonymous Writer

"Who are you? Who the fuck are you, you arrogant son of a bitch!"

De Wolfe was in tears, pulling at his thinned hair, when he stopped.

"I won't let you do this to me you, you weasel. You fucking weasel of a goddamned lout!"

And he took the letter, and his eyes scanned over it, and he felt the intelligence of it dash over him, and the envy, and the politics of it, and of how the letter had tried to define him.

But it also had the reverse effect of defining him, this so-called "Anonymous Writer," De Wolfe thought. This was a con man who had been denied by society what he possessed: money, privilege, prestige. This was a man who was after his money. This was a man who was going to blackmail him. All he had to do, him and the other two blackmailers, was set a dollar amount, and since there were three of them, De Wolfe thought, it would be an exorbitant price for him to pay for whatever information they had on Eva Durant.

"Eva ... what have you done to me!" De Wolfe said, pounding the small desk. "What have you done! What horrid thing from ... in your past!"

What did he know about Eva Durant: the World Stage?

Eva Durant was intelligent, bright, several notches above the other showgirls in that culture of glitz and glam and anything goes. And Eva Durant was the most beautiful of any girl who'd ever danced on the World Stage's stage. And he, Maxwell De Wolfe, was above any personal fact checking, vetting of background, of why young girls like Eva Durant dance in sexy costumes, become sexual tools, provocateurs. How women like Eva Durant arrive to the World Stage to tease and titillate hordes of sex-driven, bawdy men who love them for their flesh and willingness to exhibit it like forbidden fruit and not be afraid of these men's lust and loving and the sex it will bring to them tenfold, in infinite quantity. Men who admire and desire them in ways that are sick and sickening and perverse.

And it's what De Wolfe felt now, sick. Sick in his head. Sick in his stomach. He couldn't go to Eva, ask her what she'd done, what her history was, who these men were: she was being watched as well as him.

"I wouldn't call her. I wouldn't fucking dare. I can't talk to Eva over the phone, over something as explosive as this. We have never spoken over the phone. Never. Never during our two years together!"

Their life, he gave them their life. He set her up at 10 Ballad Street. He provided her with the Masthead Publications job. He was the one who tried to be with her three nights a week or step out with her to a speakeasy, and the two of them would have a reserved room they could hide in and feel somehow satisfied they were safe and free.

This "Anonymous Writer" was already impacting his life in painful, intrusive ways.

"Hell, he's right about the police. If what he has on Eva is enough to cause great scandal for me, why would I chance such a fucking, futile alternative."

But what struck fear in him more than anything was the abortion of his affair with Eva. *Of her past being so despicable I would want nothing more to do with her,* De Wolfe thought.

He had to stand. He had to make sure he could stand. That his legs hadn't suddenly rotted and that he could withstand another blow delivered to him by another outside force, not Juan Manuel who killed Emilie this time, but by this revelation concerning something totally unknown to him, that bared him, elevated him as someone once again vulnerable, who could reach a peak of emotion and forget who Maxwell De Wolfe was no matter how the world viewed him in his black top hat and the wealth he continued to amass at a rate defying any rhyme or reason or moral justification for access.

Chapter 13

"**I** can't wait to see this with my own two eyes," Dorrell said from the other side of the street, but a goodly distance away from 11 Broadway.

"I can. This shit ain't for me. You the big shot with the gripe with De Wolfe. I just want De Wolfe's fucking money, man."

"Right, right, Caesar," Dorrell said, having heard this bland recitation of his before.

"Got these damned shoe boxes you spent money for. Money we coulda used for something better than this shit."

He'd said that a few times today too. By this time it had grated on Dorrell's nerves.

"Okay, it's time for me to start heading down Broadway."

"Pretending we bootblacks. I ain't no bootblack, man. They sorry asses. Lump of do-do. Fucking bootblacks, man."

Caesar remained hugged to the building's wall as Dorrell—after spotting De Wolfe's Packard being actively parked—began making his way down the street.

"No, ain't shining no shoes, mister, I quit for the day," Caesar said, waving off what could have been a potential customer. "I ain't no dummy," he said under his breath. "I'm a fucking con man, man. Above any of that sorry bullshit them bootblacks do!"

DE WOLFE CAME OUT OF **De Wolfe & Fitch.** Dorrell saw him look up and down Broadway cautiously. He had the newspaper tucked under his armpit. Dorrell saw the red in De Wolfe's skin and knew, without a doubt, De Wolfe felt this "anonymous" someone was toying with him, having grand fun with him at his expense, and could kill him for it.

Dorrell was in a crowd of white men. De Wolfe walked down the stone steps and to the car. Dorrell chuckled.

The newspaper, De Wolfe, I see the newspaper. Don't forget to flash it, De Wolfe. Before you get in your fucking car!

And when Fagan came to open the car door for De Wolfe, suddenly, De Wolfe waved the newspaper in the air much to Dorrell's amusement.

"Good job, De Wolfe, excellent. You follow orders well. Quite well," Dorrell said to himself.

Caesar, when he saw what De Wolfe had done, turned his back to him and began walking Broadway in the opposite direction of Dorrell.

"Damn if Dorrell ain't wasting my time and his," he said under his breath. "Thought the motherfucker was so fucking smart. Should be rich by now. Rolling in dough.

"Shoulda left his black ass in Lula's Lounge with that big-ass broad he was trying to fuck!"

THE FOLLOWING DAY AT SIX o'clock in De Wolfe's office.

Ring.

"Yes, yes, is it—"

"You don't expect me to tell you my name now, do you, Mr. De Wolfe? That would be downright stupid of me."

"Who the hell are you!"

"Don't worry, sir, you'll find out at the end of this—"

"Charade, goddamnit, you're pulling on me!"

Pause.

"Oh, so this is what you think this is? What we're doing?"

"No, no, uh-uh, but …"

"Think, De Wolfe. Think."

And De Wolfe had to pause and think about the person he was speaking to, with the smooth, mannered voice, who sounded much like how he wrote: with an erudition and appreciation of words that even he had to admire.

"Thank you for your attention to detail yesterday." Dorrell laughed. "Naturally, we did expect as much from you, De Wolfe."

"You did that to humiliate me, you bastard!"

"Of course, of course we did."

"You fucking bastard!"

"You waved the newspaper brilliantly. We saw your chauffeur's reaction to—"

"You are using the pronoun 'we,' when it seems you're the only one who—"

"Shut up, De Wolfe! This operation has a hierarchy, as yours does at Fitch & De Wolfe!"

"You goddamned bastard! You know my firm's correct name. You fucking—"

"I'm in charge of the operation. I'm the smartest, the brightest—"

"What a fucking ego you have … huh … Stuck with? Is that what this is all about?"

"Don't think you can goad me, De Wolfe. Con me, even if you too, are a con man."

"Or some political agenda you've got … Why you used the term 'little people' in your letter, since you are a 'little' person so it seems, Mr.—"

"Don't make me laugh," Dorrell said, laughing, "we have the goods on you, that plain and simple, De Wolfe, and you know it: Eva Durant. Your mistress, sir."

"What has Eva done to you that's so horrible, t-terrible," De Wolfe pleaded. "That's so deplorable that it has you resorting to this kind of chicanery?"

"Not to me, De Wolfe, to you."

De Wolfe swallowed, and it was as if he had swallowed his tongue whole, the sensation he'd gotten from it.

"Have you followed our—"

"Yes, yes, I haven't spoken, been in touch with her. W-with E-Eva," De Wolfe said as if too frightened to use Eva's name.

"She's in no way involved in this situation, let me make that clear to you, De Wolfe," Dorrell said reasonably. "She'll be as shocked as you when she finds out we know about the two of you. She's your mistress."

Pause.

"H-how much do you want, you bastard! How much! The money!"

"Not so fucking fast, De Wolfe. Not so fucking fast!"

"Why! Why!"

"This game of ours is just beginning, sir."

"I'll call the cops, the police, the authori—"

"Shut up and listen! You're at the mercy of us now!"

Pause.

"I'm, I'm listening."

"You are on this island alone, De Wolfe." Pause. "You know when I was in Sing Sing, I always felt alone."

What the hell is this punk talking about! Son of a bitch!

"I didn't think it would happen to me, De Wolfe, but it does to everyone in prison. What about you, De Wolfe?"

Both knew it was a rhetorical question not to be addressed—nothing more.

"And ... you know what, De Wolfe, it must be how Eva Durant feels like locked up there at 10 Ballad Street. On that block. In that building. A fortress like that."

De Wolfe laughed. "So you're a con man with a fucking heart, huh?"

"Yeah, De Wolfe. A con man with a fucking heart. Yeah."

"Thought so after telling me that sob story of yours about Sing Sing, like I should give a good goddamn. A rat's ass."

"I'm a bleeding heart, De Wolfe, right out the pages of—"

"Take the fucking money. Just give me the amount, the figure for—"

"Ha. You're a dog chasing its tail, De Wolfe. So … good night."

"Good night!"

"A letter will arrive at your office soon, De Wolfe. When, exactly, I can't very well tell you at this delicate time and moment. But it will be soon. We don't need your money right now, De Wolfe. Don't worry, you won't go broke. We just want your undivided attention for now, at least."

Dorrell laughed.

"You, you fucking …"

And what De Wolfe heard next was click in his ear.

"Sick bastard."

THERE'D BEEN NO CONTACT BETWEEN Dorrell and De Wolfe. It'd reached day number 4. Dorrell had no idea how much longer he was going to keep De Wolfe on the hot seat. He just knew De Wolfe had to be going nuts, insane, and that he had him where he wanted: sweating bullets by the barrel full.

But Caesar wasn't buying into Dorrell's psychological paradigm: he just wanted De Wolfe's money, not his flesh. He'd told Dorrell they were moving too slowly, and though Dorrell told Caesar he'd speed things up, he hadn't.

It's why yesterday, Caesar gave Dorrell an ultimatum: either he contact De Wolfe today or he, personally, was going to blow Eva's cover—the lid off their operation.

"I'll tell Eva what you and me know, Dorrell. Her passing for fucking white with De Wolfe. And we blackmailing the motherfucker. Gonna kill her if she don't get De Wolfe to hand over forty thousand dollars. Even split down the middle!"

Just the thought that Caesar Stark could come up with something as absurd as that and present it to him drove Dorrell crazy. This was his operation, his "baby" from start to finish. Where was the guile in Caesar's plan, the intrigue and master chess moves that make the game more than a game but a series of surprises and nuance and exploitation and inescapability from the victim's disadvantaged perspective? He had De Wolfe trapped in a corner where he couldn't get out not until *he* let him.

And then there was Dorrell's patience, how he was using it to unbalance De Wolfe in daily financial dealings in the office of De Wolfe & Fitch. Dorrell keeping De Wolfe from Eva, someone who by now was worrying what had happened to De Wolfe and De Wolfe wondering what was happening to her, this ragged, unplanned event that had more questions in it for them than answers.

And then the ultimate question controlling De Wolfe's mind: what he (Anonymous) knew about Eva. What deep, dark, clandestine secret was Eva holding from him in this relationship he, De Wolfe, was bonded to and thought he alone controlled.

DORRELL HAD PICKED CAESAR UP in a car he stole an hour earlier over at Fifty-Fifth Street and Tenth Avenue, and they were parked on Fourteenth and Rand Streets, five blocks north of Ballad Street.

"I don't trust you, Dorrell. Not no motherfucking liar like you!"

"I am a liar, Caesar. You carded me right."

It was 11:13 p.m.

"I admit I've been going about our business with De Wolfe all wrong. And I want to make it up to you."

Dorrell had parked the stolen car on Rand Street, in front of a closed butcher's shop with a butchered pig (its head chopped off) painted on a red wooden sign hanging by a rusty nail.

"Man, you serious, Dorrell?"

"Cross my heart and hope to die," Dorrell said, grinning. "Remember how we used to say that crap, Caes—"

"On Underwood Avenue."

"And swear if we didn't tell the truth, something bad would actually happen to us."

Caesar laughed. "Like fucking die!"

Dorrell started the car up and turned the headlights back on.

"Where we going?"

"Over to Ballad Street. I want you to see for yourself how we're going to plan this thing out with De Wolfe. The operational part of it, okay? Where the drop-off's to occur. I promise you, Caesar, you'll get a kick out of this."

"Forty thousand right, Caesar? Split down the middle!"

"Right!"

"We gonna be fucking rich, Dorrell!"

Dorrell made a turn off Farragut Street and onto Ballad Street.

"How you gonna spend De Wolfe's dough when we get it?"

"Spend it?"

"Don't fucking play games with me. Yeah, I said spend it!"

"I don't plan on spending it, Caesar. Not a dollar of it. A red cent of it."

"What you gonna do, stick it up your fucking ass! Huh, huh!"

Dorrell neither laughed nor answered Caesar. Dorrell parked the car in front of Ballad Street's empty lot.

"By the way, what you think's gonna happen to Eva, Dorrell? Since De Wolfe's gonna throw her fanny out in the street when he finds out she's a nigger. Ain't good for shit!"

Dorrell hesitated and then said. "Maybe I'll give her some portion of De Wolfe's money. Be charitable with it. Consoling ..." Dorrell said coolly. "Who knows."

"You'd do that for Eva!"

"Why not, Caesar? Eva's earned it."

Caesar opened the car door. "So what's the lot gotta do with—"

"Oh, right, right ..."

"Man, don't be pulling no shit on me. Wasting my fucking time!"

"Uh-uh, Caesar. The lot, it's where the drop-off point or, if you prefer, the pickup point's to be staged," Dorrell said. "It's where we'll tell De Wolfe to have the money dropped off. Forty thousand smackeroos in a sack, and we'll have him put it ... let's see—"

"See, I can barely see shit out here, Dorrell, this time of night."

"Where should we have him drop it off at? Hmm ..."

"Did you hear me, Dorrell!"

"Come on, come on, we'll have flashlights tomorrow night, Caesar. You and me."

"Right, right, I forgot all about—"

"Right."

They were near the middle of the lot.

"When you gonna call De Wolfe?"

"First thing in the morning."

"You think he can raise that kind of loot that fucking fast?"

If Caesar could see the way Dorrell was looking at him in the dark, his head would snap off.

"He's fucking rich. What do you think rich men do? They call their bank. They can buy the Woolworth Building with one fucking phone call. What do you think rich people do, Caesar?"

"All because of Eva. That long, pussy-haired bitch trying to pass for white! Thought one day I'd be the one fucking your sister. Hot as the bitch was when we was young, Dorrell!"

"You know what, Caesar, I'm beginning not to like you."

"And what, you got a fucking gripe, problem with me!"

"I don't love my sister, don't even like her, but her last name is Durant."

"Who thinks she's white."

Dorrell was turning the color red. He didn't need this confrontation but was glad it was happening, that Caesar Stark, a dumb, lowlife, petty thief, had such a foul mouth and low opinion of people (Eva). It was going to make things easier for him when the situation he'd planned out arose.

"Telling me you gonna give her some of your dough. A motherfucking thief like you. You piss poor like me. We come from the same shit. Wear the same clothes to school sometimes five, six times a week 'til we wear holes in them wide as that moon in that fucking sky up there, motherfucker.

"When this caper's done with tomorrow night, you going right back to the fucking Bowery, and I'm going back up to Harlem, Dorrell. Them shiny-head niggers who De Wolfe probably spit on like all them rich blood suckers do. You ain't gonna be no better off than me. You—"

"Are you through, Caesar? Finished?"

Caesar stuck his hands in his pockets and dropped his head. "Yeah, motherfucker."

"Then I suppose we can get back to business. The business at hand. That brought us together: De Wolfe. Tomorrow night. So this is what we're going to do," Dorrell said, walking in front of Caesar enough that Caesar had to catch up with him, and when he did, he was side by side with him. His eyes were squinting.

Dorrell stepped back away from him by no less than a yard.

"Yeah, keep looking, Caesar, because I think I see the perfect pickup spot from here. The—"

Dorrell pulled a claw hammer out of his coat pocket. "MOTHERRFUCKER!"

Dorrell bashed Caesar twice in the head with the hammer as hard as he could as Caesar dropped to the ground on his knees, fell flat, and then produced the worst shrill of a scream Dorrell had heard since Sing Sing prison, when a con was knifed by another con in the Yard.

Caesar was rolling on top of the ground, in the dirt, but was still alive.

"You ain't dead yet, Caesar? You motherfucker!"

"Don't let me die like this! P-please, d-don't l-let me d-die like this, D-Dore … Dorrell!"

Dorrell pulled the knife out of his back pocket and got down on his knees. He grabbed Caesar by the neck. "Why not, Caesar!" And from behind, Dorrell stabbed Caesar once in the back and then again for good measure.

"Fuck you. Fuck you!"

Caesar's body slumped back against Dorrell's chest. He laughed. "Why, I thought it would be tough to kill you, Caesar. A big, strong ox like you. The hammer wouldn't do it, be enough, but I was foolish enough to try anyway.

"But pretty much knew it'd take this," Dorrell said, holding on to the knife handle. The knife was still stuck in the center of Caesar's back. "You fucking chump."

Dorrell dragged Caesar by his arms and through the lot's dirt and to the car parked at the curb. The passenger door was open, and Dorrell lifted Caesar's body up and onto the front seat and then shut the door and rounded the car and got in.

Dorrell looked at Caesar with the knife sticking out his back and blood dripping out the back of his bludgeoned head.

"You were playing out of your league. In the big leagues, Caesar. I had no use for you. I just let you tag along for the ride." Pause. "Ride, ride, we're taking a ride, all right—isn't that apropos. Just perfect. A short one down to the East River." Pause. "To visit the fishes.

"By the way, Caesar, I wouldn't've given you two cents of De Wolfe's money. Not over my dead body, motherfucker."

DORRELL HAD TOSSED CAESAR'S BODY into the East River.

He parked the car in front of 10 Ballad Street.

"You're inside there, aren't you, Eva. Up on the second floor waiting for Maxwell De Wolfe. I killed Caesar Stark tonight. Remember him, from Underwood Avenue? A black man, so I can blackmail a white man. De Wolfe. Your lover, for his money. Not because De Wolfe's soiled you. Or to protect your honor.

"For money, Eva. Strictly money, my dear."

The red brick building looked so silent and cold and lifeless, set apart from everything, Dorrell thought.

"The last time I saw you, damn, I'd have to scratch my head to try to remember. Hell, I can't remember. Neither you nor mother came to my sentencing seven years ago. But our paths will cross again. And it'll be soon, Eva," Dorrell said, continuing to stare at the building and breathing spastically.

"Caesar, tonight, is the first person I've ever killed. I hope I don't have to kill Maxwell De Wolfe. De Wolfe is my next victim." Pause. "But I will kill De Wolfe if I have to. Must." Pause.

"If you only knew, Eva, that I'm parked out here, right in front of your fucking building. Looking up at the second-floor window, right now."

EVA WAS STARING IN ONE of a number of mirrors hanging on the bedroom wall. She was dressed, but practically nude. She'd applied extra makeup to her face, even if she had no need for it, not someone as astoundingly beautiful as her.

"Where are you, Max? Where have you been the past four nights? What's happened to you?"

She was looking at a face marked by anguish, despair, of not knowing what was happening in De Wolfe's life. She was in something skimpy, designed for sex, for someone like De Wolfe even if he was struggling with an erection and maintaining it (even when he got one), Eva thought.

"I'm here for you, Max. You know I'm here waiting for you," Eva said, in a painful plea, her voice rising and then falling. "To have sex with you, Max. To please you. Even if it's for you, not me." She kept looking intently into the mirror.

"It can't be Emilie, can it? Can it, Max, again? It's been long enough, your agony, grieving for her, hasn't it? I know it has."

She was so full of doubt, of what could be happening in De Wolfe's life. She'd read the newspapers, hunting through them for anything she could find, especially to see if Alexandra De Wolfe might have died, but there was nothing in the obit section of the paper or in the social registry, so what was happening to them was most unique, odd. In two days' time she would visit her mother. If she didn't see De Wolfe by then, she wouldn't discuss him with her.

Eva stepped away from the mirrors and returned to the bed, picked up a pillow, and puffed it. "I, as usual, am in the dark. Have no one to talk to. And with Max, I have no one, a contact, to deliver information to me from Max. No one!" She cried out and then fell across the huge bed.

She refused to say she hated this life she was living with De Wolfe, but this was the manifestation of what she was, De Wolfe's mistress: always at a disadvantage, living on the periphery, edge of De Wolfe's life. She understood her sadness whenever she was stuck in the middle of something she couldn't find a remedy for, or resolve.

"Where are you, Max!" Eva screamed. "WHERE ARE YOU!"

And then the thought of De Wolfe dumping her for someone else dashed into Eva's mind.

"No! No!"

It was something she'd never thought to happen, another showgirl replacing her. A showgirl from the World Stage who was younger, more pretty, more exciting than her.

"You wouldn't do that to me, Max! You wouldn't!"

She ran back over to the mirrors and looked into one then the other and then into all of them.

"I'm still beautiful. I'm still beautiful, desirable. How can another woman be more beautiful, desirable than me!"

She dashed back across the floor. She flung herself back onto the bed, and her body shivered. She felt frozen in time, in a nascent nightmare. Maxwell De Wolfe could be tired of her. Bored of her. He could have had enough of her.

Eva was sobbing into her hands.

"It-it's been two and a half years. How long do these illicit things last, a-affairs last? A mistress last? A year, two years, three years? How long before another beautiful woman comes along? We're worn out? Replaceable? Ask Alexandra De Wolfe. Ask, ask her, all the other women Max has bedded. Has discarded, g-gotten rid of, r-removed from his life."

Eva was out of the bed. She'd crossed the floor again but at a slow, deliberate pace, wiping her eyes and under control until she stared into the largest mirror on the wall with confidence, but, mostly, contempt.

"Who were once me. Eva Durant."

LILLY WAS TIDYING UP THE small kitchen (as if it needed it). She was extremely nervous. It was one fifty-five, and here she was tidying the kitchen for the second time today. For most of the day she didn't know what to do with herself, her nervous energy. But to say she'd been worrying, she'd done plenty of that.

It began as soon as she awoke this morning. As soon as she knew what stood in front of her as the new day unwound, and then the unnatural would occur, but something a mother would want no matter what might come from it, good or bad, it still would be a mother's wish.

Her faith was in her heart. This Christian faith she'd held on to for all of her life, that kept her so positive and rich with hope and integrity and the goodness to want what was best for others as well as herself. It's what this day would be about for her, to keep those virtues that formed her vital and alive in the circumstance she was soon to face.

Lilly heard the knock on the door, and her face trembled, but it was two o'clock.

"I-I'll be right there."

The door opened.

"Dorrell!"

"Mother!"

Lilly just stood back and looked at her handsome tall son who was dressed so smartly and confidently. She took him around his waist, and Dorrell's arms fell across her shoulders, and they hugged.

"Harlem ..."

"Yes, Harlem," Lilly said, the two of them finding the couch near the window to sit on.

Dorrell looked around the apartment. "You haven't changed, Lilly Durant." Dorrell laughed. "Always as neat as a pin."

Tears had formed in Lilly's eyes, and Dorrell, with his hand, began wiping them, his hand holding steady.

"I-I never thought I'd see this day, Dorrell. N-not ever again."

"Me either, Mother."

"To actually hold you, darling. To actually hold you. My son, Dorrell."

The telephone call came two days ago. And to say Lilly was unprepared, for a few seconds, she couldn't speak into the phone and cried then too when she heard Dorrell's voice, the beauty and tenderness of it that transcended anything that had happened between them, their story and its complications and long lapses of communication and exchange that gave her little opportunity to be a mother to him, help guide Dorrell's life as a parent whose wisdom could furnish important substance to him.

"You look so healthy, Dorrell."

"I was much lighter when I got out of Sing Sing. I've added at least eight to ten pounds more back on top my frame, Mother." Dorrell smiled. "But you look sensational, Mother. But you always do. I have always had the most beautiful mother and sister too."

A natural twist of her mouth occurred, for Lilly couldn't help it.

"Eva, I thought of her too, Mother. In Sing Sing." Dorrell stretched out his legs and then looked directly into Lilly's eyes. "By the way, what is Eva doing these days?"

Lilly felt her pulse quicken, and her body felt nervy again, as if it might crack.

"She, your sister's working for Masthead Publications in Manhattan."

"Oh, a publication firm."

"Yes."

"Good for her."

"Yes, she's quite pleased, Eva," Lilly said with a smile pressing her face. "She visits me when she can. Always on the weekend."

He wasn't going to pursue this any longer, Dorrell thought, ask how a colored girl wound up at Masthead Publications without passing for white, or where in Manhattan she lived. He wasn't visiting his mother to make her feel uncomfortable, but he knew Eva would come up in conversation in some shape or form, and so this limited personal engagement was sufficient for him.

He did want to see Lilly. He did love her. He was the wayward son. She was not the wayward mother. He was the one who was born defective, who wanted to deceive the world, hold it hostage as he was doing now with De Wolfe, to make it pay for what he could never really grasp, he could never really strip bare to understand.

"I love you, Mother."

"I love you, Dorrell."

She took his hand. "Why wouldn't you let me cook for you? I wanted to so badly."

"I don't know why, Mother." Dorrell took a deep breath. "I don't want you to think ..."

"You aren't going to make this a habit, are you, darling? You visiting me here in the apartment?" Lilly said, lifting Dorrell's head with her fingers so she could look back into his eyes, since his head had dropped.

"I didn't come here with pretense, any pretenses, Mother. I'm not Eva. I've always been on my own. I've disappointed you enough in one lifetime. It won't happen again. I have that much dignity still left in me."

She knew Dorrell enough to know that she must not expect too much from him. Sing Sing was in his past, and she knew his defiant nature and how he thought more of triumphs than defeats and that the Sing Sing experience might have hardened him, not softened him.

"Where did it go wrong, Dorrell?"

"I don't know, Mother."

"How I wish your father—"

"That good for nothing!"

"I've forgiven him."

"Good for you, Mother," Dorrell said resentfully. "I haven't. His sorry ass deserted us. He never was a man. A colored man who stood for something."

"Your father, Francois, wasn't strong, Dorrell. He couldn't accept responsibility. That of raising a family. The three of us."

"Is he dead?"

"God only knows. God only knows what's happened to your father."

"Sometimes I-I wonder, that's all."

"So do I."

Dorrell stood. "I'm leaving, Mother."

"But why?"

"I have to."

Lilly stood along with him. "It's beginning to feel too comfortable for you, isn't it, darling?"

"Don't ask me questions I can't answer, Mother. Don't do that, be that unfair with me," Dorrell said.

"Sometimes it's like that with your sister."

"What do you mean?"

"There's something troubling her right now, and she won't tell me. Let me in on it," Lilly said, taking Dorrell's hand again. "I want to be a mother so badly to my children."

De Wolfe! De Wolfe! It's working!

"But I can't say ... I mean, she does tell me enough about her life. I do make some contribution, but what's disturbing her now, I see it on her face, Dorrell. It is as plain as day, Eva can't hide it."

"We all try, don't we?"

"That's why ..."

"What?"

"Are, is everything going well with you since your release?"

"Yes. The money. I thanked you over the phone, Mother, but I want to thank you again," Dorrell said, hugging her. "The next step is for me to find something that I'm good at. Not crime. Not something I've proved to be a failure at."

"It's just that ..."

"Yes ...?"

"You're so smart, Dorrell. Talented. There's so much that you can do if you put your mind to it, darling."

"I do feel there's something waiting for me just around the corner, uh, bend, Mother. Really not that far off. You know, on the horizon."

"But you, Dorrell, have to make it happen. You can't wait for someone to do it for you."

"Mother, you are an example for anyone, if there ever was one."

"Thank you, Dorrell."

"So when are you to see Eva again?"

"Soon, I'm sure."

Dorrell opened the apartment door. "Give her my best regards, Mother."

"I just wish, Dorrell, that—"

"It'll never happen, Mother. There's too much rotten history between us. Too much negative stuff for us to work through. We're grown. Adults. Have always taken separate paths away from each other.

"I just hope she's happy, that's all. That she has the peace of mind, the kind I'm seeking, Mother, every day of my life."

"Do you need more—"

"Money? No. It's been enough, adequate, what you were generous enough to provide me. I will do better financially, so don't you worry. I'll be all right. I'm going to make certain of it. That money's no object for me. That I've eliminated, at least, that basic, fundamental obstacle."

DORRELL WAS SKIPPING DOWN THE apartment's stone steps. He was delighted by the news he'd gathered from Lilly. He was positive now that his mother knew everything about Eva's affair with De Wolfe, knowing she was De Wolfe's mistress. Without any communication from De Wolfe, Eva was in a panic: she couldn't comprehend De Wolfe's extended absence from their love nest at 10 Ballad Street. Their relationship was hemorrhaging.

"It's working, man. One hundred percent," Dorrell said, landing down on street level. "Eva's in a fucking tizzy by what's going on in her life!"

He turned around and then looked back up at the four-story building.

The idea of Eva agonizing along with De Wolfe greatly pleased him. As far as he was concerned, she owed black folk who couldn't cross the color line, who couldn't pass themselves off for white, a piece of her flesh. She should be judged like him, for his crime against society, for what she was doing with De Wolfe. She was the one who chose to gain advantage, or was she ashamed of being a member of the Negro race and did something about it in such a frenzy of calculation, she got lost, sucked up into her own duplicity?

But now wasn't the time for analysis but action. Now was the time for both Eva Durant and De Wolfe to pay for their transgressions, Dorrell thought, even if it sounded to him like a religious rant from someone like him who did not believe in God, only in himself, much like Maxwell De Wolfe, he assumed.

Dorrell looked up 130th Street, and there were buildings galore and black people galore. He felt comfortable in this space, with Negroes, his own race. This place called Harlem. A dark place that white people—at one time—fled from. It wasn't a "jungle," but for him, a home.

Chapter 14

He'd gotten a letter from the blackmailer, the fictional Franklin De Witt, at ten o'clock. Marilyn Ochs (from past instruction), De Wolfe's secretary, had handed it to him at that exact time of the morning.

It was 2:10 p.m. De Wolfe's morning schedule blocked him from reading the letter that had produced a pound of his sweat by now, and an itchy, agitated state of mind not even Cyrille Fitch had ever witnessed in the office of De Wolfe & Fitch. There was no apology forthcoming from De Wolfe. They worked for him. He was their boss.

De Wolfe had just come out his personal bathroom, and his breathing, right now, was erratic. The letter, from this fictional character who was real not by name, only by deed, seemed to be breathing out at him with a nasty odor. His life the past week or so had changed drastically. Now he wondered how much more can it change.

"Oh my god. My god!"

He couldn't think for now, only cry out in pain and fear and desperation, and there on the desk was this thing that had to be opened, something that could alter the order of his life forever.

De Wolfe fumbled with the envelope, and his face was contorted into a twisted mask of the many days and nights he'd been fighting with his sanity, to think another man could do this to him, Maxwell De Wolfe, the power he had over the world, drop him to his knees.

And it was a con man, not a businessman, not a kingpin, a giant in the world of commerce and finance, but a common street hustler who had devised a plan so rigid that it could possibly strike at the heart of him, and too his soul.

And with the letter opener, De Wolfe was able to slit the flap open and then take the letter out of the envelope and then unfold the letter and see—

EVA DURANT IS BLACK. A NEGRO.

It was written in bold ink.

DE WOLFE SAT STIFFLY AT his desk.

This was to be the follow-up to yesterday's shock that was taken by De Wolfe as if his whole body had been riddled by bullets and he'd been bleeding from head to toe from each bullet that had punctured his flabby, copious flesh.

Yesterday's letter was brief but continued to insist that De Wolfe not contact Eva Durant and that he wait for a ring at six o'clock in his office.

Last night, the more De Wolfe thought of the blackmailer, the more he wanted to call the cops, get them in on this nightmare of his, stop it. Just stop the GODDAMNED THING!

Ring.

"You're a bald-faced liar!"

"Oh, so that's what you think of me, De Wolfe? Now isn't that nice to know."

"A bald-faced liar!"

"Still defiant, are you. Still think you control this situation and not me."

"Eva can't be black, she's too beautiful to be black. A-a Negro. Too intelligent. Too—"

"And it's what you think of black people, De Wolfe? A race of—"

"Right! Damned right! Imbeciles! Imbeciles! In-intellectual midgets, d-dwarfs!"

Dorrell didn't actually expect this, but there was no telling what he should have expected from a man so powerful and rich as De Wolfe. What hatred or defiance or deep-seated opinion on race he harbored.

"So all of this, my elaborate planning out of—"

"What the hell happened to 'we,' we!"

"May I continue?" Pause. "Planning out of this confrontation with you is what, nothing more than a prank, De Wolfe? Something done for fun by a juvenile with empty gesture?"

"You're a liar!"

"Shut the fuck up and listen to me, De Wolfe: I killed the 'we' in this fucking operation, and if I have to, I'll kill you!"

This news knocked De Wolfe back into a state of fear.

"Okay, okay! I'm Eva's brother. Dorrell Durant. Our home was Newark, New Jersey. Right across the water. Our father is Francois Durant. He abandoned us at an early age. The bastard. Our mother, I'll not mention, include her name, it's all been recorded in city records, information a powerful person such as you can easily obtain. But she is the best mother in the world, bar none."

"You killed two—"

"It was fun, De Wolfe." Dorrell laughed into the phone. "I never was going to share your money with them. They were two-bit crooks. Petty thieves. Untalented, forgettable, and discardable."

"You, you killed them in cold blood?"

"Two black men so that I could ..."

"What, what, you fuck!"

"You think I have to share everything with you, De Wolfe? Every quirk, gesture, every idiosyncrasy? I have psychological problems as well as you. You're no different or better than me. I'm black, colored, but I'm not Eva, my sister, who I'm two years older than: I never tried passing for white. Cross over the color line. Test it like her. Betray my race."

"Black, Eva's black!"

"Are you tearing your fucking hair out at the roots, De Wolfe? Out your crappy scalp?"

"I ... I—"

"So now you believe me, do you?"

"Yes, yes, I—"

"Because I hate her. Do you hear me, De Wolfe? Despise her. I always disliked her. But now knowing about you, that she's been your black whore for—"

"I love her! Love her!"

"How pathetic. Don't you sound pathetic. Pathetic coming from you, someone like you, De Wolfe. I expected much more from a great man like you. I really did, De Wolfe."

"My life, you don't know my life, how I live, y-you don't know."

Dorrell smiled. "I know all right, De Wolfe. I know the decadence of the rich as well as the poor. Except the poor are primitives, savages, and the rich, noble, refined. But you'll get no pity from me."

Silence.

"How much money do you want? Your blackmail demand?"

"How much ... seventy-five thousand dollars."

"I thought ..."

"I don't care what you thought, De Wolfe."

"Yes, I see ..."

"You know the empty lot on Ballad Street?"

"Yes."

"The money's to be delivered there tomorrow night at two o'clock. The person who's to make the drop, Fagan Dooley, your chauffeur—am I not correct, De Wolfe?"

Silence.

"Yes, Fagan Dooley, will place a sheet of canvas over the money off to the right of the lot, oh, about fifty yards in from the street."

"No-nobody travels Ballad—"

"But you and Eva." Pause.

"I bought a flashlight just for the occasion, De Wolfe. I made it easy for you."

"H-how can you do this to her?"

"What difference does it make now, De Wolfe? She's black, a colored woman, isn't she?"

De Wolfe didn't answer.

"Oh, by the way, give Eva a four-day eviction notice."

"But—"

"After all, what the hell else are you to do with her, De Wolfe, but throw her out in the street on her fucking fanny."

"Is, is that all?"

"No, I want you to make a copy of the key to the building."

"There're two," De Wolfe said, before he could catch himself.

"Two?"

"I …"

"Don't fuck with me, De Wolfe. Because if anything goes wrong …"

"I'm sorry, yes, there are two. One for the front door. The second one—"

"I get it. There's a door on the second floor I have to access. To get to Eva. The key will do that for me." Pause. "Even if I could have easily picked both locks, but it's better, neater this way.

"And of course, you can visit her in the four-day time frame to square things with her, after the drop's executed by your man."

"You …"

"It's been good doing business with you, De Wolfe."

"Y-you chose a life of crime, why?"

"It chose me, De Wolfe. This career of crime. Of schemes and dreams. Of riches."

"Don't you, why couldn't you use your brain, talent in a different way, for a different, more moral, noble purpose?"

"So now you want to reform me, De Wolfe? Or now you see even someone like me, a colored man in this world, not to be inferior to a white man, to you?"

"No, no, you bastard, I'm not saying that!"

"Of course you're not, De Wolfe. You're still fighting for your goddamn life, but it ended today. You believe Eva's black. One hundred percent believe it, De Wolfe. And when Eva finally confesses to it, you'll know why she passed for white. Why she entered your world as a white woman. Eva will explain all of it—everything to you, De Wolfe. All the dirty little details, and it still won't matter.

"She'll still be a colored girl in your eyes, De Wolfe. Black. A nigger with nigger blood. Inferior to a white woman. The white race." Pause.

"And finally, if you think you can have me killed and there'd be no way to trace Eva to you, it'll be a big, big mistake. My lady friend, who's privy to the same set of facts as me, will expose you as I have now done.

"Who would relish nailing your white ass to the wall, De Wolfe, like fucking deer meat."

WHEN DORRELL SAW THE HEADLIGHTS to De Wolfe's Packard beaming down Ballad Street, a chill of pure pleasure shot up and down his spine.

He'd stolen a car on Sixty-Third Street to get to Ballad Street, but the car wasn't parked on Ballad Street, but two blocks away on Logan Street.

De Wolfe's Packard parked in front of the lot. Dorrell knew De Wolfe wouldn't be in the car, only his chauffeur, Fagan Dooley. Dorrell was on the side of De Wolfe's building dressed in black and could see everything that happened in the lot due to the car's headlights and the flashlight Dooley carried.

Dorrell felt, suddenly, as if everything was moving in slow motion, not at the speed of reality, of life. "There he is, the chauffeur and the canvas sheet."

Dorrell saw Dooley enter the lot and then stop and then do what he thought he'd do all along, get back in the car and drive the Packard into the lot, about midway.

"Smart man, Dooley. Smart man." Dorrell laughed.

And now it was time for Dorrell to hustle two blocks over to retrieve his car. By that time, the operation should be completed, Dorrell thought. It was impossible for him to be seen from the opposite side of the block. The only light on the block was the building's, and its dimness provided limited light anyway.

When Dorrell rode down Ballad Street in the dark gray car, the Packard, as expected, was gone. Dorrell did the same thing Dooley had done; he rolled the car into the empty lot and parked it in front of the canvas sheet.

"Seventy-five thousand smackeroos is under that canvas, isn't there? Cold cash."

I must be sweating like De Wolfe was yesterday when he got my call! Dorrell thought.

Dorrell got out of the car, and still thinking of what was under the canvas, he was too transfixed by it all to even reach out and pull the canvas off the top of the money.

Then, finally, he said, "Here goes!"

A beam of light shone down on the bundled money. Dorrell knew seventy-five thousand dollars when he saw it, that De Wolfe hadn't cheated him out of a penny.

"Damn, man, I'm fucking rich!"

Back in the car, the money in the car's backseat, Dorrell pulled out of the dark lot.

"Too bad Caesar's dead. I killed him. He would've seen how my plan worked to perfection. How sweetly I fleeced De Wolfe."

De Wolfe had put the keys to 10 Ballad Street in a manila envelope.

Dorrell drove the car down the block and then executed a U-turn. He drove the car back up the block and then stopped. He looked up at the second floor.

"If you only knew what happened tonight, Eva. How I've ruined your life but made myself rich. All because of you, Eva. What a great fucking sister you are. Turned out to be, after all."

Chapter 15

Fagan sat behind the Packard's steering wheel remembering only one thing: three days ago when Maxwell De Wolfe, his employer for twelve years, told him there was seventy-five thousand dollars in cash in the trunk of the car and that he was to deliver it to the empty lot on Ballad Street at two o'clock in the morning. How seventy-five grand got in the back of the trunk, he had no clue.

Even before De Wolfe had continued, it scared the living shit out of him!

But De Wolfe had continued, letting him know about the canvas strip in the trunk, also, that he was to cover the bundle of money with it. It was said like a business deal had been transacted and then consummated between them, but he was just De Wolfe's chauffeur, in his employ, not an equal partner in crime. And all he could ask himself with the feeling of shit lumping his pants was the obvious: what the hell's going on!

But he knew he, personally, was not engaged in a criminal activity that would lead to an arrest on his part, that there was an outside agent in the world who was blackmailing De Wolfe, and it had something to do with the broad, the dish De Wolfe had stashed away at 10 Ballad Street, this mysterious woman he'd never seen but had imagined.

It's why he had not driven De Wolfe to the residence, by his estimation, for twelve days. It's why De Wolfe had been so depressed and dejected; his disposition, so it seemed, on the brink of destructive behavior. Over those past twelve days, he and De Wolfe had a different relationship, one of extensive silence between them, one of employer and employee, not of one human being to another, not like before.

And so this was the night everything for De Wolfe and his nightly pattern of late would change. For De Wolfe told him to drive him to 10 Ballad Street, to where the *woman* was, Fagan thought. To where a new chapter of the story would pick back up again, Fagan thought.

THE WALL OF SILENCE WAS deafening.

The Packard parked in front of 10 Ballad Street.

Fagan opened the car door for De Wolfe.

They followed their old, reliable routine. The one—by now—that was two and a half years old.

But when Fagan inserted the skinny key in the second door, the one to the second floor entrance, gently, De Wolfe took hold of Fagan's arm.

"I want you to stay in the car, Fagan. I am not staying the night. But I won't be long. Not like past visits," De Wolfe said in a threadbare voice.

"Yes, Mr. De Wolfe."

De Wolfe let Fagan look into his eyes, and Fagan saw a man who had grown older by some years, as if the world had fallen in on him, and the dark bags under his eyes had dragged him down to being a mere mortal, a man who would never recover from the fall.

"Thank you," De Wolfe said after Fagan slipped the key into the door and opened it.

EVA WAS BESIDE HERSELF, FOR she heard the door to the second floor open and close. She knew she had!

And then she heard De Wolfe's cane as it thumped the floor that was leading to her bedroom. And she was attired for him; as always, she was attired for De Wolfe.

"Max! Max!"

Eva grabbed him with the excitement of an abandoned child, of someone who was sick with worry and at the same time joy, admiration, and adoration.

De Wolfe wanted to say, "Take your hands off me, you black bitch! You black whore! You nigger!" but he couldn't. He wanted to feel this from Eva, this spirit of hers, this beauty he once knew but would tonight destroy with every breath in him and horror for what Eva Durant had done to him in this cocoon-like world he'd created for them and them alone.

"Oh, Max, oh, Max, you're back! Back, Max!"

And Eva began to take off his coat, when De Wolfe said, "Don't. Don't. It's not necessary."

Eva halted, and a strange expression sprang up on her face. "Don't, but why, Max?"

De Wolfe walked away from her and then turned to her, and when he saw her in the skimpy outfit, he said, "Cover yourself up, Eva. For god's sake! Put on a goddamned robe!"

"I ... but—"

"Do as I told you, you ..."

But De Wolfe wasn't able to say it just yet, now, the word he wanted to use, that he'd been eager to use only minutes earlier, in the car, when he was thinking of Eva, of the bile he tasted that had emptied out his heart and was laying as hard as plastic on his tongue.

"But, but why, Max, what have I done?"

"Do it, goddamnit! Just do it, for god's sake!"

"Yes, of course, Max. Of, of course." Eva scurried across the room to get her robe.

She was wrapping the powder blue robe around her waist when she looked across the room at De Wolfe, who stood away from her and, to her, looked so angry and distraught, so much older in the face.

"I won't let you humiliate me like this, Max."

"Humiliate you, huh ..."

"I, you've, I've been out of contact with you. You, and then you walk in here with no explanation as to why ... Every night I've waited here in this room for you, Max. Alone. Alone. Every night since—"

"I don't have to answer to you, not someone like you!"

"A mistress," Eva said sassily, her temper rising. "Because I'm your mistress, a kept woman, and suddenly, out of nowhere, when you return, you, there's no courtesy from you, no—"

"And you expect that of me, someone like me?"

Eva took a quick step forward. "W-what are you making me, suddenly, Max? How are you rearranging me? Who, what am I suddenly to you?"

"You are a liar. An imposter. Fake. That's what you are!"

"What do you mean, I-I—"

"And you've become so good at it"—De Wolfe laughed—"you don't even know what the hell I'm talking about, d-do you? You have no fucking idea. N-no fucking way to tell truth from fiction."

Bewildered, Eva stumbled across the floor and over to the bed and sat down. Her lower lip trembled, and her beautiful eyes turned blank.

"W-what h-have I done?"

"Done? Y-you piece of shit. You piece of nigger shit!"

And the shock of what De Wolfe said stabbed Eva like an ice pick.

"Oh no, no, no—"

"Yes, yes, yes. You're a nigger! A nigger. A fucking nigger!"

Eva kept screaming out in the room.

"Nigger, nigger, nigger!" De Wolfe said, jamming the cane into the floor one thrust at a time. "You're nothing but a piece of nigger shit!"

"Yes, yes, yes—"

"Nigger shit! Nigger shit!"

"I'm black, I'm black!"

De Wolfe then took the cane, when he got to the wall of mirrors, and began smashing the mirrors with it, but not all of them, for he'd fallen to the floor from his effort.

Both were crying, De Wolfe on the floor and Eva on the bed.

"I'm sorry, Max, I'm sorry ..."

"You fucking whore, you black fucking whore ..." De Wolfe said from the floor.

Eva went inward, to what had happened over the past twelve days, how her "lie" had been discovered by De Wolfe. This thing that she'd gotten away with not just with De Wolfe, but with the white world she lived in, who did not see her for who she was, black, colored, a nigger, who thought she was one of them, white, beautiful, intelligent, well spoken, sophisticated, and cultured.

"Can we talk," Eva said, stretched out on the bed, looking at De Wolfe across the floor.

"Talk, talk, I've been doing a lot of talking these days," De Wolfe said, blocking his tears.

"W-with who, Max."

"Who ... who ...?" De Wolfe's hand trembled when he pressed down his ragged beard, when he tried gaining control of himself while struggling to his feet. The veins in his neck were turning blue.

"Dorrell Durant ... do you know him!"

"No!"

"Yes!"

"My brother!"

"Nigger! A con man too!"

Eva could not imagine this happening to her, of Dorrell doing this to her.

"But he wasn't lying, no, not at all. Not one fucking bit."

"How did—"

"He knew. Ha. You'll have to ask him, won't you, Eva."

"He was—"

"In prison, the bastard, Sing Sing, I believe," De Wolfe said, gaining back his strength.

"Yes, Sing Sing, Max, Sing Sing."

"The dumb fuck. But he's smart, isn't he?"

"Yes, Dorrell—"

"He was blackmailing me. The fuck was blackmailing me. And I paid him off. Seventy-five thousand dollars. Seventy-five thousand fucking dollars!"

Eva gasped.

"So to keep his trap shut about a nigger woman! Someone with nigger blood in her! Nigger scum! Keeping you as my fucking mistress for two years! Two years!"

Eva was beginning to feel cheap, like someone who was colored, sleazy, not someone who was white, who had accustomed herself to feeling white, not colored—certainly not a "nigger."

Suddenly Eva opened her robe. "You loved this nigger flesh, didn't you, Max. This dark, nigger meat? Didn't you!"

De Wolfe looked at Eva; he lusted for her.

"Didn't you! Didn't you!"

"It, it was your weapon over me!"

"Sex, Max? Sex!"

"Yes, yes—if I had known you were colored, a colored girl with nigger blood—"

"Of course, Max, but you didn't!"

"You, there's nothing to prove. You're proving nothing, nothing at all by what you're doing," De Wolfe said, jamming the cane into the floor. "Give-giving me a hard-on!"

"To you I was white. To me I was white."

"But you're not, you're not, you're colored. Colored, Eva. A nigger to me now!"

"Then leave! Leave then! Leave!"

"How long did you think this charade of yours, you were going to get away with this, it would last, this deception of yours? This degradation you've done to the white race?"

"Fool, what a fool, fool you are!"

De Wolfe, he had to stop, pause, try to understand what he'd just said as if he were a defender of the white race, not a product of it.

"I've suffered mightily from …" De Wolfe hobbled over to one of the mirrors that had not been smashed, whose shattered glass had not littered the floor. "Look at me, Eva, look at me. I'm an old man."

And De Wolfe had thought how Fagan had looked at him too at the top of the stairs, in the naked light, that he was looking at a man who had aged by millenniums.

"What are you going to do with me, Max? Tell me, please."

"I don't want you any longer. Not one fucking piece of you. In-insult of you."

"I'll … then I'll leave 10 Ballad Street, of course," Eva said.

"Of course."

"Is that all?"

"I thought I would die at times over the past week," De Wolfe said, taking to a chair. "W-without you."

"I thought, I was worried for you," Eva said.

"Alexandra, her life just follows its merry course of events."

"Merry?" Eva scoffed.

"No entanglements, no …"

"Yes, yes," Eva said, closing her robe, wrapping it to her. "Everyday regrets she can do nothing about."

"We're all fucking trapped. You were too, weren't you," De Wolfe said, looking at Eva, "until you tried changing what fate handed you. That colored face of yours."

"I will pack my bags, Max. I will be all right," Eva said, lying back onto the bed.

"Yes, you do that, Eva. You do that," De Wolfe said, now standing, seemingly exhausted by what had happened in the room. He looked around the room. "I-I don't know what I'm going to do with this building now."

"There'll be others, Max, like me. There'll be other mistresses. Women. They just won't be colored."

De Wolfe began making his way across the floor.

"Goodbye, Max."

De Wolfe said nothing, nor did he turn back around to Eva.

"THERE HE IS!" FAGAN SAID to himself. Fagan hopped out of the car.

Watching De Wolfe walk down the short stoop with his cane, Fagan thought De Wolfe walked terribly bad.

Fagan, not offering an exchange of words with De Wolfe, acknowledging De Wolfe's state of mind, privacy, opened the car door for him.

When Fagan got in the car, it felt like a morgue, as if someone had just died. He geared the car, and immediately upon its departure from the curb, he began to think. He began to think not about tonight, but tomorrow arching across the sky and bringing him and De Wolfe a brand-new day together, another journey to take themselves on.

He didn't know when they'd return to 10 Ballad Street again, but one day they would, and when they did return, De Wolfe would be suffering as he was now in the car's backseat, De Wolfe not speaking a word, even one coming out of him, but tonight's torture buried much further in him, much more alive and strifed in his bowels.

He loved De Wolfe in his own private way of loving someone. He'd peeled so much of him away over the years that he could sympathize with him, the death of his daughter, Emilie, more than humanized him, and now a man who loved a woman whom he could never have but who must have disappointed him enough that it cost him seventy-five thousand dollars; and now more heartache, it seemed to him, than De Wolfe could bear.

ALEXANDRA HEARD DE WOLFE MAKE his way down the hallway. She removed her blinders and glanced over to the clock.

"It's over, finally over, isn't it, De Wolfe's affair. That mistress of his at 10 Ballad Street."

Alexandra was in bed. She placed her blinders back over her eyes. Seeing De Wolfe once a day, only at the dining room table, she had become more and more subjected to and upset by De Wolfe's declining mood. She did feel sorry for him but would not in any way extend herself to him in any different way.

"He would simply rebuff me. And it is not my place for that. De Wolfe's wife. I am not in his life for that role. Benefit."

When her father suffered with his mistresses, she and her mother felt it immediately, so it was not a foreign feeling for her, but De Wolfe had really invested much emotional capital into this mistress he kept at 10 Ballad Street, who it seemed had broken his heart.

She should say good riddance to her but wouldn't. The pain in De Wolfe had settled into the mansion, into its walls; and it would take a good washing to cleanse it, to remove its awful stench.

Alexandra heard De Wolfe's bedroom door close.

"My father. He taught me well, didn't he. Everything I should know about this untidy state of affairs. I was raised to be who I am. Taught well, yes. It was a valuable lesson to learn."

DE WOLFE HAD HOBBLED ACROSS the bedroom floor. He'd gotten over to the mantelpiece without the aid of room light to guide him, only his bruising, persistent pain and his heart screaming as if it could spit out at the world in red.

"I can't change her color. I can't do it. I am not powerful enough to do that, rewrite history." De Wolfe began laughing in a mad, bizarre way. "There's so much I can change, but not the color of a man's skin. Or, or what travels in his blood. I don't make the laws of nature or of this land, this country I live in. I just follow the law, even me, Maxwell De Wolfe."

De Wolfe felt lost within a constitution, lost within a law that judged Eva to be black by her nigger blood's content, count. And so it's how he had to regard her, but not when she was white, or when he was in bed with her, or having sex with her, or sharing his sorrows and triumphs with her when Eva Durant was his mistress.

De Wolfe was trying to understand why Eva had done what she did: cross the color line, pretend to be white. Those gorgeous showgirls at the World Stage, so many of them wanted to be something else, De Wolfe thought, not just show off their gorgeous gams or grind their fannies for a gallery of older men driven by their voracious sexual appetites, but actresses.

"I do recall that. Someone saying that regarding Eva. Was it, yes, yes, it was from Amy Dawkins, Eva's roommate. An actress. A fucking actress. It was Eva's ambition. It's why she was passing for white."

She was burning with the ambition of being an actress but, for two and half years, was able to hide that aspiration from him too, like he had to hide himself from the public, from what rich men do, the other life they live, that brings them joy until one day they lose it.

"I would have dismissed it anyway. Thought it childish. Acting. The very idea of it. Eva, Eva would not have gotten a word of support, token of support from me if she … Damn you, De Wolfe! D-damn you!" De Wolfe cried out.

He began stabbing the cane into the floor as if he were stabbing his heart and then crumpled to the floor. He wanted to call Helga, but Helga wasn't on duty. He wanted someone to help him up from the floor. For someone to help him rise up, again, to his feet.

Someone.

Chapter 16

The next day.

Eva was lying on the bed. She was drowsy, for she'd been resting. She reported to Masthead Publications today. At Masthead, she'd laughed to herself for a goodly portion of the day: they still thought she was white.

But once she stepped back into the building, back into the bedroom, she was quickly reminded of the trajectory her life had taken last night, what course it was on. All she had been thinking of while resting was De Wolfe, his rage and hatred.

She refused to feel sorry for herself, for she and she alone had chosen to live with deceit and extravagant falsehoods, to take such a giant leap in a country that loathed her kind, yet she was living among them as one of them.

She laughed, but it was a hollow laugh, for she did feel sad. She did feel the sting of De Wolfe's rejection of her: that she was just a "nigger" to him and nothing more.

Eva's eyes shut.

She'd been lying on her back for a few minutes, when she thought she'd get up to pack, for she'd asked for tomorrow off, and Masthead Publications granted it but said she would have to make up for it when asked to: she agreed.

Eva stood, and she wanted to fall back on the bed and cry but looked straight ahead to her closet of clothes, finery, and tried not to let this heavyhearted feeling of sadness sap her emotionally to the point of—

"Who ..." Eva had heard the movement of the hallway's door, someone in the hallway. "No ... it ... it can't be. It can't be!"

She was running to the bedroom door.

"Max! Max!" she screamed. "You've come back. You've come back to me, Max! Everything's all right, over with. Every—"

The door flung open.

"Dorrell!"

"Hi, sis!"

"Dorrell!"

"Come, give your big brother a kiss!"

"How, how ..." Then Eva stepped back, for Dorrell had barged into the bedroom.

"So this was your rendezvous. Your cozy little love nest, you and De Wolfe's." Dorrell looked around the bedroom. "Fancy. Fancy. But then, of course, my imagination has designed and redesigned this place a thousand times over."

Dorrell looked at Eva's fresh bodily impressions on the bed. "Sleeping alone these days, are you, Eva?"

Eva walked away and toward the bed.

"And to answer your earlier question, De Wolfe made copies of the keys for me, needless to say. I asked him to. It was better than breaking in. It was a part of the—"

"Blackmail."

"Why, yes, of course, Eva."

Dorrell strutted across the floor and then stopped. "We have never talked face-to-face, De Wolfe and I. Only by phone. And then there were the letters, strictly from my end, not his. It was pure pleasure, though. Outwitting De Wolfe. Keeping the old fuck on edge," Dorrell said. "On the hot seat." Dorrell cleared his throat.

"Money not an object then, Eva, only cunning. Mine, not De Wolfe's. His power, useless to him. Vacant."

Eva took a closer look at Dorrell and saw how beautifully attired he was, and of course, she thought, he was always beautiful to look at, like her, like all the Durants who shared the same bloodlines.

"You were quite excited, Eva. Just now."

Eva felt ashamed, embarrassed.

"But De Wolfe's not coming back, my dear sister. He wouldn't waste seventy-five grand on a nigger like me, or you, his mistress."

She hated him more than ever, his sarcasm, his gloating, his aloofness. He was a brother who always talked down to her. Someone who tried to be the absent, surrogate father in her life even if he was but two years older, but who thought himself wise, able to provide all the answers to life's questions. But he was nothing more than a con artist, someone who stole for a living and who broke their mother's heart.

"Caesar Stark—"

"Caesar Stark!"

"Oh, you wonder what he has to do with this nasty little caper of mine? Someone from Underwood Avenue, the old neighborhood. But just goes to show that you never know who's watching you, Eva," Dorrell said, pulling up a chair and sitting.

"Caesar spotted you a few weeks back, making your way down Ballad Street, so he decided to follow you, Eva. And what Caesar saw …"

Eva covered her mouth.

"But the dumb ass didn't know how to run this big an operation, went way over his head with this one. So he found me up at Lula's Lounge in Harlem. Probably the smartest thing he's ever done in his life." Pause. "Dummy.

"Know the place, Eva, Lula's Lounge, or is it below you, not highbrow enough being it's a colored Harlem hangout. Not your kind, white. Even if De Wolfe kept you on a short leash, I suppose you'd call it, huh, Eva?" Dorrell laughed.

"Too bad Caesar didn't live long enough to see how I pulled—"

"Why not!"

"Because I killed him. It's how come. Then dumped his dumb ass in the East River!"

"No!"

"Yes! Killed him in the empty lot across the street where De Wolfe's chauffeur dropped off the seventy-five grand. Knifed Caesar Stark in the fucking back." Pause. "De Wolfe turned me into a murderer too!"

"No, Dorrell, it's your evil that killed Caesar, Caesar Stark!"

"You think so! I tried to help you when you were young, wet behind the ears. I tried, Eva. But you'd never listen, and so you became a white man's whore. A black bitch but called herself white!"

"I wanted to be an actress, it's all I ever wanted!"

"Something you can't be—it's what you mean. Not the kind of actress you want to be. Glitz and glam. On top of the world. With your beauty, good looks. But that's not for a black girl. The silent screen!"

"De-De Wolfe found me at the World Stage. I don't know how it got to where it—"

"Became an affair? Because De Wolfe was in love with you, silly girl. It didn't take long. Not with your beauty. De Wolfe did all of this for you. And you let him."

"I …" Eva was crying.

"All of it was going to end sooner or later for you."

"But, but you had no right—"

"They all do, tasteless trysts like yours." Pause. "And as for De Wolfe, he was nothing more than a 'pigeon,' as we say in the trade. An 'easy mark.' And you were the bait, Eva. The lure. Sell you, my sister, down the river … it was easy. Easy as hell."

"Why is it that you hate me so much, Dorrell?"

"I do, don't I?" Dorrell brushed back his beautiful black hair. He shut his eyes. "Do, should I blame it on you, or … I don't know …

"You, when you were born, came along, all the attention shifted from me to … No, it wasn't any of that fucking psychological crap, bullshit, like the next thing I should do is see a fucking shrink. Lie on a fucking couch and … I'd still tell the world to go to hell!

"But at least I still love who I am, not like you. Who's chosen white over black!"

"Get out, Dorrell! Now!"

"You're the one who's confused about who you are, not me." Dorrell's voice softened. "It's just killing Caesar Stark, a brethren, a black man to accomplish my goal, what I assessed best for me at the time, that disappointed me some. The opinion I had of myself as a con man, not a murderer." Pause.

"But once you go down that road—"

"You're sick, Dorrell. Sick. Yet, yet—"

"What, fucking what, Eva!"

"Mother worries about you. She loves you. Prays for you. I don't know why, but she does."

Dorrell stood. "And what did she think of you and De Wolfe, may I ask? Your dirty, sordid fucking affair with De Wolfe?"

"She detested De Wolfe. She detested the life I was living. And me, passing myself off for white."

"Then we've both made mother unhappy. Have brought her grave pain."

"Yes."

"But now, I'll never have to ask mother for a penny, a cent of her money, not ever again."

"I-I hope not, Dorrell."

"That I promise, Eva. Never again."

She was still looking Dorrell dead in the eye and hoped what she saw was sincere, not another con job he was pulling on himself, this time.

"And you'll never hear from me or see me again, Eva."

"I don't want to, Dorrell. Not you. I couldn't handle it."

Dorrell saw the shattered glass on the floor, something he saw the instant he'd entered the bedroom. "Upset, was he?" Dorrell laughed. "Maxwell De Wolfe?"

Eva walked over and picked up a sliver of glass. "But I refuse to let myself clean it up," Eva said.

"After all, you were De Wolfe's mistress, not his maid. He would've paid you maid wages if that were the case." Pause.

"Goodbye, Eva. Have a good damned life."

Dorrell walked out the door.

Eva dropped the piece of glass she was holding in her hand to the floor.

"Thank, thank you."

ONE WEEK LATER.

Dorrell was in the New York Public Library on Forty-Second Street. It was a behemoth of a library, and the Rose Main Reading Room with its high ceilings was as marvelous and spacious as every physical aspect of the library.

A book was in front of Dorrell, but he wasn't actually reading it, for Dorrell was in the room to write Lilly Durant. He gave the impression he was reading from a book and copying its contents, in a room where much research was done, there being no nonsense about anyone's intent in keeping within the library's strict discipline and seriousness.

Dorrell felt comfortable in this room lined with thousands of reference works. His brass lamp had been turned on for no more than a minute. This was a peaceful spot, not like the Bowery, in the fleabag hotel he still stayed in, had not moved out of, despite De Wolfe's seventy-five thousand dollars, despite him being rich, something a thief such as himself dreams of, one day, successfully attaining: scoring the big hit.

His rationalization, to himself, was that he had to begin acclimating himself to being rich gradually, a black man with money, therefore, substance. This was the more sensitive, urgent issue for him now, making the leap from poverty to wealth.

The money had been deposited in various banks. Some of the bank accounts in his name and others in fake names with him using, of course, bogus ID. Once a con man, he thought each time he assumed a new identification, always a con man!

He was at a loss right now as to how to begin the letter to Lilly, as Dorrell looked out into this stellar space of sturdy wooden desks, and the urgency of book pages turned in a rapid rhythm attributed to the insatiable thirst of knowledge the library provided its thousands of regular users.

And while thinking, Dorrell thought of himself, Eva, De Wolfe, and what was to become of their lives. Would Eva ever become a legitimate actress? Would De Wolfe ever get over her and become the De Wolfe of old, a greedy bastard who wanted to own things in the world for acquisition only?

And what about me? Dorrell thought. *Had I learned anything from the Sing Sing experience after six years of being locked up and then released?*

"I don't know," Dorrell said under his breath.

Because he still thought like a con man (every waking minute), not someone who could change. He was still thinking of the next scheme, the next new heist or big caper. It was in his blood. It was all he knew. De Wolfe's money had not changed his mental state.

He could not imagine Dorrell Durant not waking up each morning without trying to beat another poor sap out of a buck. *The world's full of them,* Dorrell thought. *They're everywhere. A dime a dozen in this fucking world.*

Lilly didn't know what to think, looking down at the letter in her hand she received in the post from Dorrell, but one with no return address. Straight off she'd noticed it.

Lilly had carried the letter from the kitchen to her bedroom and sat in an old wooden rocker and let the remaining daylight serve as her light. She'd gotten in from a long stint of domestic work that had started at six o'clock and ended at four o'clock, nonstop.

"What have you done now, Dorrell? Or is it money again, darling?" Lilly's cheeks sunk in when she'd said it, the word "money."

Dorrell had just visited her, the first time in seven years, and told her there was no need for her to give him more money. But it wasn't the money, she would give him every penny, cent she owned if he needed it. It was just that there was no return address on the envelope, no way to contact him; that bothered her, that made the prospect of reading Dorrell's letter troublesome for her.

Lilly retrieved her glasses, put them on, and then adjusted them.

Dear Mother,

I write you this letter as a son who loves you more than anything or anyone in the world. You have struggled in this world we live in with great patience, personal pride and dignity. You have continued that struggle for fifty odd years of your life with no break in stride or hope, in some way, for a better day.

I write you this letter because I no longer feel worthy of being your son, and because I will finally disappear from your life. Actually, unburden it in a way. This I know will be painful on you, but selfishly, for me, it is the best thing I can do for you without you fully understanding my motive as to why.

Can you trust me, mother? Can you, for the first time in your life, really trust me that what I am saying is best for both of us? I have done something very bad, very disturbing, but whereas I have some small remorse, it is not enough to make me say I wouldn't do it again to someone else, if such opportunity

219

arose. I would take full advantage of it, mother, I know I would.

I bid you goodbye in the only way I know how, by telling you I love you. Above any sin in life I've willfully committed, any crime or immoral, indecent, adverse act, I have always loved only one person in my demented and abject existence, and that is you.

Love,

Dorrell

"D-disappear, vanish from my life?"

Lilly removed her glasses while sobbing. This was the last thing she expected from Dorrell.

"It-it's not prison again, is it, Dorrell? Is it!"

It was the only thing Lilly could think of that would precipitate Dorrell to do something like this.

"What am I to think? Dorrell's back in prison. Sing Sing. My son. 'Disappear.' He said disappear, didn't he?"

Eva did not mind the tiny, confined hotel room or the plaid drapes at the one window; she felt free. It took but two days for her to reach this level of euphoria, but it's how she felt the second day she came in from Masthead Publications and slipped the room key into the splintered wooden door that greeted her. She was staying, temporarily, in the Emerald, a cheap midtown hotel in Manhattan. She was still passing for white.

It was hard for her to leave 10 Ballad Street. She used a taxi to haul her things off to the hotel. It took three trips on the taxi's meter. There wasn't adequate closet space in the room for all her things, but the Emerald was to be her temporary dwelling. It's why most of her clothing was piled high on the floor. She didn't need or want De Wolfe's money. She had the jewelry he'd lavished on her that would start her hocking it tomorrow and allow her to come away with a pretty penny. Eva had to become practical about her life now, make things work, financially, as best she could, since she had to stand up on her own two feet again.

She thought the opinion of herself would alter because of De Wolfe, his abusive, hateful verbal tirade, but to her surprise, it hadn't happened. In fact, she was sitting in the hotel room with a hand mirror and looking at her face.

It had begun to feel like a prison for her at 10 Ballad Street and her, consequently, becoming its prisoner. That's why before the taxi pulled away from the building, she felt relieved that she was leaving Ballad Street to never return.

She liked the Emerald Hotel's noise, the action in the hotel.

This was her eighth day of living a new life away from Maxwell De Wolfe. She had serviced De Wolfe with sex, and he had made her life comfortable and free of stress. There were days when she thought of De Wolfe, but she never loved him.

"It would be a sad day when a mistress falls in love with her lover," Eva said with a seasoned sense of experience. "My heart's not made of stone, not at all, but De Wolfe wasn't a man a woman falls in love with, not under any circumstance."

She did leave De Wolfe a personal letter before she left. She left it on the bed. She wrote it because she did have a tenderness in her heart for him but nothing more affectionate or prolonged.

Maybe Dorrell had done me a favor, Eva thought. *Maybe his timing was perfect. I needed to escape. I needed my freedom. De Wolfe was an encumbrance to me.*

She wouldn't tell her mother about her and De Wolfe's breakup. Her mother had gotten used to De Wolfe in her life, comfortable with him. There would be new worry in her, a responsibility that she must help her financially and emotionally when neither was the case, if she was told she and De Wolfe had broken up: the affair with him had ended.

As for her name, she would change it. Not be so sentimental and innocent and careless this time. Soon she would become Antonia Hall, not Eva Durant, but Antonia Hall, Eva thought. It would still be a great stage name for her to work under.

And she would not cross back over to black. She was white, not black. There were privileges, advantages to being white. She held no hatred toward her race, blacks, but had descended too far down into a white world to find escape, maybe from De Wolfe, but not from the white world. And she would bury herself more into the white world with her new name and credentials. She didn't want to abandon the Durant name before but not now: she had learned her lesson, and well. There would be no more obvious mistakes by her.

The hotel's desk clerk, the white men who saw her in the Emerald, were visibly dazzled by her. But if she ever told them she was colored and not white, they would call her a nigger like De Wolfe had, something so hurtful, degrading, that it'd cut, at times, every human characteristic out of her, every human element all because of her skin coloring, Eva thought.

"All because my mother's blood bled into me and I have her bloodline and have been born into a human history." And now she was no longer a human being, but a burden born to an inhuman species, an inferior race of people of no worth.

"But I am beautiful," Eva said, looking into the hand mirror.

"I am beautiful and white. Not black. But white. Antonia Hall."

Chapter 17

Six days later.

De Wolfe had pulled the armchair over to the wall of mirrors and sat. Eva's letter was in his lap, but he had yet read it. The letter was unexpected, for he thought she hated him; it's how their two-and-a-half-year affair had ended between them, with her hating him.

De Wolfe's cane lay on the floor, among the shattered glass. There were three mirrors still left on the wall. The three mirrors his cane had not smashed into bits and pieces. It was like his affair with Eva Durant never happened in this room, as if it were a fantasy he lived with and he was the only one left lamenting it.

"I miss her. I love her. I am a broken man," De Wolfe said. "I will never be the man I was. The De Wolfe I once knew."

He was not sure of Eva's letter, what it might say; it's why he had not wanted to read it in the bedroom at 10 Ballad Street, but in his mansion, where the walls would protect him, make Eva Durant a distant, faraway figure—but not in this room, where he saw, clearly, her waiting for him in the bedroom's bed, and him lusting. He might not ever leave the room but die in the chair and rot away, his power stripped from him, and him holding on to an illusion, a vision as if it were real, as if it could bring Eva Durant back to him.

DE WOLFE WAS IN HIS bedroom and at his fragile little desk. The lamp's light shone down on Eva Durant's letter to him. De Wolfe began reading it. When De Wolfe finished reading Eva's letter, he stood.

Melancholy drenched his bones. De Wolfe badly needed the cane's support; it had to get him to Alexandra's bedroom and then back to his.

Tap.

"Mr. De Wolfe?"

"De Wolfe, Elsie." The bedroom door opened. "Thank you."

"You are welcome, Mr. De Wolfe," Elsa said, shutting the door behind her after leaving the room.

De Wolfe paused and then looked down at the letter he'd carried into the room.

Alexandra was in her favorite armchair reading a thick book.

"I've come," De Wolfe said after Alexandra's acknowledgment of his presence in the room, "to you with a letter I wish you to read, Alexandra."

Alexandra rested the fat book down in her lap.

"My behavior the past month osr so, particularly the past week … I was at 10 Ballad Street. It is why I did not dine with you this evening."

Alexandra took the glasses off her longish nose. "I have no interest in what goes on at 10 Ballad Street, Maxwell. You are aware of that. We have covered this ground before. You will not bore me with your dalliances or your worries or fatigue with your personal affairs.

"I am exhausted by them."

"Yes, Alexandra, I-I am tired. Weary. A broken man." Pause. "It's what I keep repeating to myself over and over, futilely, uselessly. Don't I look it, without feeling pity for myself?"

"Pity? There's no need for me to look at you, Maxwell, for what godforsaken reason? You are an old man. It's what you—not that many nights past—confessed. And I am an old woman. We both are. We both have lost our youth. Our vitality."

Alexandra laughed like winter mocking spring.

"It's what we've become. We are relics, Maxwell. Decaying. No longer vital or important. Simply objects of decay. Museum pieces. But not to be admired or cherished by anyone. Tolerated, yes, and then one day ignored."

De Wolfe looked at her and then placed Eva's letter on the side table next to her.

"I am done with it, Alexandra. The affair."

Pause.

"I will be in my room, Alexandra. Waiting for you."

Alexandra picked up the book but then felt annoyed by the letter De Wolfe had left for her on the side table.

"You fool! You arrogant, egotistical fool, De Wolfe!" Alexandra slammed the book shut. "I will not read this damned letter of yours from your mistress. This vulgarity. I will not stoop so low. I would rather rip it into a thousand l-little pieces—be done with it!"

Seconds later.

"All right, De Wolfe! All right! Have it your way!" Alexandra shrieked.

Furious, and yet curious, Alexandra picked up the letter.

Dear Max,

I do not hate you for what you have done to me. You have helped to mature me because you have forced me to look at my life with a renewed passion and determination to become the woman I will one day become.

The sex we had did not fulfill me, only you. This you knew without me telling you, but I performed my role as your mistress well. I have that much talent.

You will be the one with the broken heart, not me. I am not saying this in a mean or spiteful, invective nature, but with the honesty you taught me when you spoke of your family life at home with your wife, Alexandra, the lack of love between you.

That life will always be yours. I have no idea of what my life will be without you. But when I walk out this building at 10 Ballad Street today, I will know a better, kinder day will greet me. I will be able to breathe again and to feel whole.

I have belief. Belief. Belief.

Affectionately yours,

Eva

"My god!"

TAP.

"Come in, Alexandra. I have sent Helga off to her room."

Alexandra entered De Wolfe's bedroom. He was sitting upright at his desk as if he'd been propped up in the chair.

"I read the letter, Maxwell," Alexandra said, placing Eva's letter on De Wolfe's desk. "Did you love her?" Pause. "This girl named Eva?"

"Yes," De Wolfe said.

Pause.

"Do you love her still?"

"Yes."

Alexandra turned and walked away. She opened the bedroom door and then closed it behind her.

De Wolfe dropped his head down onto the tiny desk.

"Eva, I love you. I do, still … Eva."

Printed in the United States
By Bookmasters